*Where the Magic had taken him—or when—
he had no idea.*

Where or when it had taken *them*.

Abby lay in his arms, her legs entangled with his. Warm, soft, and invitingly naked, her skin caressed his, seriously impairing his ability to concentrate on their surroundings.

"I know this place." Abby's voice came from just above him in a breathless whisper. "I've seen it a hundred times in my dreams. Where are we? How did we get here?"

When he opened his eyes, a dull gray light filtered through the room, emanating from the early morning sun shining through a crack in the wooden shutters high up on the wall. He knew the place as well.

"This is my own bedchamber."

MELISSA MAYHUE

"An author with a magical touch for romance."
—*New York Times* bestselling author Janet Chapman

(*Turn the page for rave reviews of
Melissa Mayhue's enchanting romances.*)

Highlander's Curse is also available as an eBook

Also by Melissa Mayhue

MELISSA
MAYHUE

Highlander's
Curse

POCKET STAR BOOKS

New York   London   Toronto   Sydney

Pocket Star Books
A Division of Simon & Schuster, Inc.
1230 Avenue of the Americas
New York, NY 10020

This book is a work of fiction. Names, characters, places, and incidents either are products of the author's imagination or are used fictitiously. Any resemblance to actual events or locales or persons, living or dead, is entirely coincidental.

Copyright © 2011 by Melissa Mayhue

All rights reserved, including the right to reproduce this book or portions thereof in any form whatsoever. For information address Pocket Books Subsidiary Rights Department, 1230 Avenue of the Americas, New York, NY 10020

First Pocket Star Books paperback edition April 2011

POCKET STAR BOOKS and colophon are registered trademarks of Simon & Schuster, Inc.

For information about special discounts for bulk purchases, please contact Simon & Schuster Special Sales at 1-866-506-1949 or business@simonandschuster.com.

The Simon & Schuster Speakers Bureau can bring authors to your live event. For more information or to book an event contact the Simon & Schuster Speakers Bureau at 1-866-248-3049 or visit our website at www.simonspeakers.com.

Cover design by Min Choi
Cover art by Alan Ayers

Manufactured in the United States of America

10 9 8 7 6 5 4 3 2 1

ISBN 978-1-4391-9032-6
ISBN 978-1-4391-9038-8 (ebook)

A third Hero is born . . .
Welcome to the World, Kaden Kyle!

Somewhere in the Mysts, my dad is grinning ear to ear,
knowing he has three great-grandsons now!

Acknowledgments

Thank you to Elaine Spencer, a fantastic agent as well as a fantastic person. It's so great having you in my corner!

And

My sincere thanks to my wonderful editor, Megan McKeever, for helping me see the forest *and* the trees! You're the best!

Prologue

─── ∾ ───

This hardly looked a proper cottage at all, let alone the home to a seer of Thomas the Rhymer's fame.

Colin MacAlister hesitated a moment to survey the ruined shack confronting him before dismounting.

Not even his own mother's claim that his actions were those of a brash, untested youth had prevented this quest, so certainly he wouldn't allow something as minor as the unwelcoming appearance of this abode to deter him.

False bravado, she'd accused. Have a care for the Fae, she'd warned. Respect the danger they represent.

He'd show her. His bravery was real. And as for the Fae? It was contempt he felt for them, not respect. He'd seen them with his own eyes this past year when they'd all but killed his brother. Drew's body might have survived, but his heart, his spirit, they'd shattered that part of his brother.

There was nothing to fear from the Fae in this place anyway. They were too entrenched in their own arrogance to inhabit a place such as this. No, if the seer was here, he'd be alone.

Colin filled his lungs, slowly and with purpose, before forcing the air out again and with it, the doubt that plagued him. His determination bolstered, he tossed his reins over a low branch and headed for the door of the little hovel.

Perhaps the old man he'd spoken to back in the last village had been mistaken. Why would a man such as Thomas Learmonth leave his manor at Ercledoune for a heap of crumbling sod such as this?

No matter the appearance of the hut, he still had to try. He must find Thomas. He'd ridden too far and risked too much to give up now.

He'd but lifted his hand to knock on the door when it opened. A woman so old she looked as if her skin wrinkled in on itself stood before him.

"I seek Thomas of Ercledoune. Is he within these walls?"

She moved toward him, forcing him to take a step backward.

"What is it that a strapping lad like yourself would have of poor auld Thomas?" She scratched her chin, staring at him with one eye squinted shut. "Not that I'm saying he's here, mind you."

"My business is with him and him alone. I'd warn you no to be playing games with me, woman. I've no the time or patience for it." He hadn't the luxury of time to waste on some lonely old crone.

"You've some nerve about you, lad," the old woman

cackled in her oddly accented voice. "Lonely old crone, you've pegged me, have you? And after the grand sum of no more than a mere moment's acquaintance? You base that assessment on your vast years of experience and hardship, do you?"

A chill raced the length of Colin's backbone as he at last met the old woman's eyes. A green as dark as the hidden depths of the forest stared back at him, capturing him, holding him immobilized.

He'd not spoken those words aloud. He'd only thought them.

"You're all too easy for me to read," she murmured, the color in her eyes swirling as she spoke.

"What takes you from me, my love?" a man's voice called from beyond the door, breaking whatever power had bound Colin's attention to the woman.

"Out of my way," he muttered, the impetuousness of youth bolstered by need allowing him to push past her and into the room beyond.

What he found when he entered was in stark contrast to what he'd seen from the outside. The room itself was bathed in a warm glow of light coming from a large fireplace off to one side. Nearby, an old man sat in a richly cushioned chair, his hands resting on a polished table next to a stack of the finest, whitest paper Colin had ever seen.

The old man held a quill between ink-stained fingers, dipping it first into a little pot and then touching its tip to the sheet in front of him.

"Thomas of Ercledoune?" Colin demanded, his tongue suddenly heavy in his dry mouth. It could be no other than the great seer himself.

"Aye," the old man answered slowly, turning a watery gaze in Colin's direction.

At last! Joy sparked in Colin's heart.

Legend had grown around Thomas of Ercledoune, a seer who had accurately predicted the death of Alexander III. A man who, if those legends were to be believed, gained the gift of sight from the Faerie Queen herself.

"You must tell me, True Thomas, will Edward the Longshanks be pushed back or will all of Scotland fall to his armies? Is there any hope for our freedom? I must know."

"Leave him be," the old woman ordered stepping around Colin to place a protective arm over Thomas's shoulders. "Your petty concerns of this world are of no consequence. Can you not see he's exhausted and ill?"

"All the more reason I must speak to him now, before it's too late." This might be his last chance to learn what the future held.

"I order you to leave him be," the woman stubbornly insisted.

"Away with you!" Colin yelled, surprising even himself with his outburst. Whoever she was, she had no right to give him such orders. He wouldn't be denied the knowledge he sought. Not now. Not after all he'd gone through to find True Thomas. "I must know my destiny. I'd hear it from his lips!"

In front of him, the air around the old woman glowed green and her form shimmered as he watched. He rubbed his eyes, unable to believe what he saw as her shape shifted from old woman to child to maiden.

"Neither crone nor maiden, young upstart, but a queen who confronts you now."

Colin leaped away, grabbing for the sword on his back as he did so. To his amazement, he found himself unable to move, as if his hand had frozen to his weapon, his feet firmly stuck to the floor. He could not move any part of his body. He could, in fact, do nothing but watch the shimmering beauty draw close, her anger pulsing around her like a living rainbow.

"It's your destiny you'd have, is it?" Her eyes flashed as her hand slammed down on the table beside them. "So self-important you are, you'd not even take care for the feelings and health of an old man? So self-important, you'd be rude to a helpless old woman. You should be ashamed of yourself."

She didn't understand. It wasn't really like that. He wasn't really like that. He'd explain it all if only he could make his tongue work.

Her eyes widened as if in surprise when she came close and placed her fingertips against his chest, directly over his heart.

"And you, with the blood of the Fae coursing through your veins. Your behavior would be bad enough from a Mortal, but from one of my own?" She shook her head in disgust. "Well, pup, you'll receive more this day than you bargained for. If it's destiny you want, then by all means, it's destiny you shall have."

The air he breathed went cold, his nose stinging like he'd stumbled into the glen on a snowy day. Around him, the room shimmered and wavered and his eyes tinted over with a green film as if he were trapped within a colored, pulsing sphere of light. He heard the woman's words reverberating from somewhere outside that sphere.

"You ask after the destiny of Scotland, but that's not what you truly want, boy. No Fae's destiny can ever be complete without finding his one true love, his other half, his Soulmate. Surely you've learned that much of your own people."

She was wrong! He was a warrior by nature and training. A warrior by choice. All he'd ever dreamed of was defending Scotland. By sheer force of will, Colin fought the Magic binding him, managing at last to move his lips.

"No!" His voice was little more than a whisper. "Dinna need love." Love was for women, gathering like hens in a warm solar, not for warriors like him. He had a much higher calling.

"Oh, you think so, do you, my rash child?" The Faerie Queen's laughter tinkled around him, bouncing off the green sphere and echoing inside. "Well, we'll just see about that higher calling of yours. Seems to me you're but a youngling Fae in need of a lesson. And a lesson you shall have, a history lesson of your people. In the long ago, in the battle that split Wyddecol from the Mortal plain, Soul pairings were ripped asunder, leaving each soul a jagged half, crying out for its missing piece until it could once again find its own match. Only when the two halves are once again joined will a Fae feel complete. That finding is the true destiny of all Fae. A destiny you'd deny as you stand here before me."

Lifting her arms, she placed one hand on either side of his head. "I call on the Magic lying dormant in your blood to rise up and I give you this gift, young Fae: from this day forward, you'll feel all those Souls, each and every one. You'll feel their sharp, jagged edges, seeing their anguish in your mind's eye. You'll feel their pain as they blindly call out for one another, even as your own need calls out, the need you deny exists. You'll see the Souls that fit together. All of them. All except your own, that is, since you claim your own need is of no importance to you."

"I ken yer anger, my love, but such a burden as you put upon the lad will drive him mad." Thomas's voice floated through the haze. "Can you no see yer way clear to provide an escape from the millstone with which you weigh him down?"

"Very well, love, for you." The Queen's tone, caressing and warm, chilled as she turned her attention back to Colin, the green of her eyes swirling like a boiling cauldron. "Only by joining with your own Soulmate will you cease to feel the horror and pain of the great wanting."

The Faerie Queen's voice seemed to pierce his body, as if her words dived through his skin and into his very bloodstream. When at last she stopped speaking, the silence echoed in his head, beating against the inside of his closed eyes as loudly as the anxious pounding of his heart.

She released him then and he fell limply to the floor, lying there weak as a newborn babe when she walked away.

"Come, my beloved," he heard her say over the scraping of a chair against the floor. "I've indulged your desire to stay in this world long enough. It's time we returned to Wyddecol where your youth and vigor will be restored."

Just as he thought himself alone, he felt her close, whispering in his ear. "I granted you an escape only to please my Thomas, and though you've angered me greatly with your impudence, I feel the need to tell you the whole of it, youngling. Since you swear you've no need for your own missing half, it should come as no serious disappointment to learn she'll not be found in this lifetime. Perhaps my gift will allow you to learn the true importance of your destiny before your paths cross again."

And then she was gone, the sound of his own shallow panting his only company in the stillness of the room.

How long he lay there, unable to lift even a finger, he had no idea. Perhaps he slept, but he couldn't be sure. At last, his eyes flickered open and he pushed himself up to sit.

The room around him was dark and dank, smelling of animal dung and wet hide. The table and chair he'd seen earlier had disappeared, a roughly hewn wooden bench setting in their place.

He rose to his feet and stumbled outside into the light of afternoon to find his horse exactly as he'd left him, his reins still draped over the low branch.

With one last glance back at the little hut, he hefted himself up onto his mount and turned his horse away, back toward the village. Disappointment in his failure to find the answers he'd sought closed in on him, shrouding his thoughts.

Whether he'd really found Thomas of Ercledoune or only imagined the entire incident, he might never know. For the moment, he wanted to believe it had all been some bizarre nightmare brought on by sleepless nights and lack of food.

He had almost convinced himself that was the case.

The first twinges hit him just outside the village proper, sharp pains cutting against his consciousness. Jagged impressions of brightly shining lights, like broken sunbeams gone horribly wrong, they flittered through his mind. So many of them, one piling in after another until he lost count of the different shapes battering inside his mind, each of them pulsing, seething with the unrelenting agony of their own unabated loneliness.

He kicked his horse's sides, demanding speed through the village and beyond until at last the images began to fade.

It was then he knew the truth of it.

Those shards of light had been the Souls of the villagers. Just as the Faerie Queen had said he would, he'd felt every single one of them calling out for their missing half. He'd felt their desolation and pain.

His meeting with Thomas of Ercledoune had been no trick of his imagination. Nor had his encounter with the Faerie Queen been a fantasy. They were all too real.

As real as the "gift" she had given him.

As real as the curse he'd bear for the rest of his days.

One

~

*H*ere's to Abby, our archaeologist extraordinaire!"

Abigail Porter lifted her glass, clinking it against the ones held by her friends before bringing it to her lips and downing the colorful contents.

The shot was liquid candy in her mouth, heating her chest as it rolled down her throat.

She was so going to regret all this tomorrow morning.

"Hey ya, honey!" Lauren waggled a finger at the passing waiter. "Another round right here, just like the last one."

"At this rate, I'm gonna feel like shit on that plane tomorrow." Casey wiped her index finger into the narrow opening of the empty little glass to catch up every last drop. "But it'll be worth it for one last Girls' Night Out!"

Last time. Abby shook her head, trying to clear the fuzz from her brain. Her whole life would change after tonight.

She'd met Lauren and Casey on her first day of college

and they'd been inseparable ever since. After Casey had taken her dream job and moved to California, they'd still managed to see each other every few months when Casey would fly through Denver on her business trips. Not even Lauren's getting married and moving to the East Coast had ended their friendship, though it had meant their Girls' Nights Out were fewer and farther between.

But nothing lasts forever.

"We'll still see each other, Case. Just maybe not as often and I'll probably be dragging kidlets along when I come. They'll need to get to know their aunties, after all." Lauren nodded emphatically as she spoke.

Abby felt her lips peel back in a grin. The minute Lauren had stepped off the plane this morning she'd announced that she and Greg had decided to have a baby. She had it all planned. Six months to eat healthy and give up everything that was bad for her and then she'd get pregnant. Just like Lauren to expect her life to go according to a timetable.

And knowing Lauren, it probably would.

"Here you go, ladies. Nobody's driving tonight, I hope?"

The waiter's features seemed to blur a little as he held the tray in front of him and placed each little glass and an accompanying large one together on the table.

"Nope. Staying right here at the hotel," Lauren assured the young man. "Got early flights out."

Abigail blinked hard, reaching with an unsteady hand to pick up her shot as her friends did the same.

Lauren and Casey were both staying at the airport hotel tonight, but since she lived in town, she was going home in a taxi.

"No matter what you say, Lauren, it won't ever be the same again." Casey shook her head, her drink untouched. "Sam keeps talking marriage and family and we all know it's just a matter of time before I cave to the pressure. Abby's going off on this dig thing this summer and now that she's a big mucky-muck international archaeologist, she'll end up all famous and giving lectures on the Discovery Channel. And you! You're going to freakin' have kids, for God's sake. We won't ever be the same again. We'll be officially grown up."

"Not an archaeologist yet." The words rattled around in Abby's brain until she finally managed to blurt them out loud. Granted, she had her undergraduate degree, but the year she'd taken off to work before pursuing her master's had slowed her down. With money an issue, she'd had no choice. Just the thought of her student loan debt made her reach for the glass of beer sitting in front of her.

"You will be. And you'll be the best one ever, too. Nobody can find stuff like you can."

Abby only wished she could feel as certain of her future as Lauren sounded. It had been her life's dream from the time she'd been old enough to know there were ancient cultures waiting to be discovered. Her only goal in life was to follow the voices calling in her head and to make a success of it. She hadn't the slightest doubt that her destiny lay in finding something ancient, something wonderful meant for only her to find.

"Absolutely she will," Casey agreed. "And didn't you say this new archaeology job is everything you'd hoped for?"

Everything and more. Like manna from heaven this opportunity had dropped in her lap. Some wealthy archaeologist wannabe was footing the bill for a three-month dig in Scotland trying to prove some theory of his about original inhabitants that would get his name immortalized in archaeology textbooks around the world.

All Abby cared about was that they'd be excavating the site of an ancient stone circle. It was a chance the likes of which she'd only dreamed of in the past. Like chocolate syrup on top of a sundae, Mr. Wannabe Famous was paying a generous salary to the candidates he chose.

And, wonder of wonders, he'd chosen her as one of them.

How an introvert like her had made it through the interview process and actually gotten on the team, she had no idea. She'd been a nervous wreck when she'd met with the representative. All she knew was that she'd received a letter yesterday welcoming her onto the team. Being selected meant that four months from now she'd be flying to Scotland and starting the most exciting thing that had ever happened to her in her entire life.

"Does Craig know you're leaving the country for two months?" Casey tried unsuccessfully for an innocent look, batting her long lashes over the rim of her beer glass.

"No." Why would she tell him? That relationship had been over and done with more than a year ago. "He's moved on, Case. Last I heard he's engaged or something now."

"It could have been you he's engaged to, you know," Lauren accused. "You could have had that one if you'd tried a little harder."

"Didn't want that one. Craig's a nice enough guy and all, but he's just not . . ." Abby stopped, thinking of the man she'd come so close to marrying. He really was a decent guy. Handsome, wealthy family, good job. Craig was pretty much perfect. Perfect hair, perfect manners, perfect smooth, clean hands that were softer than hers. He was perfect, all right. Perfect for someone other than her.

"Oh, let me guess. He's just not The One," Casey finished for her, dramatically wiggling her fingers in the air to signify quotation marks.

"Exactly," Abby agreed with a shudder. "Besides. Like I need a man to complicate my life right now? I'm totally fine on my own, you guys. Totally."

That was the story she was sticking to with these women. The parade of horrible blind dates her well-meaning friends had subjected her to after her breakup with Craig was all too clearly etched in her memory.

"Oh, yeah? Well, I think a man is exactly what you need," Lauren responded. "If we get you and Casey both married, then we could all do the mom thing together. Our kids could grow up and maybe even get married to each other. We could be our own in-laws! How perfect would *that* be?"

The idea sent the three of them into a fit of giggles as Lauren twirled her hand around her head like a cowgirl with a lasso, signaling the waiter for another round.

"Last one for me, girlies. I got to get me some z's or I'll never make that plane in the morning. Correction. *This* morning." Lauren grinned wickedly as the waiter delivered their drinks. "So let's make this a good one. Just like old times. We have to drink to our heart's deepest secret wish. Casey?"

Casey lifted her drink first. "My secret wish. Okay. Since it's you guys, I'll admit this. In spite of all my crap about not ever getting married, I'm really not going to mind so much when I let Sam talk me into it. My wish would be that since I'm getting home just in time for Valentine's Day, he asks again so I can surprise the shit out of him and say yes this time."

"Good one. No real secret there, but good, none-theless." Lauren grinned and lifted her drink. "My turn. I want twins. I'd wish for two girls so I can name one after each of you. Greg has already agreed. Now you, Abby. Your deepest, most passionate wish."

Abby lifted her glass, trying to focus her thoughts through the alcohol haze, horrified when she blurted out the truth. "I do want to find The One. Not some soft-handed man. I want a real man's man, you know? The sooner the better."

"What happened to our Miss I-don't-need-any-man?" Lauren started to giggle, holding her perfectly manicured fingers in front of her lips. "Oh, honey, I wondered when you were finally going to admit it to yourself. Frankly, I'm amazed that the girl who can find anything hasn't already found her perfect man."

"Wait, wait. I know exactly what she needs," Casey interrupted, setting her glass down and leaning forward. "Total alpha male, just like in those romance books you read, Abby. All hot and bothered, right there in your bed, muscles rippling with every move, just waiting for you to jump his bones."

"That's perfect for her! An honest-to-God hero in all his naked glory," Lauren added with another giggle.

"Exactly. That's what I wish for. I want to find The One," Abby agreed, nodding her head as she tried to picture that mysterious Soulmate who lived only in the dark recesses of her imagination. She lifted her glass and clinked it against those her two friends held. "I wish that all our wishes come true."

For an instant, the lights in the room seemed to dim, casting a green glow over them, and the empty glasses on the table rattled.

"Whoa, those planes must be flying low tonight," Lauren laughed. "Here's to us, ladies. May all our wishes come true."

"May all our wishes come true," Abby and Casey echoed.

They clinked their glasses together again and emptied them, sitting quietly for a few minutes after their laughter died away.

"Won't you change your mind and stay here with us tonight, Abby? It'd be like old times," Casey offered as she and Lauren rose to their feet.

"Yeah, you really should. There's no reason you need to drag your butt home at this time of night . . . or morning," Lauren agreed.

"Nope." Abby stood, hugging each of her friends in turn. "I'm on the schedule to work at the museum this afternoon. I'll just finish my beer and then grab a taxi home. No big deal. Really. I should be able to get a few hours of sleep before I have to get my day started. You guys have good flights out tomorrow. And call me when you get home."

Another round of teary hugs accompanied by promises to stay in touch, and Abby sat back down, watching her friends disappear through the door toward the elevators. It had been so much fun to spend the day with them. If only she hadn't ruined it by stupidly admitting her desire to find that one perfect man. She suspected she'd be dealing with the fallout from this evening for quite some time.

She downed the last of her beer and then fumbled in her purse for cash to leave as a tip. The waiter had more than earned it by putting up with them all evening.

Two steps away from the table she grabbed for the nearest chair back to steady herself. Those cute little drinks might taste like liquid candy but they sure packed a wicked punch.

She headed for the lobby and the front doors, grateful that though the room spun lazily around her, at least she didn't feel like she was viewing the world through a glass of green liquid as she had earlier at the table.

Maybe if she was lucky, Lauren and Casey would be in as bad a shape as her. Maybe, just maybe, they wouldn't even remember her whole I-want-to-find-the-perfect-man debacle.

"Yeah, right," she snorted to herself, causing the doorman to jump as if he hadn't realized anyone approached.

She was so screwed. Those two women would never forget. And they'd never let her forget, either. Both Lauren and Casey would be scouring their lists of single men the second they got home, searching through every possible candidate. They'd be pushing every single man they could find her direction until she was old and gray. A future filled with scores of crappy dates and Not The Ones lay before her thanks to that one little slip.

Oh, yeah, there was no doubt that she was so going to regret tonight in the morning.

Two

A foreign anxiety rumbled around in Colin's stomach as he sat astride his warhorse watching King Robert's army calmly set about preparations for a night's encampment. His mount tossed its head in response to the noise wafting up from the men scurrying around below.

"Easy," he murmured, giving the animal a pat on the neck. He knew exactly how the horse felt. It was beyond him to understand why the Bruce had agreed to wait until tomorrow to take the castle at Perth. In addition to being one of Comyn's kinsmen, Aymer de Valence was wholly devoted to Edward and not to be trusted. And camping their entire army here at Methven? In the open like this and only miles from Perth? The whole of it seemed a frustratingly foolish move to him.

Apparently his companions felt similarly vexed.

"I canna believe we're no even to set guards for the

night." From his left, Simeon MacDowell's mutter was the only sign that he felt as frustrated as Colin.

Alasdair Maxwell sat his mount on Colin's right, unusually solemn. "I'm no at all easy in the chosen encampment. We're too exposed down there. Our king is too trusting by far. Wallace would never have done such."

"Wallace is gone. It's Robert we follow now." Colin agreed with his friend's assessment of their situation, but he'd allow no criticism of their new king.

From their perch on the small rise it looked like the entire of Robert's army was laid out across the rolling land, as if served up on a giant trencher, ready for the feasting. In contrast, the larger hills looming off to the west held a promise of safety. A promise of respite from the mass of men below.

"It's because yer a Highlander, Dair," Simeon offered softly, breaking into Colin's thoughts. "This place is home to farmers. The land here rolls with her hills. In truth it's no so flat though it may appear so to yer eyes. Yer spoiled by the hiding places offered up in the nooks and crannies of yer mountains."

"Mayhaps," Dair murmured. "Or mayhaps I just prefer the tactics of Wallace. He'd no have laid us all out in the fields below like easy targets at tournament. We'd have been scattered among the trees, at the very least."

"His tactics dinna fare so well at Falkirk." Simeon spoke without taking his eyes from the troops below. "Though in this particular instance, I find I must agree with you. I've no love for what we do here."

"It's of no matter now." Colin dragged his eyes from the distant hills to once again survey the army below. "We've no course but to accept that Wallace is gone.

Longshanks has seen to that. We've pledged ourselves to the Bruce. He's our rightful king now and we'll do what we can to aid him in his fight for Scotland's freedom."

"So we shall," Dair agreed, tugging his reins to turn his horse from the view below. "But that disna change the fact that this place echoes in my bones with foreboding. I'll no lay my head to rest down there with that lot. No in the open like that."

"And where do you think yer going?" Sim questioned, all the while urging his own mount to follow Dair.

"Into the trees, just off this direction. It will no be so far as to be left behind on the morrow, but I'll feel better with a bit of cover around me. I prefer my eyes, rather than my back, turned toward Perth."

With one last look over the army encampment, Colin followed along behind his companions. Overly cautious perhaps, to his way of thinking, and yet Dair's sense of caution had rarely steered them wrong. The man had an uncanny ability to sniff out danger.

Besides, placing some distance between himself and all those men down below was more than desirable. In the years since his foolish encounter with the Faerie Queen, he'd learned to erect the mental barriers that shielded his mind. Even so, this many souls simultaneously crying out for their mates relentlessly battered even his best defenses.

Not to mention that, like Sim, he happened to agree with Dair's tactical assessment. There was something about this place that felt eerily wrong, like treading over sacred ground. Even now a tingle of apprehension rose up his backbone and prickled his neck, as if every hair on his body stood on end.

When they entered the forest, his horse suddenly halted, pricking up its ears and pawing the ground nervously. A wave of dizziness swept over Colin and, as if the sun had settled below the horizon, the light dimmed to a pale, indistinct green cast.

Ahead of him on the path, Sim turned in his saddle to look back.

"By the saints!" Sim exclaimed. "What's happening to you?"

Colin's arms and legs refused to follow his commands as if he had turned to stone, and he could only watch as the faint green glow turned to a wavering emerald sphere surrounding him.

Like a swarm of angry midges on a late summer day, tiny dots of multicolored lights flashed and dived around his head, careening into one another and bouncing off the walls of the decidedly solid sphere. They moved faster and faster until they were but a blur, their brightly lit tails streaking out behind them.

Sim strained in his direction but Dair held him back with an outstretched arm. His words were barely audible over the buzzing and hissing of the manic lights.

"Stay yer ground. It's the Fae."

The Fae! Dair must have the right of it. Nothing of this world could bring about such as he experienced now.

The walls of the sphere shimmered and solidified to the point Colin could no longer see through them. In the next instant, his stomach plummeted to his toes, leaving him weightless as if his body were being tossed through the air into a great, black chasm.

By the Fates, what more could the damned Fae possibly want of him now?

Three

―∾―

His hand, large and callused, stroked up her thigh to rest on her hip. She snuggled back against him, as if she could melt into the hard chest and powerful arms that held her. He drew her close, one strong hand slipping down to cover her breast. Her entire body tingled in response to his touch, her senses crying out for more. This was it. He was The One. She'd found her perfect man, her Soulmate.

Abby awoke slowly, keeping her eyes closed against the sun that filtered through her bedroom curtains. Dregs of the dream she'd been having still fogged her mind, not yet giving way to the reality of her waking world.

It had seemed so real she could still feel the heavy warmth of the man who'd held her in her dream. Still feel his arms around her. Still feel his roughened hand covering her breast.

Abby's eyes flew open and she steeled herself not to move, not to scream.

The large, warm hand covering her breast was no dream.

Oh, damn! What *had* she done last night?

Scenes of her evening out with the girls flipped through her mind as if she were scanning through a Rolodex. Nothing. There wasn't even an inkling of any man in her memory.

This couldn't be happening. She never did anything even remotely like this. Not picking up strange men, and certainly not forgetting that she'd even done it.

Though she wasn't foolish enough to deny she'd been about as drunk last night as she'd ever been, she still would have sworn she'd come straight home and gone to bed—alone! A quick glance down confirmed that she was wearing the boxers and T-shirt she thought she remembered putting on last night before climbing into bed. Alone.

And yet . . . here he was, his big, warm body cuddled around hers like he belonged here.

How could she remember dressing for bed but not remember climbing in with this man?

She shoved at the panic crawling up her throat, fighting to rationalize her way through this. Men didn't break into houses just to climb into bed for a good night's rest. They murdered you, or attacked you, or at the very least robbed you and then left. They didn't just go to sleep. No, there had to be a logical explanation for the man warming her bed.

Like being totally drunk and dragging some stranger home with her? A stranger she couldn't even remember meeting?

After a moment of indecision, she carefully slid out from under his hand and rolled to her side to have a look at the mystery man in her bed.

Okay. Time for a new dating rule. From now on Drunk Abby got to pick out all the new men to date.

This one was something to behold with the covers draped low across his hips. From the dark copper hair that brushed against his shoulders, to the shadowed line of his strong jaw, right on down to the solid wall of muscle that masqueraded as a normal man's chest, this guy was exceptional.

And, unless he was wearing some amazingly low-cut underwear, he was also exceptionally naked.

Abby's heart pounded in her chest. A naked Adonis in her bed. One who apparently spent the better part of his life in a gym, too, from the looks of him. Those arms were magnificent. If she didn't think she'd risk waking him, she'd hunt down a measuring tape just to prove how truly magnificent they were.

She swallowed hard and glanced back up to his face only to find herself staring into the bluest eyes she'd ever seen. They were so mesmerizing it took her a delayed moment to realize that not only was he awake, he'd also obviously caught her ogling his body.

Well, what could he expect? He was in her bed, after all. A man who looked like that? And wearing nothing but skin? Oh, yeah. A man like that was going to get stared at anywhere. He should be used to it.

Rationalization or no, her cheeks still heated. "Good morning." She tried to ignore the nervous squeak in her voice. "Sleep well?"

Hell's bells. She sounded like some inexperienced old maid trying to make small talk after a one-night stand.

"Aye," he answered, his deep voice reverberating in her chest. "I suppose I did at that. Where am I?"

Gorgeous, built like the proverbial brick outhouse, and on top of all that, he even spoke with a brogue. That was it. She was never going to even attempt to meet another man without ten or twenty pretty little candy-flavored drinks under her belt.

"My house in the city. Denver. Colorado. You just flew into town last night? I guess we met at the bar, huh? At the hotel out by the airport?"

Great. Now she was babbling like some total idiot. So much for smooth and sexy morning after. Classy way to break the news that she had no earthly idea who he was or where they'd met. Wonderful impression she was making. No doubt he'd think she was some hotel-stalker sleazebag who picked up strange men on a regular basis and then dragged them home to . . .

Damn. What *had* she brought him home for? She had no idea whether they'd done anything other than actually sleep. She couldn't even remember his name.

"Colorado." He rolled the word around in his mouth, stretching out every vowel. "How did I get here?"

Apparently she hadn't been the only one drinking more than her fair share of alcohol last night.

"Taxi?" She found herself helplessly shaking her head as she climbed out of bed.

"Taxi," he repeated, his tongue caressing the word as if it were an alien concept.

"Taxi," she confirmed, much more confidently than she felt.

What was with him anyway? He ran his hand in a slow caress, back and forth across the sheet where she had lain only moments before, his eyes darting about, scanning the room as if he wanted to miss nothing.

To hell with it. She couldn't keep pretending like this, especially since there didn't seem to be any way she was going to pick up enough clues from her overnight guest to figure out who he was. Honesty wasn't just her best choice, it was shaping up to be her only choice. "I don't seem to remember very much from last night. I was out with friends and then I guess I must have met you? I know this is probably going to sound like a line, but I don't do things like this. Not ever. This really is beyond embarrassing, but I don't remember bringing you home with me. I don't even remember your name."

He sat up and the covers pooled in his lap, his hands scrubbing over his face.

"Colin," he mumbled through his fingers. "Colin MacAlister."

God. Even his name was beautiful. Especially when uttered in that deep, rumbly brogue of his.

"And you, lass?" His gaze captured hers again. "What are you called?"

"Abby," she answered, feeling unreasonably hurt that she'd made so little impression on him that he'd forgotten her name as they slept. "Abigail Porter."

Just when she'd thought the moment couldn't get any more awkward, a tiny click sounded from the alarm sitting on her headboard, followed by an ear-splitting blast of music.

Colin sprang from the bed as Abby dived for the clock, slamming her hand down on the little button to silence the offending machine.

"Sorry about that. I keep it really loud because I have a hard time waking up in the . . ." The words dried up in her mouth as she turned around. It was as if her brain had forgotten what words even were, let alone how to string them together to form sentences.

Colin hovered at the bedside, naked. Completely, gorgeously, take-her-breath-away naked. Head lowered, legs flexed, arms lifted, poised as if he were single-handedly ready to take on an entire army of bad guys.

The only thing at odds with his perfect Spartan warrior pose was the look of confusion on his face.

"That noise is meant to waken you?"

"Hello? Alarm clock." She managed at last to drag her eyes back into her head and turn her back to him. "Jesus. You need to put some clothes on." Really, really needed to. Either that or she was going to make a complete fool of herself by jumping him right here in the middle of her bedroom.

Heaven knew, he looked ready to be jumped. Every hard bit of him.

"I canna seem to find my plaid," he muttered from behind her.

His what?

She waited, back turned, arms crossed tightly under her breasts in an effort to keep her hands to herself. "Did you leave your things in the bathroom?"

Her stomach tightened even as she asked the question,

the answer assaulting her mind. He'd left nothing in her bathroom. She knew it in the same way she always knew where to look for artifacts on a dig site. She just knew. Neither his clothing nor any of his other belongings were anywhere in her house.

Good Lord. Had they climbed out of the taxi with him stark naked? If any of her neighbors were peering out the shades, they must have loved that. By now the taxi people probably had her name and address posted at every taxi company in town warning drivers to avoid her at all costs.

"Whatever," she mumbled, as much for herself as for him. There was no way anything she had would fit him. Not even her biggest sleep T's.

A *whoosh* sounded behind her, and she risked a peek to find he'd swept the blanket off her bed and was even now wrapping it around his large frame.

"What's the day, Abby?" Though he spoke to her, his attention had been completely captured by the touch-activated lamp at her bedside. The light repeatedly blinked on and off in reaction to his finger tapping against the metal base.

Surely they had similar lamps in Scotland.

"Friday." How long did he think he'd been here?

Once again his startling eyes rose to capture hers. "What year?"

Perfect. She should have known he was too good to be true. Proof that Drunk Abby wasn't any better at picking men than Regular Abby. Naked as a jaybird and asking what year it was; this guy was apparently as mental as he was attractive. Either that or he was suffering from the world's worst hangover ever.

She decided to keep it light. "No matter how your head feels, it's still the twenty-first century." Maybe that's what happened when you combined massive quantities of alcohol with jet lag.

"Twenty-first," he muttered, striding to the window and pushing aside the draperies. "Then I must find Mairi. She lives somewhere in this Colorado."

Yep, perfect. Abso-freaking-lutely perfect. Not only had she brought a strange, possibly deranged man home with her, on top of everything else, he turned out to belong to another woman.

If her life got any better this morning, she'd simply scream.

Nothing to be done now but to get this nightmare over and done with. She might as well swallow her pride and get on with it. "Does this Mairi of yours have a last name?" She could only pray her question hadn't sounded as snarky to him as it had to her.

"MacKiernan." He couldn't seem to tear his eyes away from the street in front of her house long enough to look at her when she spoke. "No!" he called as she started out of the bedroom. "She was to wed. Her name would be Navarro now."

As if a two-ton weight had been lifted off her chest, Abby breathed in a great gulp of air. He didn't belong to another woman after all.

Wait a minute . . .

"Mairi MacKiernan Navarro?" She'd taken a class in medieval studies with the woman a couple of years ago. Professor Navarro had known her subject matter so well, it had quickly become one of Abby's all-time favorite classes.

"Aye, that's my cousin's name."

His cousin. Humiliation on top of humiliation. Fate and Coincidence must have been drinking at the table next to her in the bar last night, just sitting around with nothing better to do than plot this bizarre fluke in her life. Now she'd get to call up a favorite ex-professor to confess she'd snatched the woman's cousin from the airport hotel and spent such a wild night with him that all his belongings, including the clothes off his back, were completely missing.

Abby pushed a tumble of hair out of her face and headed into the living room to look up Professor Navarro's phone number.

Come to think of it, she'd be best off to skip the whole wild-night thing.

Colin's mother had always told him there were no coincidences when the Fae were involved. That being the case, he could only thank the Fates for what little favor they'd shown him. Like allowing him to remember the name of the place where his cousin Mairi had told them she lived. Like remembering what century she inhabited.

Most of all, thank the Fates that this woman in whose bed he'd found himself had been able to contact Mairi on that tiny box of hers.

Little else might make sense to him at the moment, but the one thing he didn't doubt for an instant was that the Fae had sent him here, to this time, to this woman, for a reason.

Though as to what that reason might be, he hadn't a clue.

And as to the woman?

He scratched his stubbled chin, feeling the smile that spread over his face. He'd found little in life quite so pleasing to his senses as Abigail Porter. And for a fact, nothing had ever felt so good in his arms.

Too bad she seemed to have no better idea as to why he was here than he did. Less of an idea in truth, since she'd apparently managed to convince herself he'd gotten here in some normal way, brought by something she called a *taxi*.

"They should be here soon."

Unable to help himself, he stared at her as she stood in the doorway, a short, fluffy garment covering her, neck to knees, her hair wrapped in more of the same strange material.

"Feel free to help yourself to breakfast while you wait. There's cereal in the cupboard next to the stove and I just picked up milk at the store yesterday, so it's fresh. You're welcome to whatever else you find in the fridge."

Fridge? He shook his head in refusal, unwilling to admit he had no idea what she talking about. Mairi and Ramos would arrive soon, and they would help him make sense of this world. Until then he'd simply sit here on this amazingly well-padded chair and say as little as possible.

"You're sure you don't want coffee? Oh, duh!" She lifted the heel of her hand to the side of her head. "You're a Scot. Of course. Tea? Would you like tea?"

"Nothing, thank you, my lady."

With a shrug of her shoulders and a confused little frown, she disappeared back into the chamber she'd called her bedroom, closing the door behind her, leaving the scent of flowers wafting in her wake. The smell was new so it must have something to do with the *shower* she'd said she was going to take.

He sat quietly, allowing his eyes to explore all the mysterious wonders in this room, chief among them shelves and shelves of books.

"Okay." She sounded breathless when she at last returned to the room and hurried to the window, as if she'd been rushing.

Her hair, brown and shining, had been pulled back from her face on either side. While the bulk hung down her back in long curls, one soft tendril lay over her shoulder.

His hand fairly itched to feel those curls sliding through his fingers.

"I'm sure they'll be here any minute now." She tugged on the curl at her shoulder, winding it around her finger nervously. "So. Where in Scotland are you from? I'm actually going to get to go there this summer."

"My home is called Dun Ard." And if he closed his eyes, he could almost imagine her standing on the great staircase there.

"Dun Ard," she repeated. "Sounds lovely."

She'd crossed her arms protectively under her breasts, a stance she'd taken repeatedly over the course of their morning together, and fixed her gaze out the window.

"I'm sure they'll be here soon."

It was likely nerves that kept her repeating those words, as if meant to reassure them both, a suspicion confirmed when she began to chew at her bottom lip.

"Unless my directions were . . . wait. Maybe this is them now."

Colin rose and moved across the room to stand beside her. "It is."

Ramos stepped out of one of the strange carriages he'd seen earlier through the window and walked around to the other side to open a door, allowing Mairi to emerge. Both of them looked as if they'd hardly aged a day since Colin had seen them last, nearly eleven years ago.

"Okay. So, I guess you'll be on your way. You know, before you go, I don't quite . . . um . . . know how to ask this without sounding like a total idiot but . . ." Her eyes cut up to his and quickly away as her cheeks colored an attractive red. "I'm not sure what, if anything, happened between us last night. Would you by any chance remember if we . . . uh, you know, *did* anything?"

She worried that he'd dishonored her?

"No, we did nothing."

"Yeah, but . . . I mean, no offense, but if you didn't even remember my name, how can you be so sure you'd remember anything that happened between us?"

So innocent and lovely, her face all but flaming as she spoke. Without thought, he opened himself to her, allowing himself to see the outline of her soul blazing around her.

Golden with ragged edges.

Lifting a hand to her neck, he urged her to look up at him before he responded. "I can assure you I would no have forgotten something as rare as coupling with a woman like you. To my great regret, it dinna happen. You may believe me, lass."

He lowered his lips to hers, surprising himself as much as it might have surprised her. And yet it was as if there was no way to avoid it. Not even what he'd seen in that glimpse of her aura could stop him. He simply had no choice.

Even more surprising was her response. It was as if she melted into him, parting her lips when his tongue demanded entry. She tasted sweet, like honey and mint, and he had to force himself to break the kiss and step away.

"My thanks for yer kind hospitality, Abigail Porter, and for the loan of yer bed cover."

Backing away from her, he opened the door and stepped outside to meet his cousins as they approached.

"Colin!" Mairi hurried forward and threw her arms around his neck. "Good Lord, what are you wearing? How did you get here? I want to hear everything."

Ramos clapped a hand on his shoulder before the two of them hurried him off toward their odd transport.

Once seated inside, Colin looked back toward the dwelling to see Abigail standing in the open door, her fingers pressed to her lips.

He resisted the urge to lift his hand in farewell or to call out to her. It was not his right to do so. It was clear from the golden color he'd seen in her aura that she'd already met her Soulmate. Met, though they'd not yet joined. The ragged edges of her aura confirmed that.

And yet, in spite of this knowledge, he felt inexplicably drawn to her. Perhaps it was because whatever reason the Fae had for ripping him from his own time had something to do with her. At this moment, he simply had no clue as to what that reason might be.

One thing he was sure of, though. He knew in his bones that he would see her again. He would learn the reason for his being here and he would see Abigail Porter again.

Selfishly, foolishly, he hoped her aura's edges would still be ragged when next he laid eyes on her.

Four

The past fortnight had been the longest of his life.

Colin stared out the window of the speeding automobile, watching the unfamiliar scenery whip by.

"If there's any who can figure out a way for us to get you home, Pol is definitely the one." Mairi reached back from her spot in the front passenger seat to pat his knee. "Try no to worry yerself so, Cousin."

All that was important to him hung in the balance and his only hope was Pol? How could he not worry? Considering his inability to return to his own time, worry was all that was left to him. This Faerie ancestor they were to meet at the home of Mairi's brother today was his last chance; this same Faerie ancestor who'd ignored him each and every time he'd gone to the Glen to plead for the ancient Prince's assistance.

The lives of Alasdair Maxwell and Simeon MacDowell,

the two men who had grown to be as much brothers as friends to him, would forever be on his head were he unable to return. Their lives and the lives of the four thousand men he'd left behind in that field at Methven.

Dead. So many of them would be dead.

Only days before as he'd tried to distract himself from his worries, he'd discovered the room his cousin called her research library, filled floor to ceiling with wondrous shelves of books, finer than any he'd seen in all his life. One tome in particular had caught his eye, a history of Scotland's Wars of Independence. Scanning the index, one name in particular had stood out: Methven. He'd hurriedly flipped the pages to read about the Battle of Methven, named for the place where he'd last seen his friends and fellow warriors. What he'd found there in those pages had shaken him to the depths of his soul, haunting his dreams.

"Without my return, they'll likely die. Sim and Dair both. I have to go back. I must warn them and alert the Bruce to move his men before they're slaughtered as they sleep."

"That's something you canna do, Colin." Mairi's eyes brimmed with pity. "Even if Pol is able to send you back, you must not go to yer king with what you've learned. Believe me, I, of all people, understand how you feel. But you canna change what's to happen. Yer no to ever tamper with the flow of what's been. It's Faerie law."

So she'd explained when she'd found him reading through that *history* book of hers.

"To hell with yer Faerie laws, Cousin. I've no a care for the Fae. They've done naught but make life difficult for all our kin. They've brought naught but misery as far as I can see, so I've no care for their foolish laws."

"It's not just about a Faerie law," Ramos interrupted, his eyes fixed forward as he slowed the vehicle to a stop in front of a large house. "It's about the reason for that law. You've no idea what adversity could result from your actions. Even the most well-intentioned change could have disastrous consequences down through the generations."

Mairi nodded her agreement. "An all too real concern. But even more important, Cousin, you've no the right to tinker with what has already happened. It's no yer history to be changing. History belongs to the world of Man."

It would do no good to argue with his stubborn cousin. They'd been through this before when she'd slipped that amazing book from his hands and tucked it back into its place on the shelf.

Instead, he unfolded himself from the backseat of their car and straightened. Ahead of him, standing in the doorway, his cousin Connor waved. Though he'd heard stories of Connor from his mother for as long as he could remember, he'd first met the man only last week when Connor's wife and daughter had attempted to assist Mairi in sending him home.

Attempted being the key word.

"He's waiting." Connor spoke over his shoulder as he led them down the hall and through an archway.

The pain hit before Colin had both feet in the room. An all-encompassing, punch-to-the-gut, take-your-breath-away pain that doubled him over.

"Colin?"

Mairi rushed to his side but he waved her away, stumbling blindly to take a seat.

"I'm fine."

He'd be fine in a few moments, anyway. It was his own fault. He'd been so wrapped up in his own selfish troubles, had grown so comfortable in the presence of his cousin and her Soulmate, he'd completely forgotten his need to erect the barriers he normally used to shield himself from the world.

It was the intense pain of a broken Soul Pairing that assaulted him now. Someone in this room had known life with their true Soulmate. Had bonded with that person and then had them torn away before their allotted time.

Even as Colin hastily erected the internal barriers he'd developed against such feelings, he raised his eyes to scan the room for the source of such pain.

The hunt was short. Even though only one person in the room was unknown to Colin, it would have been no challenge to find the person he sought.

The man sat in a large chair, his back straight, his expression shielded. But Colin's second vision saw more than what was on display. Pain emanated from the man in shards of blazing red light, the shredded edges of his soul raw and pulsing.

Pol, High Prince of the Fae and Colin's own ancestor.

Colin shuddered as he met Pol's piercing emerald gaze, his mind scrambling to shut out the vision as well as the pain surrounding his Faerie ancestor.

He knew the legend, the story of Pol's having been forced to leave his one true love. He'd heard how Pol had watched helplessly from his side of the curtain separating the World of Man from the Fae as his love had been rejected by her family and had slowly withered away.

But knowing the legend and seeing the man were two completely different things. What he'd just seen, what he'd felt, explained so much. He understood now why Pol hadn't bothered to respond to his blustering demands for answers when he'd visited the glen.

Considering how Pol suffered, it was a wonder the prince could function at all.

"It has lessened over time."

Colin had no doubt Pol spoke directly to him.

"It's quite disconcerting, you know," the prince continued. "I've rarely encountered any with the gift of Soul Vision."

"Gift?" Colin shook his head. "Curse is more like it. Courtesy of the Faerie Queen herself. Her own particular way of teaching me to respect my elders."

A bitter lesson forced on a headstrong, impetuous youth. A lesson, in truth, he might never have learned any other way.

Pol tipped his head and, for a moment, his eyes glazed over as if he were lost in some ancient memory. Then he blinked rapidly, turning his clear gaze to Mairi, picking up the thread of an earlier conversation as if no interruption had occurred.

"Cate tells me the Magic refused to heed your call no matter what you tried."

Mairi nodded. "Exactly as I described when I called you, Grandfather. Cate and I tried everything we could think of, even including Rosie's help, all to absolutely no avail."

"How did he come to be here?" Pol continued the annoying course of speaking to others about Colin as if he weren't sitting there within reaching distance.

"We don't have an answer to that," Ramos responded, taking a seat next to his wife on the sofa. "Though it's quite a coincidence he ended up with someone who actually knew Mairi, a former student of hers."

Colin sat back in his chair, folding his arms. *Fae.* He might as well have stayed in Mairi's library for all the good he was doing here. It certainly didn't feel as if they needed him at all for this conversation.

"When it comes to the Magic, there is no such thing as coincidence." Pol shook his head. "You've investigated the woman? The one who found him?"

The woman? Colin looked up, scanning the faces around him. They were speaking of Abby.

"Aye." Connor nodded from his spot by the doorway. "There's no much to tell. Seems a decent enough lass. Working and going to school. Coryell assigned surveillance to her right away."

Surveillance? Someone spied on his Abby? He struggled to tamp down the anger this knowledge spurred. It wasn't as if she was actually *his* Abby. He knew that. Still, she was more than just some random stranger into whose home he had fallen. Of that he had no doubt.

If not, why had she haunted his dreams from the day he'd first encountered her? Even after learning about the Battle of Methven, in his nightmares filled with screams of the dying men he'd left behind, always she was there, a presence at his side, her hand reaching for his. One sweet, gentle touch to his fevered skin and no matter how hideous the scene before him, he found the strength to move beyond it all.

In spite of dreams, he understood that she didn't belong to him and that he likely had no right to the anger he felt welling in his chest on her behalf, but if not him, who?

"Who is this Coryell?" Colin demanded, unable to leash his tongue any longer. "And by what right does he act as watchman over Abby?"

"No a *who*," Connor explained. "Coryell Enterprises. It's the company we work with, owned by Cate's family. We've called on their services to help us determine how Miss Porter fits into all of this."

Regardless of their intent, the idea of strangers watching Abby's every move didn't set well at all with Colin. "Leave her be. She's nothing to do with any of this."

"She's everything to do with this," Pol corrected, turning his attention back to Colin at last. "We simply don't know how or why. At least not yet."

"Ridiculous," Colin grumbled, leaning forward in his seat. "Yer saying she's the key to my returning to my own time? What? You think her a witch? You believe she magicked me here with her evil powers? No. It was Faerie Magic what brought me here. I ken enough about the way it feels to say that much for a fact."

Abby was naught but an innocent victim who had nothing to do with this. She'd been more confused than he had by his appearance in her life that morning. Her reaction had been too honest to be an act. There was no way she was responsible for his being ripped from his own time and deposited into this one. He simply couldn't accept that. Wouldn't accept it.

"Of course it was Faerie Magic," Pol agreed. "But the Magic does nothing without purpose. Granted, it is the Magic's own purpose, but never doubt for a moment, purpose it is. It brought you to this time for a reason and it dropped you into that woman's home for a reason. Until we can determine what that reason is, you'll remain here. Until you fulfill the Magic's purpose for you, you'll not be allowed to return to your own time. The Porter woman is the key to what's happened to you."

For the second time today, Colin felt as if the breath had been knocked from his lungs.

"You speak of the Magic as if it's a living, thinking creature."

Pol steepled his fingers in front of him, obviously taking his time to carefully consider his words. "In a way, my son, that's exactly what it is. Not a creature perhaps, not a thing, but a living entity nonetheless. Magic is the life force of Wyddecol, flowing from the Earth Mother herself."

"And from personal experience, Colin, I can assure you the Magic does not bend to our will." Ramos clasped his wife's hand between his own two. "We bend to the will of the Magic. No matter how well we might think we understand a thing, no matter how we might struggle to reach our own goals, once invoked, the Magic will have its way."

As if he, of all people, needed to be told that little fact. He'd experienced firsthand the *will* of Faerie Magic for ten long years, ever since that day when as a brash youth he'd offended the Faerie Queen.

But this? This was a thousand times worse.

"Then what shall I do? You say I canna force the Magic to my own will, but how am I to stay here? I dinna belong in this place. I ken nothing of the ways of this time. I'm but a simple warrior." A warrior with no hope. A warrior whose comrades had been left behind to fight and die without him.

Silence greeted his question, until at last Pol spoke up. "Come home with me, my son. Home to Wyddecol. Our generals always have use for a good warrior. We'll teach you the ways and the dangers of this time even as we train you to combat them."

"And while yer learning those things, we'll search for the reason yer here and how Abigail is connected to it." Mairi reached across the empty space between them, placing her hand over his. "We won't give up until we find out something for you, Colin. You have my word on it."

What choice did he have?

"So be it."

Colin agreed to their proposal, leaving those around him to work out the details. He'd go to the Faerie homeworld. He'd learn whatever they asked of him, do whatever was necessary to make it possible for him to return to his own time.

Most especially, he'd learn if it was at all possible that Abby could be connected with his being here. And if it turned out these people were all correct in their accusation of Abby's involvement? Then he'd find Abigail Porter and demand to go home.

For now, though, he simply needed to see her again.

Five

⌐◦⌐

"Just you dinna forget that all this is yer idea."

As if his harpy cousin would let him forget. Colin unfolded himself from the passenger seat of Mairi's automobile, quietly making his way around to her side of the vehicle.

"Dinna fash yer bonny head, Cousin. Yer husband will never have cause to ken what we've done this night. And if he does, I'd no allow you to take the blame for it. Just you sit tight until I return."

"Yeah, well, just you remember to own up to it if he does find out," she grumbled behind him. "And hurry up. It's cold out here."

He didn't bother to respond now any more than he had the other twenty times she'd muttered the same on their late-night journey to this quiet location. A *neighborhood*, Mairi had called it.

Abby's neighborhood.

Keeping to the shadows was no problem on a moonless night such as this. Nor was the light snow that had started to fall a short time ago. Distinguishing between the seemingly endless number of buildings was another matter. It was all so very different from what he was used to, the homes of the masses so very much larger. So very much nicer than those of his time.

Life had certainly changed in the past seven hundred years.

Rounding the corner, he spotted Abby's home immediately, the tidy house framed by two large trees in the front, light streaming from the large windows.

Though he'd debated what he'd do when he reached this spot, he had no better idea now than when he'd first approached Mairi with his request to come here. He knew now only what he'd known then, that he felt compelled to see Abby one last time before he traveled to Wyddecol.

He hesitated there in the shadows, reluctant, now that he'd arrived, to make his way up to her door. He might not know what he wanted from this visit, but he did know that whatever it was, it concerned only him and Abigail.

Somewhere out here in the dark at least one other lurked: the spy sent by Coryell to observe Abby's every move. And though the man might well be a craftsman at his work, Colin had no intention of allowing his visit to be observed and reported back to his cousin's employer.

That alone ruled out simply walking up to the front door and knocking.

Decision made, he backtracked past several houses

before crossing the street to locate the entrance to the alleyway behind. From here it would be easy enough to slip over the low fence surrounding her property and make his way to the door he'd seen leading out of her kitchen.

Approaching the back of her home, he quickly realized he'd need to shift his plans yet again. The door opened and he dropped to his knees, hugging close behind the bramble of leafless bushes that lined her yard.

Abby herself stepped out into the night, her figure in sharp relief against the light shining through the opening. She hovered around a massive wooden box that sat just outside her door, moving quickly from one corner to the next, leaving little flickering lights wavering in her wake.

Candles? It made no sense to him why she'd be needing the poor illumination of the wax pillars when she had access to that fine, bright light shining through her door.

All thoughts of candles fled a moment later, replaced with visions of witchery when she lifted the lid on the great box and clouds of smoke billowed out into the night. Short-lived visions, since her next move robbed him of his ability to think at all, leaving him grateful he was already on his knees.

The fluffy robe she wore opened and fell back, pooling at her feet as if in worship, just as he might have if he were at her side. Under the robe she wore nothing. Or, more accurately, next to nothing. Two brightly colored strips of cloth, hardly enough to cover her most intimate parts.

She paused, looking out over the yard before tilting her head to the side as if she listened for something. Apparently satisfied, she reached inside the door and, with the flip of a switch, the lights went out, leaving her barely visible as she climbed up what looked to be a small ladder before descending into the candle-ringed box.

Though the incident had lasted only seconds, the image was forever imprinted in his mind of Abby standing there, bereft of clothing, snow drifting down around her. It took no effort to imagine the icy flakes coming to rest on her soft skin, melting together to form droplets that would roll down the heated curves and valleys he'd witnessed only moments before.

He wiped a hand over his mouth and onto his chin, more undecided than ever as to how he should proceed. Surely this was some intimate ritual he had no right to interrupt and yet he needed more.

Slowly, he lowered his barriers, allowing the magic to flood his senses. He flinched, his breath catching in his chest as the pain of hundreds of souls cried out their need all around him. Meticulously, he filtered through them, blocking them in great swaths until all that was left was Abby.

Pure and golden, her aura surrounded her, its ragged edges revealing she'd not yet bonded with her Soulmate. The relief he felt was short-lived.

"What do you think yer doing?"

Mairi's hoarse whisper unnerved him. Intently focused on Abby's aura, he'd completely missed her approach.

"They've a name for this," she hissed over his shoulder and into his ear. "Peeping Tom is what they'd call you. And they'd arrest you for it and haul yer arse off to jail. And wouldn't we be in a fine mess then, trying to explain who you were and where you came from? Come on with you now."

Reluctantly, he allowed his cousin to lead him away, back down the alleyway and to her automobile, neither of them speaking again until they were seated and she'd started the engine.

"When you said you'd a need to see that woman again, I thought you meant you wanted to speak with her." There was no missing the accusation in his cousin's voice.

He'd thought so, too. Had, in fact, had every intention of doing just that. But he'd been wrong. As it turned out, he'd needed only to see her again, to simply reassure himself, after all the dreams, that she was real. Having seen her with his own eyes, he could leave for Wyddecol, satisfied that one day soon they would meet again.

Abby sipped from her glass before sinking down into the relaxing bubbles of the hot tub. This one feature more than any other had convinced her to come up with the extra cash to rent this place last year. Steamy wisps danced up to meet the falling snow, carrying her frustrations with them.

Maybe half an hour in here and a large glass of wine would relax her enough that she might actually get some sleep tonight. Peaceful sleep, uninterrupted by dreams. Or at the very least, uninterrupted by dreams of *him*.

The thought of her mysterious Highlander had her upending the goblet.

What was it about that man? As if it wasn't bad enough she'd dragged him home with her in the first place, now her subconscious tormented her with visions of him, serving him up in one dream after another, night after night. It had gotten so bad, in fact, she was beginning to expect him to actually show up again.

Expect or hope?

Hope was more like it. Just tonight she could have sworn she'd felt him somewhere nearby. Too bad her weird ability to find things didn't extend to people.

She lifted the glass to her lips again, only to realize she'd already emptied it.

"Damn."

Just as well. It was already late and she needed to be at the museum early in the morning to start work on organizing the new Celtic exhibit she hoped to have up and running before she left for her summer on the dig. With barely over three months left to prepare, she hadn't the time or the energy to waste on anything that wasn't absolutely essential.

The exhibit this month, meeting with the organizer of the dig next month, and then training her replacement— those were her priorities. She had a million things to do before she was ready to board that plane to Scotland.

A million things, none of which included wasting time on some schoolgirl crush, moping over a gorgeous Highlander who'd walked out of her life as quickly as he'd entered, all without so much as a backward glance.

The next three months couldn't be busy enough to suit her. The more hectic, the better. Because busy and hectic would surely push Colin MacAlister completely out of her thoughts.

Six

DENVER
MAY
PRESENT DAY

Now *this* was the way an evening with a potential Mr. Perfect should go. An elegant dinner in an exclusive dining establishment with a handsome, attentive man sitting across the table. A perfect evening with a perfect man. This was so much better than dragging some stranger home in a fit of drunken amnesia.

Not that this particular man was in the running for The One.

Abby set her crystal goblet back on the table without so much as a taste and smiled briefly at the perfectly handsome man in question before darting her gaze away and around the stylish restaurant. She found herself unable to meet his intense green stare for more than a second or two without the butterflies in her stomach gearing up for their Riverdance impression.

"Is the wine not to your liking?"

"No, it's lovely, Mr. Flynn, thank you." She hurriedly caught up her glass again and sipped, trying to back up her false claim with another smile.

Her new boss was likely paying through the nose for the bottle nestled in ice, if the waiter's reaction to his ordering it was any measure of cost. Certainly it wasn't Jonathan Flynn's fault that her tastes tended more toward bottled hops than grapes.

"Jonathan," he corrected with a smile. "No need for such formality between us, my dear."

"Jonathan," she murmured around another bitter sip.

Maybe he didn't see a need for any kind of formality, but Abby wasn't so sure.

From the long white limo that had arrived to pick her up tonight to the exquisite rose Jonathan had handed her when he'd introduced himself, the whole evening felt about as far from a work-related experience as she could imagine. It felt, in fact, much more like a first date than a meet-and-greet with her new boss.

An incredibly uncomfortable first date, at that.

"That's better. After all, we'll practically be living together in another month." He flashed a brilliant smile in her direction just as their appetizer arrived.

"Mushrooms stuffed with crabmeat, lightly sprinkled with aged Romano cheese," their waiter intoned, as if announcing that the president had just entered the room.

Wonderful. Two of Abby's least favorite foods on the face of the planet, paired for her dining pleasure. There wasn't enough aged Romano in the entire world to cover that up.

She picked at the food on her plate, washing each bite down with a tiny sip of the wine.

"I never miss an opportunity to visit this restaurant when I'm in Denver." Jonathan broke the silence that had filled the space between them. "The only thing better than this appetizer is the entrée I've arranged. I trust you're not displeased with my having ordered for both of us? I simply wanted to share my favorites with you."

"No, it's fine. Everything's lovely. Thank you." Very upscale. Very classy. Definitely an evening fit for the Perfect Date category if she'd ever seen one. Even though it wasn't a date.

"Good. I take it everything is in order for your departure next week?"

"Absolutely." This was a topic of discussion she'd have no trouble warming to. "I can hardly wait. I am so excited about the opportunity you've given me to be a part of this dig. It's like a dream come true. I'm really looking forward to meeting the rest of the group."

"I have no doubt you'll be a valuable part our team, Abigail. Ah! Here's our entrée."

The waiter returned, sweeping plates off a rolling cart and onto their table, once again announcing their food like an honored guest. "Kobe tenderloins on a bed of truffle-laced mashed potatoes, ringed with beluga caviar. Cooked to a perfect one hundred and twenty degrees, just as you requested, Mr. Flynn."

Abby forced a small smile as the plate came to rest in front of her. She might not be a gourmet herself, but she didn't need to be to know that the meat on that plate was what she'd consider raw. One cut confirmed her suspicion as bright red stained the potatoes under the steak.

Visions of the cereal she'd be having later tonight

danced in her head with appealing clarity as she forced down her first small bite.

"I wonder, Abigail, would you mind satisfying a point of curiosity for me?" Jonathan smiled again, reaching across the table to brush his fingers across the back of her hand, his touch soft and smooth against her skin.

"If I can." At least it would keep her from having to take another bite for a little while.

"One of the professors who submitted a letter of recommendation for you to join our team, a Dr. Oldham, indicated that you had an uncanny ability to find whatever you searched for. *Magical* was the word he used, if I remember correctly. Could you tell me more about that?"

Magical? Maybe so. That was what her dad had always said, too. All she knew was that when she searched for any object her mind just sort of connected with it, as if the item spoke to her. No way was she saying something as crazy as that out loud, though. Jonathan Flynn still had a week to cut her from the dig team and she wasn't taking any chances by making him think he might have chosen some sort of crazy woman for his project.

"Dr. Oldham exaggerated, I'm afraid. Yes, I did have an exceptionally high percentage of finds when I interned under him, but honestly, that was only because I worked very hard and I put in a lot of time. There's not much magic to that."

"As you say, perhaps not."

Jonathan's eyebrow rose and then that smile returned, an expression that sent a shiver up Abby's neck. Not a smile, she realized, but a mask of a smile, not once reaching his eyes. Silence reigned once again, stretching out as she toyed with her food, moving small bits around on her plate. Perhaps it was that uncomfortable lack of conversation between them that sent the frisson of heat dancing over her skin, setting all the hair on her arms to stand on end.

That or guilt over not eating what had to be an amazingly expensive dinner. Even now she fought an intense urge to take another bite, as if her mind tried to force her into doing something her mouth definitely did not want.

She laid her fork across her plate and grasped her water glass, surprised to see how her hand trembled in response to what had to be nothing more than nerves.

"Would you be terribly disappointed if we skipped dessert?"

Abby jerked her eyes from her hand to meet Jonathan's gaze at his question.

"Not at all." At the rate this meal was going, she had little desire to see what the officious waiter might deliver to their table next.

"My schedule is rather more hectic for this visit than I would have liked. If it's acceptable to you, I'll have my driver see you home."

"Oh, absolutely. Of course." The guy was a zillionaire or something. It only made sense he had more business in town than just having dinner with her. "I appreciate your making time for us to meet."

"I wouldn't have missed it, Abigail." Their server appeared at the table, check in hand, and waited as Jonathan signed the slip. "Let me walk you out to the car."

The trip from their table outside to the waiting limo was a blur. Abby's only real awareness was of the sensation of Jonathan's hand against her lower back, the gesture one of familiarity, almost possessive in nature.

As the driver hurried to open the door, Jonathan grasped her fingers and lifted her hand to his lips, flipping her palm up at the last second.

Abby fought the urge to pull away as his lips grazed over her wrist, lingering for what felt like the longest second of her life.

"We have many more dinners in our future, Abigail. Of that you can be sure."

Forcing her mouth into a smile, she ducked inside the limo and scooted back in the seat, feeling a modicum of relief only when the vehicle pulled away from the curb.

She wiped a hand over her forehead and laid her head back against the soft leather. Maybe she was coming down with something. That might explain the bizarre way she'd felt back there in the restaurant.

Here she'd had the perfect evening. An evening women the world over would kill for. Chauffeured around in a limousine, wined and dined at maybe the most exclusive place in town, accompanied by an exceptionally attentive and handsome man; what more could she ask for?

As if in answer to her question a picture formed immediately in her mind. Auburn hair, not blond. Blue eyes instead of green. A rolling Scot's brogue instead of a cultured British tongue.

It seemed that not even a Perfect Evening with a Perfect Man could drive that damned Highlander from her thoughts.

* * *

Flynn O'Dannan raked his bottom teeth over his tingling lips as he stepped back from the curb, watching the limo disappear into traffic. It was as though he could still feel the steady flow of blood through the delicate skin of Abigail's wrist.

He brushed back a lock of hair from his forehead, smoothed one hand over his chest, and turned to reenter the restaurant, heading straight to the bar this time.

The Bloodlust gripped him like an addiction. An addiction he fully intended never to indulge in again.

"Cognac," he demanded as he slipped onto the high padded stool.

He'd spent the last three years carefully planning, setting up the intricate web necessary for him to assume the identity of Jonathan Flynn, to put together this excavation. Finding the likely candidates, locating an abandoned stone circle, obtaining the proper papers and permission; all of it had cost him a small fortune.

Money accumulated over several lifetimes. Money well spent.

Of the women he'd chosen to be part of this so-called archaeological expedition, Abigail Porter seemed the best candidate on which to concentrate his time. Her actions tonight demonstrated that she would be pliable and easy to manipulate through her emotions. Though she had resisted his best attempt to place a Compulsion on her to eat the foods he knew from his background investigations she least liked, that meant little.

Two of the others had failed that step. They wouldn't be joining his team in Scotland next week.

Unfortunately, her resistance wasn't proof in itself. There were a few strong-willed Mortals who had the ability to resist, though they were rare.

Just a taste. Her blood can't deceive.

No! He pounded back the useless alcohol, enjoying the burn in his throat. Signaling the bartender for another, he slammed the glass to the bar with shaking hands. What he wouldn't give for a draught of Faerie Nectar.

No. Control returning, he denied the Bloodlust more calmly now, knowing all too well the effects of tasting blood. Indeed, through the blood it would be impossible to hide any trace of Faerie heritage from him. The sweet tang of Magic would pulse through his veins even as it flowed through hers.

Giving in to the craving would provide the knowledge he sought, but there would be a price to pay. A heavy price. Ingesting blood resulted in the loss of his invincibility. The loss of control. And as desperately as he desired the exotic caress of the Magic, he equally despised feeling the vulnerability of a mere Mortal. It was a trade he was unwilling to make. He was strong enough to fight the addiction's siren call. He wasn't a power-hungry monster like the masters he'd served all the years. His only desire was to go home.

Soon enough he would know for sure. If, as he suspected, Abigail was a Faerie descendant, she'd locate the Portal he sought and he'd be well on his way back home. Back to Wyddecol, the home of the Faerie, where the Magic would flow through him for the rest of his days without any negative consequences.

He was a patient man. After waiting all these centuries, what did a few more weeks matter?

Seven

Terror slithered up and around Abby, spreading and tightening until it covered her like a second skin. It seeped deep inside her body, oozing in a foul black sludge as it merged with her bloodstream, polluting her river of life.

Horror tingled through her, holding her captive as she fought for her next breath until, at last, she forced herself to break free. To run.

Harder and harder she drove herself, one heavy footfall after the other, pounding down onto the ground she covered. The sound hammered against her ears before echoing away, lost in the endless black emptiness through which she traveled.

The terror was close now. Gaining on her. So close she could feel its icy fingers graze her shoulder, feel its fetid breath waft across her cheek.

"No!" she screamed, pumping her arms to force herself to run faster through the disorienting black void.

Running away.

Running toward that distant patch of light. Toward her haven of safety.

Toward him.

She could see him in the distance, the mysterious Highlander who haunted her dreams. Dreams that had turned to nightmares of late.

Even the realization she dreamed did nothing to lessen the grip of the hideous terror.

Forward she pushed, her chest burning with her effort as she swallowed great gulps of air. Forward, on toward the light. On toward safety. On toward him.

The instant her foot touched the circle of light, relief flooded her body, leaving her weak, drained, as if she'd given all she had to reach this spot.

She pitched forward, falling, falling endlessly into the bright nothingness.

And then she was in his arms.

Strong arms lifted her, enfolded her, drew her against the chest made of steel.

His lips, warm and gentle, grazed over hers, stealing her breath away.

"We must leave this place, Abby."

No. She struggled to refuse him, not remembering why it was so important to her to refuse. She didn't want him to go. She wanted . . .

Wait! He'd spoken?

Abby's eyes flew open, the rolling brogue of Colin's speech still rumbling in her ears as if she'd actually heard the words.

Though she'd dreamed of the man almost every night

for the past four months since she'd met him, this was the first time he'd uttered a single word in her dreams.

"I'm turning into a total freakazoid."

She spoke the words aloud as she pushed up to one elbow and swung her legs over the side of her small bed. Something had to give and pretty darn soon, too. Dreaming about this guy every single night was making her crazy. What she'd originally thought was some simple infatuation had lingered until she'd begun to worry that it was morphing into obsession.

How was she supposed to concentrate on her work at the dig site if she couldn't get more than two or three hours' sleep without that man running around inside her head? This opportunity was way too important for her to blow it over some guy she'd met only once in her life.

Not even the soothing sound of rain pattering against the window would lull her back to sleep now. She glanced over to the clock, counting the hours backward on her fingers to determine the time difference before she grabbed up the phone. It might be five in the morning here in Scotland, but in Los Angeles, it was barely even bedtime.

"Hello?"

"It's getting worse." Without preamble, Abby launched into her tirade, sounding as frantic as she felt and not caring one little bit. If anyone could help her think this through, it would be Casey.

"Abby? Is that you? Damn, girl. Isn't it like, middle of the night or something over there?"

"Five a.m., not that it matters. I can't sleep. Every time I shut my eyes, he's there. I'm losing it, Casey. I'm even hearing his voice now."

Just over a month ago, she'd confessed to Casey all about the mysterious Scot she'd dragged home after their last Girls' Night Out in Denver. She'd told her about the dreams, too.

"Is he still in your bed? Still making love to you?"

"Not by the end of this one." She probably shouldn't have shared that, in the dreams, Colin was always in bed. Not that it took much effort for her to rationally explain that part away. It was likely only because the first time she'd ever seen him, he *had* been in her bed. What she couldn't rationally dismiss was that the bed and the room she saw in her dreams were definitely not hers. In fact, they looked like something straight out of a museum re-creation. "And, anyway, I told you, we don't ever actually *make love* in the dream, it's more like—"

"Oh, excuse me," Casey interrupted. "Wild foreplay, then. You and I both know where those dreams are leading, girl. If you ever finish one out, you *will* be making love, trust me."

Not at all true. She'd just gotten much closer to finishing one and she'd ended up in the mother of all nightmares.

"I'm telling you, it's that wish we made," Casey insisted. "I don't know how, but that has to be it. You ended up with a naked Mr. Perfect in your bed and the day I got home, Sam and I set the date for a Christmas wedding so you'd be back in time and then Lauren called just yesterday to say her doctor confirmed she's pregnant. I know it's crazy, Abby, but I'm convinced this guy is haunting your dreams because he's the one you've been waiting for your whole life. You wished for him, you got him, and then you let him slip through your fingers. Now you've got to go hunt him down, girl. There's no question about it. He's The One."

"No way," Abby muttered halfheartedly, all the while remembering how the lights had gone that crazy green color when they'd made their wishes that night. "Besides, I wouldn't even know where to begin to look for him."

Unless she contacted her ex-professor in Boulder, but there was no way she was going to humiliate herself like that again. It had been bad enough calling the woman up the last time to ask her to come get her cousin. Professor Navarro probably already thought she was some sleezy barfly psycho. What would she think if she got a second call? *Hey, remember me? The one who had your naked cousin in my house? Um . . . speaking of Colin, could you tell me where to find him?*

Not happening.

"Not a single idea where to look for him," she repeated insistently.

"Yes you do. Didn't you say he told you where he lived in Scotland? Think, girl! You're right there. I mean, the whole country probably isn't much bigger than Colorado. Hunt him down. Go see him. You have to do this, Abby. It's like fate or something. It's way bigger than you. Besides, you want to be able to sleep again, don't you?"

Abby caught herself nodding along as her friend spoke, knowing from the roiling in her stomach she'd already made her decision. Fool that she was, she was going to do it.

"Okay, fine. I'll Google him as soon as we get off the phone."

"Then we're off the phone now. You call me as soon as you meet up with him again, you hear? I want to know absolutely everything! Now, go."

"Bye, Casey. Thanks."

Her words echoed back from the dead line, her friend already having disconnected.

"All-righty, then," she attempted to reassure herself, crawling out of her bed and padding across the uneven floorboards to the old end table she used as a desk in this little room.

Not that she'd dream of complaining about her accommodations. She knew how lucky she was the dig organizers had found this wonderful old bed-and-breakfast so close to their dig site. Swan House fairly resonated with history. And having access to a wireless internet connection, even as unreliable as it sometimes was, was a rare and unexpected blessing.

"Dun Ard," she murmured, her fingers flying over the keys.

To her surprise, it popped up on the first page of entries. Not a town at all but instead, an ancient family holding turned into a rustic-looking hunting lodge. A quick MapQuest search informed her that the lodge was within a few hours' drive from here. With the rain, there would be no site work today and because of that, no reason she couldn't use one of the vans.

She didn't have a single excuse not to do this. None except her own cowardice, and that was the one excuse she simply wasn't willing to accept.

Less than an hour later, freshly showered and more determined than ever, Abby stepped into the hallway and headed down the stairs. She refused to allow herself to dwell on what would happen once she reached her destination, instead focusing on the journey itself.

Too much thought on what she'd do when she actually came face-to-face with the inhabitant of her dreams, and her determination might well evaporate before she even got started.

"Abigail!"

Her footsteps faltered as she recognized the voice of her benefactor, Jonathan Flynn, the man responsible for her great fortune in being chosen for a coveted spot on this dig.

"Where are you headed so early this morning, my dear? I thought the rain delay would have everyone sleeping late."

"Sightseeing. I thought rather than waste the day, I'd take in some of the countryside." The lie fell from her lips as easily as if it were truth.

"What a marvelous idea." Flynn's face creased in a smile as he approached. "I'll join you on your explorations, if you don't mind. I've been wanting to get out and about a bit."

"I'm sorry, Mr. Flynn. I'd really prefer to go alone. I've begun work on my initial findings report and I need some time to think through what we've found so far and what the implications are."

Abby hoped the lie would satisfy him because, truly, she didn't want to hurt his feelings. But considering the fact he'd made it obvious on more than one occasion that his interest in her wasn't entirely confined to the professional arena, somehow, confessing she was off to hunt for a man who haunted her dreams didn't seem a wise idea.

"Jonathan," he corrected, any real emotion masked by the false smile he so often wore. "We're far too close for such formality, Abigail. It would mean so much to me if you'd but use my given name. As I've asked you before."

"Jonathan," she murmured in response, a ripple of guilt troubling her conscience. Yes, he'd asked before. And, yes, she'd ignored the request, not wanting to lead him on.

"That's better. Here, then." He reached in his pocket and pulled out a set of keys. "Take my car. I'll feel better knowing you're driving it rather than one of those lumbering site vans."

"Thank you, Jonathan."

She reached for the keys, surprised when he captured her hand.

"My cellular phone is lying in the passenger seat, just in case you need anything. You have the number for Swan House with you?" He paused, not continuing until she nodded her affirmation. "Very well. Be careful, my Abigail. The roads are wet and narrow. I'd be quite distressed should any harm befall you." With that warning, he lifted her hand, brushing his lips against her wrist before letting go and walking away.

Abby let out a shaky breath and all but ran through the big front door and down to the car park. Once in the vehicle, she wiped the rain from her face, fastened her seat belt, and leaned her head back against the plush leather headrest.

Was this whole road trip a huge mistake?

With a last glance back toward the house, she started up the engine and pulled out onto the road. She hadn't seen Jonathan standing in the parlor window watching her, but she was sure he'd been there. It was as if she could feel his eyes following her.

Jonathan Flynn was a great guy, the kind of guy most women would give their eyeteeth to have show an interest in them. Perhaps it was only that his interest in her was *so* obvious—and the teasing she took from the others on the team as a result of it—that made her uncomfortable.

He certainly had been blessed with all the prerequisites to classify him as a perfect catch. He was wealthy, handsome, intelligent, and generous to a fault. She knew that she should be feeling lucky to have caught his eye.

Instead she simply felt uncomfortable.

Again she sighed, tightening her hold on the steering wheel.

More the fool, her. Here she was, driving away from perfect catch material, headed toward some mystery dream man she'd met only once. One who'd never bothered to try to see her again after spending that one night with her.

Which probably should tell her something important about her own mental state, not to mention what kind of guy this Colin MacAlister really was.

Abby chewed on the corner of her mouth, considering for a moment whether to turn the car around and head straight back to Swan House.

No. She had to do this. It was the only way to get Colin MacAlister out of her system. And without a doubt, she'd reached a point where getting him out of her system was the only way to save her sanity.

Eight

⟨⟩

"Will you be wanting yer tea here in the sitting room, Mr. Flynn?"

Flynn O'Dannan turned with a start toward the elderly hotel keeper, shaken by her use of his name. Of course. She thought it his surname. Not for the first time he silently acknowledged the foolishness of his having used any part of his real name in this charade.

"Yes, thank you. Over by the fire will be fine."

He turned his back on the woman, stroking his thumb and forefinger against his chin as he peered through the ruffled curtains to watch Abigail drive away.

Abigail. So trusting. So innocent. So absolutely desirable. The latter realization had come as a pleasant surprise over the last couple of weeks. Having her turn out to be the one he sought would certainly bring an unexpected bonus. But was she the one? Was she all Mortal or was it the Faerie blood rushing through her veins that called to him?

She's Faerie! Every one of his instincts screamed the accusation every time she came near. And though his instincts rarely let him down, he wanted proof before he made any drastic moves. Absolute, irrefutable proof.

But how?

Just a taste. Her blood can't deceive.

No! With a snort of disdain, he turned his back on the window to take a seat by the crackling fireplace. He would not allow the demon Bloodlust to lure him down that path again. He had more than enough poor choices haunting his past without adding another.

Joining the rebellion against the Earth Mother had been only his first mistake. His second, choosing to follow Reynard Servans, had been equally unwise.

As always when he allowed himself to dwell on the past, fear and regret curdled in his stomach as if it had been only yesterday.

His poor choices had resulted in his being exiled from his home world, banished forever to the Mortal Plain, his precious magic stripped from him.

Drawing on his inner discipline, Flynn loosened his grip on the arms of his chair and reached for the now cooled cup of tea.

That was all behind him now.

Once he'd faced the truth of his reality, he'd found the power to move forward. He wanted nothing so much as to go home to Wyddecol. Not to rule, but simply to live peacefully in the home of his ancestors, bathed in the glow of Faerie Magic.

Lo, but he missed the feel of the Magic coursing through his body!

Just a taste.

His grip on the cup tightened as he fought to ignore the ever-present demon.

There was a better way, though it required time and patience. A female descendant of the Fae could locate and open a portal to the Realm of Faerie. He needed only to find such a woman and convince her to help him. The woman he needed was Fae, but she was Mortal as well.

In Abigail Porter, he hoped to have found such a one as he sought.

Mortals were, for the most part, easily manipulated if you were clever and patient. Take the time to win a Mortal's heart and she'd do anything you asked of her. Winning Abigail's heart should be an easy enough task. In his experience, Mortals were vastly materialistic. He had only to shower her with her heart's desires to win her over, and that was something he could certainly do.

Once he was sure she was the one.

Too often he'd seen the results of mistaking some woman for what she was not. And as for him, he was through making mistakes.

Flynn reached into his pocket and pulled out a small black case. One glance inside assured him the GPS tracker in his cell phone was functioning properly, giving him an accurate record of wherever Abigail traveled on this little jaunt of hers. He'd worked far too hard to find her to carelessly allow her to slip away now.

Not that he actually thought she'd run away. Already he could feel her molding to his desires. Even on a day off, she chose to spend her time working on his project, to make it better, to please him.

Rising to his feet, he walked back to the window, staring off into the distance, thoughts of Abigail filling his mind. Filling his senses.

Just a taste.

Once again he rejected the lure of the Bloodlust. There was a better way. Win Abigail's heart, and she would do his bidding without question. A better way, and though it would take time, he had all the time in the world.

Nine

———⌒———

The rain had turned to a fine, light mist by the time Abby pulled into the car park at Dun Ard. Her stomach knotted into a tight little ball as her foot hit the crushed gravel and she fought the urge to turn around and run as she made her way down the walk and up the massive stone stairs.

This was it. In a matter of moments, she'd be face-to-face with the man she couldn't seem to escape. Though she'd played that meeting over and over in her mind as the miles had slipped past, now that she had arrived, she still had no idea what she'd say to him.

Hi, remember me? We slept together that one time. You kissed me good-bye and my lips tingled for a week. I've dreamed about you making love to me every single night since then.

Yeah. Probably not. If he didn't already think her a stalker, that little speech would push him over the edge.

At the top stair, her stomach flip-flopped again. What if he didn't remember her? What if he wasn't here? What if they'd never even heard of him?

A fine, prickly layer of perspiration broke out on her skin, and she dragged a hand over her forehead before opening the door and stepping inside.

"Good day, Miss. Welcome to Dun Ard." A smiling, ruddy-faced woman stood up from her seat behind a large antique desk, extending her hand in greeting. "I'm Margaret MacAlister. Are you looking for lodging?"

"No. I'm ... uh ..." Abby gulped in a breath, hoping to steady her shaking voice. "I'm actually looking for someone. Colin MacAlister. Is he here?"

The woman's smile disappeared, a suspicious frown wrinkling her brow as she clasped her hands at her waist, looking for all the world like the disapproving headmistress in an old English movie.

Oh, lord. That didn't look at all like the "I've-never-heard-of-the-man" face.

"And just what might you be wanting with my Colin?"

Her Colin?

A new suspicion hit Abby like a tidal wave, a suspicion that made her feel as if she might be sick all over the carpet in this lovely, ancient-looking lobby.

What if he was married? This woman did say her name was MacAlister.

"I ... uh ... he, that is, Colin ..." Abby's tongue felt remarkably as it had the time she'd visited the dentist and he'd had to give her Novocain twice to deaden her gums. "I met Colin a few months ago when he visited Denver. I only wanted to stop by and say hello."

Not true. She'd wanted much more than hello, though even to herself she couldn't say what, exactly.

Almost immediately Margaret's face brightened. "Well then, Miss, it's no my Colin yer wanting. He's no ever stepped foot in the States."

"I beg your pardon?" Oh, his feet had been in the States, all right. Not only had they been in the States, they'd been in her bed. This woman might not want to believe her husband had been there—hell, *she* didn't want to believe Colin had a wife!—but it was fact.

Clearly, she trod a fine line here. It might be best for everyone if she said nothing more. Just turned around and walked away. There was still a chance for her to save face before it was too late.

But, as if controlled by a force outside herself, the words slipped from her mouth. "He told me his home was Dun Ard."

"Did he now?" Margaret's smile broadened before she turned her head to call loudly over her shoulder, "Bella! Fetch Colin out here to the desk for me, please."

He was here! Somewhere back beyond that doorway where even now she could hear running footsteps.

The hard, tight little ball that had once been her stomach suddenly sprouted butterflies. Big, hairy-assed acrobatic butterflies, from the feel of it. All wearing steel-toed boots and marching in lockstep formation across her intestines.

The seconds dragged by in a fashion Abby would have denied was possible before now. Just as she'd decided she could stand it no longer, that she'd make some wild excuse and beat a hasty retreat, a small boy no more than eight or nine burst into the room. He ran straight to Margaret's side, stopping to frown up at the woman.

"What do you want of me, Mum? My show's on telly. I'm missing it," he complained.

"Mind yer manners, lad." With her hands on his shoulders, Margaret turned the boy around. "I'd like you to meet this nice lady who's come for a visit. This is my son, Colin, and this is . . . begging yer pardon, miss. Did you give me yer name?"

"Abby," she offered, almost forgetting herself in her surprise as the boy politely shook her hand. "Abigail Porter."

This was Colin MacAlister?

"Run along back to yer telly, Colin. Sorry to have taken you from yer show."

With a shy smile, the child took off running and disappeared through the doorway.

"Now, Miss Porter, do you still think it was my Colin you met?"

Abby could only shake her head, waiting for her brain and her tongue to catch up with one another. This was altogether just plain wrong.

He'd lied to her.

He'd come home with her, climbed his naked butt into her bed, and lied to her.

"I apologize for troubling you, Mrs. MacAlister. I was so sure that . . . but, obviously, I was mistaken and I'm sorry for taking up your time."

He'd lied. To her. God only knew who he really was.

Her face burned with embarrassment and anger. The pitying look on Margaret's face only made it worse.

"Dinna you worry yerself over yer mistake, lassie. MacAlister's a common enough name in these parts. Likely you misunderstood the gentleman as to the name of his home."

Yeah? No, not likely at all. He had lied to her. Plain, bold-faced lied.

Abby's breath caught as she made her way down the stone steps toward the spot where she'd left the car. The cold mist stung her face, helping her to concentrate on something other than the tears blurring her vision.

Now what? This had been her last hope for getting him out of her head. Now she'd never find him, and that could mean she'd be haunted by him for the rest of her life.

She climbed into the car, slammed the door shut, and leaned her head back against the leather headrest. "Liar!" She spat the condemnation into the empty car as if she confronted him.

Damn him! He'd had absolutely no reason to lie to her. It wasn't like she was going to turn into some psycho stalker who'd come looking for him.

She stuck the key into the ignition, biting back a bitter laugh as she realized that was exactly what she'd turned into. She'd traveled over four thousand miles to Scotland and spent the whole of today trying to hunt the man down.

No wonder he'd lied to her. A great-looking guy like that probably had women stalking him on at least two continents. And clearly she had turned into one of those stalkers.

"Thanks a whole hell of a lot, Casey."

No, that wasn't fair. This wasn't any more her friend's fault than it was her own. It was *his* fault.

Margaret had said that MacAlister was a common name here, so his telling her his name was *Colin MacAlister* could well be the Scottish equivalent of introducing yourself as John Smith, for all she knew. He must have thought himself pretty clever pulling that one on her.

Didn't that just serve her right for picking some stranger up in a bar? All things considered, she had absolutely no right to feel so horribly betrayed. After all, he was nothing more than that: a stranger.

And yet betrayed was exactly what she felt. Hurt, betrayed, lost, and gullible.

"And stupid," she muttered. That's really what she was. She certainly couldn't leave off her growing list how utterly, completely stupid she felt.

With a deep sigh, Abby put the car in drive, pausing before she moved forward to wait for the dark blue car idling across from her to pull out of his space. When the driver simply stared at her but made no effort to move his vehicle, she pulled forward.

"Men," she fumed aloud, casting an indignant look his direction. "That one's likely so busy trying to figure out a fake name he could give some poor woman, he's just sitting there like a lump on a log." Well, too bad for him. He'd have to follow her now. Hopefully, wherever that woman was, she'd be smarter than Abby had been. For her own part, she sure as heck wouldn't be fooled by that trick twice.

Abby nosed the car forward but slammed her foot on the brakes as one little detail slipped into her mind.

How could she have forgotten something so important?

Behind her, brakes squealed and gravel flew as the driver of the car she'd seen earlier slammed on his brakes to avoid rear-ending her.

Their eyes met briefly in the reflection of the rearview mirror and Abby mouthed a quick *sorry* before pulling forward again, her mood too lightened to allow her to dwell on feeling guilty for her little driving indiscretion.

Colin might have lied about his home, but he hadn't given her a fake name and she had proof.

She'd spoken to his cousin on the telephone that day to arrange to have him picked up from her house. She'd seen Mairi MacKiernan Navarro, a woman she knew personally, drive up in front of her house and take him away.

He might not be from Dun Ard, or at least not *this* Dun Ard, but that didn't mean she'd never be able to find him. All she had to do was call up her old professor and ask where her cousin was now.

Simple.

Of course, before she made that phone call, she'd have to find the nerve to do it, and that would be the tricky part.

Ten

Liar!"

From somewhere in the endless black void, the accusation flew at Colin, pummeling his body and his soul with its inherent anger.

"He lied to me."

Colin shivered as the plaintive whisper rolled over him. The pain in Abigail's voice hit him harder than the accusation alone ever could have. Like some vicious beastie, it clawed its way into his heart, leaving an empty, gaping hole in its path.

He awoke from his sleep and sat up on the narrow cot in his quarters, one hand clasped to the wound on his chest to hold back the flow of blood.

Only there was no blood. Indeed there was not even any wound. It had all been a dream.

"By the Fates," he muttered, dragging a hand over his sweat-slicked forehead. All hope of sleep forgotten, he slipped from his bed and crossed to a small window facing out over the Hall of the High Council's magnificent courtyard.

He'd never experienced a dream so real. Not even the others he'd had regularly of the woman in whose bed he'd landed when he'd been pulled from his own time.

And dream of Abigail he did. Almost nightly now. Exactly as he just had. Dreams of her melting in his embrace, her body warm and inviting under his eager hands.

At least that had been the flow of the dreams before tonight. Before Abby had disappeared into the black void and this entirely different experience had overtaken him.

He scrubbed a hand over his face, trying to wipe away the lingering emotion brought on by her plaintive cry.

Why? Why would he dream of her being so distraught with him? Granted, he'd not told her everything, but how could he possibly have told her more? At the time, he hadn't understood what had happened himself. He still didn't completely understand, if the truth be known.

But he'd never lied to her. He would never have willingly caused her such pain as he'd heard in her voice.

Grabbing up his plaid, he wrapped it around himself and stepped out into the indigo-hued night. The dream had been more than a dream, of that he had no doubt. It had felt—still felt!—too hauntingly real.

The time had come.

With purposeful steps, he made his way across the

courtyard and slipped through a small side door leading into the Great Hall itself.

He crossed the eerily empty enormous hall to take the great marble staircase two steps at a time. Without conscious thought, he willed himself to move silently, stealthily, as he'd been trained to do here in this place. Not until he'd wound his way through the labyrinth of corridors to stand in front of a massive carved wooden door did he stop to consider the man behind the door.

Like as not, Pol would be sleeping.

Too bad for him. Colin needed answers and he needed them now.

He fortified his defenses in preparation for the mental onslaught his ancestor's shattered Soul always presented and then pounded his fist against the wood, surprised when the door swung open at his first touch.

"Come in, my son. Join us."

Across the room, Pol sat facing him, with Dallyn, High General of the Faerie Realm, standing at his side.

"I must speak to you, your highness." If there were answers to be had, these were the men who would have them.

Pol rose to his feet, the golden robe he wore flowing around him like liquid sunlight as he gestured to a chair next to him. "Grandfather," he corrected on a sigh. "As my descendant, Colin, you're entitled to address me as grandfather."

"As long as no one else is around," Dallyn murmured.

Colin chose to ignore them both in favor of dealing with the matter at hand.

"You asked that I come to you if the dreams changed." Though how his Faerie ancestor had known he was having dreams of any sort was another of those mysteries beyond his understanding. "They've changed."

Pol nodded knowingly and sat back down, pausing to hold Colin's gaze for a long moment before he spoke. "Describe the change in the dreams to me."

Describe the change?

The new dream tore at his gut like something reaching deep inside him, stripping away little pieces of his very being. But disclosing the full extent of what he felt? Absolutely not. That would be worse than acknowledging the pain of training, or the fear before battle. A warrior did not admit such weakness.

"I feel Abby's presence more . . ." He paused, struggling to find an honorable description. "More vividly. She is upset. Upset with me." An adequate compromise of terms. "I believe I should go to her."

"No," Pol rejected, turning his attention to his general. "The Coryells still have her under surveillance for us, do they not? Have we learned any more of this man who is responsible for her presence in Scotland?"

Colin felt as if the air had been sucked from the room. It was the first he'd heard of Abby's traveling to Scotland and definitely the first he'd heard of any man. He focused his attention on Dallyn, waiting to hear more.

"She is still being watched, Highness, but we've yet to learn much more about Jonathan Flynn. What records they've found seem to indicate a wealthy, eccentric recluse."

"Yet not only is he behind the expedition for which he personally chose Miss Porter, he's also participating, accompanying those he has hired. An eccentric recluse, out in the open, freely associating with the masses." Pol paused, his eyes fixed on the ceiling. "Nuadian, do you suppose?"

"Unknown," Dallyn replied. "But the layers of secrecy around him make it a distinct possibility. Is it time, do you think, that we send in a Guardian? To verify and neutralize?"

"Send me." Colin could not contain himself any longer. He was a Guardian. He wore their mark on his arm as proof. Besides, the idea of some stranger spying on Abby didn't set well at all. Nor did the idea that some man traveled with her. Especially some man that might well be a Nuadian. His education in the evils of the Nuadian Fae had been most thorough.

"No." Pol turned his gaze back to Colin. "You're not ready. Your training is not yet complete."

"No ready? I'm a warrior. I was born to it. It flows in my very blood. I've learned the way to recognize yer Nuadians. I ken the danger they represent." He had, after all, faced them as a young man when they'd tried to take his sister. "What more is there?"

"You've barely scratched the surface of how to blend into this time." Dallyn shook his head as if he were saying something he considered obvious. "You'll need to learn much more to enable you to fit comfortably into your new life."

Pol rose from his seat and in two steps reached Colin's side, placing a hand on his shoulder. "Patience, my son. You will leave here when the time is right. For now"—he turned his gaze toward his High General— "let us hold off on sending a Guardian. Give Coryell Enterprises time to learn what they can."

Colin ground his teeth to refrain from making comment, managing enough self-control for a brief nod of his head before he made his way from Pol's quarters.

They dared counsel him on patience? On fitting into his new life?

Patience and a new life were luxuries he could ill afford. Though he'd yet to read the whole of the wondrous book he'd taken from his cousin's library, he had made his way through enough of it to know that even should his friends survive the carnage of Methven, they'd have precious little time to recover before they'd be set upon at Dalrigh. Their lives depended upon his return and here he sat in Wyddecol, spending his days in practice of swords and playing at being a school lad with daily lessons.

Patience! He'd bide his time well enough, but for his own purposes, not theirs. Certainly not for learning to fit into a new life in this time. He didn't belong here and he had no intention of remaining. His plan was to go home. To his own time. Home, where he was needed. And nothing—*nothing!*—would keep him from that goal.

Not even the wounded voice of Abigail Porter, still echoing in his head.

"Do we err in pushing him too hard?" Dallyn at last moved to take a seat, perching on the edge of the chair as if even in sitting he somehow managed to remain at attention.

"No, my friend. We do what is necessary." Pol walked to the window overlooking the courtyard. "He is a strong one. Strong enough to face what is already inside him. The blood of the Royal line of the House of Fae courses through his body."

"Tempered by the blood of Mortals," the High General reminded.

Pol lifted a hand, waving away Dallyn's suggestion. It was too late to worry about that now. His own mother had seen to that when she'd chosen to enchant Colin, drawing out his Fae powers and enhancing them.

It had been bittersweet knowledge to learn the old queen yet lived. He'd known only that she'd been exiled somewhere within Wyddecol after the Great War when the Earth Mother had seized power. That she'd retained the power to move between the worlds had come as a complete surprise. Like as not, the High Council and the Earth Mother would find it equally surprising.

If they knew.

As surprising as they'd likely find Colin's powers to be.

If they knew.

But they'd not learn any of it from him. He didn't serve them. The Royal family had always served Wyddecol. They'd served the Magic.

The Magic itself had chosen Colin and nothing in their power could change that. It fell to him now to do his best to prepare the young man for whatever lay ahead.

Behind him, Dallyn cleared his throat. "The Porter woman, she's a Fae descendant, do you think?"

Pol nodded his agreement. It seemed the only reasonable possibility.

"That would increase the possibility that the man with her is Nuadian. She's likely in great danger," Dallyn murmured.

"Likely," Pol agreed. "And it's every bit as likely that Miss Porter is Colin's Soulmate."

"If you believe that, why didn't you tell him?" Dallyn had hesitated before the question, obviously working to reason out the answer on his own.

"Precisely because I believe that, my friend. The Magic grows stronger and with great speed. It grows tired of waiting for us to reunite the broken Soul Pairings. Until we know what it has planned next, we have no choice but to prepare as best we can." No choice but to prepare those who had been chosen as best they could be prepared.

Below him, Colin crossed the courtyard, his figure all but blending in with the shadows.

"When Colin is sent to the RoundHouse on the morrow, I want only waters from the Fountain of Souls to be used for his training. No dilution."

"Begging your pardon, Highness. Do you think that wise?"

"Wise or not, I believe we've diverted this young man from the course set by the Magic for as long as we're able." Pol nodded to himself, continuing to watch the subject of their conversation disappear into the door of his quarters. "Make it so, General."

Wisdom was no longer a consideration; only expediency mattered now. Colin would be leaving them soon, he could feel it. He wanted his young descendant fully prepared when he did go.

"Cautiously, of course," he added, turning to meet his general's gaze.

"Of course," Dallyn replied.

He hesitated to voice his next request. Still, it was necessary. "Someone must go to the Temple of Danu to invoke the spirit of the Earth Mother. Perhaps General Darnee?"

"No." Dallyn's lips tightened, his face devoid of all emotion. "I'll go. No one else should be involved. In case."

"In case," Pol agreed.

"And now"—Dallyn rose to his feet—"if you'll excuse me, Highness, I've arrangements to make." With a formal nod of respect, his general crossed to the door and let himself out.

Arrangements to make.

Pol smiled to himself, turning back to stare out over the empty courtyard. A most delicate way of putting it.

Though use of the Fountain's waters was forbidden by the High Council and the Earth Mother herself, Pol had no doubt Dallyn would find a way.

His only doubt, in fact, was what effect those waters would have on Colin.

Eleven

*I*f only the sun would chase away the dark, heavy clouds, it might yet turn out to be a decent day.

Abby shivered and pulled the zipper on her jacket all the way up to her chin, huddling into herself against the early morning chill. The rains had finally stopped early yesterday, but the clouds hanging low over the dig site looked ready to burst open at any moment. Summer in the Highlands.

"Okay, people. Gather round so we can go over today's plan of action." Mackenzie Lawrence tapped her pencil impatiently against the clipboard she held. "Come *on*, people! Mr. Flynn doesn't have all day for us to waste."

Puh-leeze. Abby forced herself to stare at her own feet so that no one would see her eyes rolling in irritation. As if every single person out here this morning wasn't every bit as committed to this project as that annoying little harpy.

Like Abby, most of the others were so excited and grateful to have been chosen to participate in this dig, they'd all minded their manners and deferred to Jonathan Flynn's every word.

Not Mackenzie. She'd quickly appointed herself their benefactor's right-hand woman and clearly considered herself head and shoulders above the rest of them because she'd been working as some professor's assistant for the past year.

Big frickin' whoop.

Pretty pushy, in Abby's estimation. Especially for an undergrad. Abby herself had no illusions that Ms. Lawrence knew more than any of the others. She didn't. It was only that none of them—including Abby— worked so hard at trying to be in charge.

Or at kissing Jonathan Flynn's butt.

Besides, they'd been over this same little speech so many times, Abby could almost give it herself. After all these weeks, she seriously doubted that the item Jonathan sought was even here to be found.

Her head snapped up when she realized Jonathan had already launched into his description, only to find his eyes fixed on her as if he spoke directly to her.

"I have faith in your ability to locate the stone marker we seek, even though it likely will be in small pieces since the site has been so thoroughly damaged by time."

Damaged by time? Abby was willing to bet a full month's salary there was more than time that had gone into the deteriorated state of this particular site. With an undergraduate degree in archaeology, she'd seen thousands of photos from more than her share of ancient sites located all over the world. This one looked like none of them. Granted, she had never been to the British Isles before, but she had firsthand knowledge of dig sites all across the southwestern United States and she'd never seen any in this shape. In fact, this site looked as if a wrecking crew had been here with sledgehammers, paid to pound the place to dust.

The effects of a thousand years of warring tribes and wet weather, according to Jonathan. That might well be, but Abby had her doubts. This destruction looked intentional to her. Intentional and absolutely complete.

She tuned out the drone of Jonathan's voice and began her mental preparation for the day's work. As she always did, she visualized herself sending out delicate tendrils of fluorescent green energy. They curled across the ground, lashing out like lizard tongues testing the air. They probed the rubble and beneath, deep into the earth under her feet, determinedly seeking their prize, the Marker Stone.

According to Jonathan, centuries ago the stone would have stood as tall as a man, its surface engraved with strange Pictish markings. He'd shown them a rough hand-drawn sketch of what he expected to find based on his research. The drawing had reminded Abby of a snake curling around a Do Not Enter sign.

She filled her mind with the image of the drawing but, again today, she felt nothing other than her own frustration. If the marker was here, it wasn't in the location where she was assigned to dig today.

Their standard pep talk ended, Abby made her way to the spot where she'd been working for the past week and stepped gingerly into the taped-off square. Down on her knees, she laid her hands on the dirt, spreading her fingers in her own private ritual.

There were archaeological treasures somewhere below her hands. She could feel them. Lovely bits and pieces of past lives, clues to a people long gone, calling to her to expose them to the world once again.

But no Marker Stone. Nothing with the design Jonathan sought.

Neither was her own special treasure here.

For as long as she could remember, she'd wanted to travel to Scotland on an excavation. Something here had called to her. Something ancient. Something special meant for just her to find.

Ah, well. There were still two months left. She might yet locate that special something.

The locals had told them there were a few small caves in these mountains and she had hopes that she'd have a chance to explore those areas to see what they might hold. Who knew? One of them might hold the treasures she sought.

For now, though, their dig site was centered in this little glen, which was just as well, really. As much as she wanted to see what history the local caves might hold, the idea of actually going inside a small, dark hole in the ground made her almost physically ill. It was that fear of small, dark places that had led her to study early Native American and Ancient Celtic peoples rather than to venture into Egyptology.

The whole idea of being sealed in a pyramid was more than she could bear to entertain.

In a matter of moments, her mind filled with variations of what might await her on this particular day. As always, she was lost in her work, completely absorbed in digging away the thin layers of dirt and debris separating her from the treasures calling to her.

"Give me your opinion on this, Abigail?"

Abby dragged her attention from the little trowel in her hand, so completely immersed in her work it felt as if she were swimming up from the bottom of a deep, dark pool into the bright sunlight.

When had all the clouds burned off?

Jonathan towered over her, clutching some small find in his hand. Light glinted off the sunglasses he'd pushed up on his forehead as he smiled down at her and held out a hand to help her to her feet.

He really was an attractive man. Tall and broad-shouldered, with long blond hair pulled back and tied at his neck, he looked like he belonged in a commercial for expensive big boy toys. If she squinted just right, she could almost picture him standing on the deck of a yacht with some fancy drink in his hand.

And yet, here he was, smiling down at her, his shirtsleeves rolled midway up his forearms, some muddy little prize clutched in one hand as he reached out to her with the other.

She accepted the help willingly, realizing as she stood that she had no idea how many hours she'd spent on her knees, only that, from her stiff legs, it had apparently been a good long while.

"What do you make of this, love?"

Her cheeks heated as several sets of eyes turned in

their direction and, not for the first time, she wished he'd stop calling her that. Initially she'd assumed he used the endearments for everyone simply because he couldn't be bothered with remembering their names. But it had quickly become apparent that not only did he remember everyone's names, he used them. It was only her he singled out for the pet names.

She took the small dirt-encrusted stone from him and rubbed her thumb over it to examine it more closely.

"I don't see . . ." Anything. Nothing at all. It looked like just a plain old stone to her. She ran her thumb over the surface, detecting no irregularity of any kind.

"Don't you think that could be a bit of engraving?" He pointed the tip of the little gold pocket knife he held at a particularly mud-caked spot. "Just there. On the edge."

He handed her the stone, pointing to a spot with the tip of the little knife. There might be something there. She shifted the stone into the palm of her hand just as he scraped the long edge of the knife against it.

"No!" He hissed the word as the blade slipped from the stone and sliced into the palm of her hand.

Both stone and knife fell to the ground unheeded.

Abby gasped, staring at the spot where the skin splayed open, feeling strangely removed as the crimson of her own blood oozed out and the sting of the wound registered in her brain.

It had all happened in the blink of an eye, and yet it was as if time had come to a stop, the sound of her own heartbeat echoing loudly inside her head as if heralding some momentous occasion.

Thub-Dub.

"No," he denied on a whisper, clasping her hand between his own as if he could undo the accident.

Jonathan held her hand fast in his, her strength no match for his when she tried to pull away. Murmuring a string of unintelligible apologies, he lifted her palm to his lips.

Thub-Dub.

Shock stiffened her body when his tongue stroked over the wound in her palm an instant before she felt the unmistakable pressure of his sucking against the site. Their gazes locked in the moment and a second shock tingled down her spine, this one tinged with an unreasonable fear, strangely reminiscent of the way she'd felt in the dream she'd had the night before she'd gone to search for Colin.

Thub-Dub. Thub-Dub.

His eyes, usually masked to hide whatever he felt, glittered now. The green of his irises seemed to sparkle with some emotion she couldn't begin to identify.

Thub-Dub. Thub-Dub. Thub-Dub.

She tore her gaze away, focusing instead on the little gold knife he'd dropped at their feet. She stared first at the silver blade, a streak of her blood covering its edge, and then at the fancy little letters engraved on the handle, as if memorizing the scripted *F.D.A.* could somehow transport her away from this moment in time.

"Jesus, what happened? Snakebite?" Mackenzie stooped to retrieve the knife, her shrill voice bringing the ordeal to an end, thankfully releasing Abby from the horrible spell she'd felt herself under.

"No. I'm afraid my penknife slipped as I tried to clear a bit of dirt from a stone I was showing to Abigail."

Jonathan's voice shook in a way that left no doubt he was upset by what he'd done, and yet she simply could not bring herself to meet his eyes again. Whatever emotion it was she'd seen there before, she knew only that she didn't want any part of it.

"Oh, well, for crying out loud. That's why we don't use things like this." Mackenzie closed the blade on the knife and handed it to Jonathan, her irritation evident. "Put that in your pocket and keep it there. And you don't suck the blood out of knife wounds, okay? Honestly, Jonathan. Do you have any idea how many germs live in the human mouth?"

"Sorry," he murmured, his eyes glazed. "I didn't mean to—"

"Look," Mackenzie interrupted. "I know this is your project, okay? But nothing is running to standard here. I know you're a researcher, okay? A paper-and-pen and stacks-of-books kind of guy, okay? So please just leave the field work to those of us who know what we're doing. You should go get yourself a bottle of water from the cooler and rinse your mouth out, too. Gross." Mackenzie jerked Abby's hand from Jonathan's grasp, sparing him a glare before peering down at the cut. "That's not so bad. You'll be fine. It doesn't even need stitches. Come on over to the van. There's a first aid kit in there and we can wrap you up. After we clean it out."

Abby nodded mutely, trailing gratefully along behind her bossy younger coworker.

A glance back over her shoulder revealed Jonathan unmoving, as if in shock. She should probably say something to him, tell him she was fine and not upset with him at all.

But she couldn't bring herself to lie to him, not even to save his feelings. She wasn't fine. She was rattled as hell. Whatever had just passed between her and Jonathan frightened her. *He* frightened her. All she wanted was to get as far away from him as possible.

Turning back, she fixed her gaze on the young woman marching ahead of her. She might have considered Mackenzie a pain in the ass from the first day they met, but that all changed as of right now. Having Mackenzie within eyesight just might be the smartest thing she could do as long as Jonathan Flynn was around.

Flynn breathed in deeply, slowly, waiting for his equilibrium to return. The Magic had hit him hard, flooding his body with its own sweet tang.

It had all happened so quickly. An accident, to be sure. But then, as the blood had oozed from Abigail's wound, the Bloodlust had taken hold and he'd been unable to resist touching his tongue to that magnificent nectar. Once he'd done that, he was lost, desperate for more.

It was glorious. *She* was glorious.

He watched Abby walking away from him, unable to tear his gaze from her. To the eye, she was little more than an everywoman, certainly not a classic beauty by the standards of this time. And yet, everything about her called out to him and he wanted her more desperately than he'd wanted any woman in a very long time. He wanted all of her. Her body, her blood, her Magic.

That glorious Magic! It rippled through him like a burst of electricity.

He'd been right about her. The blood of the Fae flowed in her veins, and along with it the pure, sweet essence of his beloved Magic. Even now its power tingled through his body, sparkling in the synapses of his brain like fireworks.

All around him, it was as if small, insistent voices tore at the edges of his awareness, all demanding his attention in a sensory-battering cacophony.

Here! The pen from Mackenzie's clipboard lay buried in a tall clump of grass off to his left.

Here! An earring somewhere beyond in the grove of trees, lost over a decade past.

Here! A shard of pottery, buried beneath his feet, centuries ago forgotten.

It was too much all at once, hundreds of voices spilling over one another in a flood of noise. So many, they drowned one another out, masking the individual words, turning the sound into an indistinguishable mass of writhing colors pounding in his brain.

Flynn lifted his hands to his ears in a fruitless effort to block the flow. How could anyone profit from an assault such as this? It would be impossible to isolate any one item from the whole.

Unless he could learn to filter the noise, to sift out that which he sought.

He stalked into the grove, slowing to snatch up a discarded trowel on his way. Once beyond the sight of his companions, he dropped to his knees and plunged the blade of the trowel into the soft ground.

Here!

Clawing into the earth with his fingers, he shoved away a handful of rotting leaves and mud. He alternated between trowel and fingers, digging like a madman until at last one of the voices ceased to call. He splayed open his hand, pushing through the clump of dirt he held until he found it, the earring that had called out to him.

What a magnificent gift the Magic had bestowed! He needed only to figure out a way to isolate the individual voices he sought, those of the Portal pieces.

Dropping the worthless trinket to the ground, Flynn closed his eyes, fighting to ignore the many in favor of the few. He filled his mind with the Portal as he imagined it would have looked, willing his mind to go deeper and deeper into the whirlpool of flowing color that was the noise.

How long he knelt on the damp ground he had no idea, nor did he care. All he was aware of was that it was working! Gradually, one by one, the voices receded, layers of color peeling back, leaving him alone in a dark cocoon of silence.

"Come on, people! Doesn't look like the rain is going to let up this time. Let's wrap it up for the day!"

Mackenzie's voice pierced his awareness, drawing him back to the present. Somewhere along the way, the clouds had returned, bringing with them the rain that splattered against his face in large, cold drops.

Already the Magic was beginning to fade.

Slowly, Flynn rose to his feet, acutely aware of the spots within him which would soon be empty again. He'd not found any trace of the Portal, but he had found something perhaps just as good.

Abigail was descended from the Fae. Now that he had his proof, he was more determined than ever to proceed with his plans.

Fighting the emptiness left behind by the initial rush of the Magic, Flynn made his way out of the grove and into the clearing, his eyes instantly drawn to Abigail.

He might never find his way back to Wyddecol, but perhaps he could live with that now. He would have her, and through her he would have the Magic. As much and as often as he desired.

Twelve

Heat radiated off the stone RoundHouse in great sparkling waves, a promise of the physical misery to come.

"Here is your robe, Guardian." The tall Fae waited only until Colin had taken the garment before turning his back. "As usual, you may leave your . . . wrapping on the stool by the door."

"I've no a need for yer scrap of cloth, Odirn." Colin grinned as he accepted the robe, tossing it to the stool before unwinding his plaid. "I've no a problem with my own body."

Surprisingly for a race of men who seemed to Colin more than ready to swive every female who crossed their path, the Fae were unaccountably modest about their own nudity around other men.

"You may have no problem, but have a care for the

rest of us. Wear the damned robe. Why must we go through this every time, Guardian?"

Why? Because teasing Odirn was one of the few things that amused him here in Wyddecol. As always, Colin held his own counsel on the matter, grinning more broadly at the old fellow.

The Fae placed his hands together as if in prayer, closed his eyes, and bowed low. "Blessings for a fruitful Communion, Guardian."

"Blessings, my arse," Colin muttered, pulling open the door.

The wet heat blasted him as he stepped inside, stinging his eyes and nose. He closed the door behind him but moved no farther into the small room, waiting instead for his eyes to adjust to the gloom of the interior. The room itself was a perfect circle, its smooth surface broken only by a fire pit set against the wall, its top glowing red with coals. This was the only light source in the cramped space. Steam hissed from a massive kettle of water placed over the fire pit, rolling into the room and filling his lungs with each breath.

In the exact center of the round room, smooth stones had been carefully laid to form a circle within the circle of the room.

The Fae loved their circles—from the standing stones they'd left in the Mortal world to their ceremonial buildings, stone circles were the rule. Even their most precious Fountain here in Wyddecol, where the Souls of Fae and Mortal alike danced as they waited their turn to reenter the living world, was encircled by a ring of massive stones.

Colin stepped into the circle and seated himself on the floor to wait out the next few hours.

This might well be some sort of religious experience for the Fae, but for him it was nothing of the sort. The only positive as far as he could see was that while he was inside the RoundHouse, it was if the curse that had plagued him for ten years no longer existed. He neither felt nor heard a single soul calling out for its mate. It was the only place he'd ever found where he could let down his barriers and completely relax without fear.

For that reason alone, he almost looked forward to this experience.

As before, to his left a covered pottery bowl held fresh drinking water. He lifted the lid and scooped the accompanying cup inside, downing a long drink.

The water was unusually cold, sliding soothingly down his already parched throat. Apparently Odirn had changed it just before his arrival. He knew from experience it would be warm soon enough, so he enjoyed one more cupful before it too absorbed the heat of his surroundings.

The oppressively hot moisture closed in around him as if he were breathing underwater. He already felt the drips of liquid clinging to his lashes and nose hair. Though he'd initially had a difficult time believing how thirsty he would be in this room, after months of this he now knew from experience it would be so. It was the warning he'd been given before his first Communion and the one he'd quickly seen the wisdom of obeying.

Drink the water.

Preparations made, he laid his palms on his crossed legs, closed his eyes, and forced his mind to empty as he'd been taught.

Unlike in his prior Communion experiences, the void filled his mind almost immediately.

As if he were actually in another place, he could feel the enormity of the dark surrounding him while he floated, weightlessly suspended in a vast nothingness. Beside him, a river of sorts flowed. A river not of water but of writhing, swirling colored mist, so thick it looked as if he could capture it with his bare hands.

The river enticed, beckoning to him, and he moved toward its bank without thought.

"Stop right there!" A voice rang out in the dark, its sheer strength of will forcing his compliance. "The Time Flow of the All Conscious is not meant for you at this time, Guardian."

Before him, silvery strands of mist gathered and swirled, gradually coalescing into the wavering shape of a woman.

Colin found himself unable to focus on her face, as it continually morphed from child to maiden to crone and back again. His breath caught as he remembered when he'd seen the like of this before.

"Yes," the apparition sighed as if it had read his mind. "Regretfully, I am the one who taught her that trick."

"Who . . ." He paused. Not a *who*. Too powerful to be a *who*. "What are you?"

"I am the Earth Mother, Guardian. I've come to see to your guidance personally."

"Yer no her. You canna be." He'd seen the Earth Mother as she'd walked the parapet of the Hall of the

High Council, council members trailing after her like ducklings behind their mother.

"That one?" The apparition laughed, the sound like a thousand tinkling bells. "She's but a physical representative of me in her world. A holder of a title, much as one might name a queen or a princess or even a general. She's naught but a mere woman. I *am* the Earth Mother, the goddess, the very one they think to honor with the title they have given that one. Waste no more thought on her. She is of no importance. Now, what knowledge is it you'd seek from me?"

There was only one question, really. "How do I return to my own time?"

Now. Quickly. Before the lives of his kinsmen were forfeit.

Again the laughter like bells. "Only she who summoned you has the Magic to take you back."

"She who summoned me," he repeated slowly. Abby? How? Why?

"You try my patience, Guardian. Have the Fae grown so weak in my absence?" The mist shimmered, the silver shifting to gold and back again.

"I'm no a Fae," Colin insisted, chafing under the accusation of weakness.

"So you like to claim. But we both know you're as much Fae as you are Mortal. Your veins run strong with the blood of my chosen, the Royal House of Wyddecol. Could it be you're simply incapable of reason?"

"I reason quite well, my lady." Colin stiffly held his temper in check. This Earth Mother person could insult him all she liked. Of all the things he might be, he was not a slow learner. One round with the Faerie Queen had taught him all he needed to know about minding his tongue in the presence of this kind of power.

"Oh, very well. I see your mind is but ill informed, not incapable of reason. And, as you acknowledge, you have already demonstrated the ability to learn from your mistakes." The mist shifted closer to his face, wispy tendrils caressing his cheeks. "She needed you, Guardian, and she wished you to her side."

Abby had wished him to her side? With Magic. Faerie Magic. This changed everything. If Abby had the power of the Magic, and she'd used it to bring him forward to her time, she had to know it. Her pretense of having no knowledge of how he'd gotten into her home, into her bed, was just that. Pretense. Which left him only one question for which he needed an answer.

"Why?"

"Why, why, why, indeed! You have so much to learn, Guardian." The apparition sighed impatiently. "You question me like a small child would question his mother. Perhaps, as any good mother should, I will simply show you and allow you to learn for yourself. The lessons we experience for ourselves are our best teachers, are they not?"

In the space of a heartbeat, the apparition was gone, leaving him floating there in the vast nothingness. Alone, with the great roar of absolute silence pressing in on his ears.

Silence, broken by a gasp.

It was his Abby, he knew immediately. He heard the beating of her heart as if his head lay nestled against her breast.

He felt her.

"Abby!"

His hand fisted as a stinging pain sliced into his palm, but he knew instinctively it wasn't his pain he felt, it was hers, just as it was her fear speeding up the beat of his heart.

She was frightened and in pain.

The Earth Mother's words floated to him again. *She needed you and she wished you to her side.*

She'd needed him enough to call him to her, and he'd abandoned her. Now she was frightened and in pain because he'd failed to aid her, just as he'd failed to aid his kinsmen.

Colin's eyes flew open on a roar of rage.

Someone had dared to hurt his Abby!

The door of the stone RoundHouse flew open and Odirn leaned inside. "Guardian?"

Colin ignored him, instead reaching for the bowl at his side and tipping it up to his lips. The shock of the cold water running down his cheeks and onto his neck banked his anger but did not extinguish it.

He rose to his feet, pulled off the now-soaked robe, and tossed it to the floor before stalking out the door to claim his plaid.

He'd made it halfway down the path before he glanced at the hand he yet held in a fist.

There, in the center of his palm, the skin splayed open, strangely white against the crimson of his own blood oozing out.

Someone had dared to hurt Abby. And whether or not she'd tricked him, what was important now was that she needed him.

No one in either the Fae or Mortal world had the power to stop him from going to her this time.

Thirteen

How long he'd stood motionless in the shadows of the woods he couldn't be sure. What Colin did know was that Abby had gone into the large house at the edge of the forest well over two hours ago and though all those who had accompanied her inside had reappeared and headed into the center of the village, she had yet to come back out.

An unaccustomed sense of indecision rolled over him in a wave, and he briefly considered going inside to find her for himself.

No. He had a plan and he'd stick with it. He'd wait here as he'd originally decided he would until she came outside. Then he'd confront her, preferably with others around. He'd reasoned it would be harder for her to angrily refuse to talk to him if there were observers.

Not that he had reason to suspect her of being irate

with him other than what he'd experienced in the visions that had plagued him prior to his decision to confront her.

But since so very little had gone according to his expectations in the past few months, he felt the need to err on the side of caution.

He'd fully expected Pol to insist he remain in Wyddecol, but once he had shared his vision from the RoundHouse, Pol had surprised him by handing him a packet of paperwork detailing all they'd learned in their investigation and showing him exactly where to find Abby.

He'd expected a fight and gotten none. He didn't want to blunder into the reverse here.

The front door of the big house opened and at last Abby emerged. Her long brown hair was pulled up and fastened at the back of her head, the curls jauntily swinging back and forth. She looked to be in a hurry, the thin shoes she wore flapping noisily against her feet with each step she took.

As she reached to open the gate, he prepared to step out into the lane but stopped when the door to the house opened again.

"Abigail! Wait a moment!"

Jonathan Flynn. Colin recognized him immediately from the surveillance photographs included in the packet Pol had given him. This was the man who'd arranged for Abby to be in Scotland. The man Pol suspected of having ties to the Nuadian Fae.

"Abigail!" He called out again, a big smile creasing his face as he drew close to her. "I feared I'd missed you and I wanted to chat about our next move on the site."

For Abby's part, her entire posture had stiffened at the man's first hail. It appeared obvious to Colin that she had no desire to speak to her employer at this moment.

"Hi, Jonathan." Abby dropped her hand from the gate, crossing her arms in front of her. "I'm just headed down to the pub for a bite. I'll be back in an hour or so and we could talk then, if you like."

As for Flynn, he didn't seem to be picking up on the silent messages Abby was sending. In fact, he seemed a tad too determined altogether for Colin's liking.

"I'll join you. We can take my car and drive over to Aviemore for a nice dinner, just the two of us. How does that sound?"

"I can't." Abby appeared as surprised by her hasty refusal as Flynn.

"Why not?"

Insistent bastard! The lady had said no. Why she refused was none of his business. Enough of this.

Colin stepped from behind the shelter of the trees, silently making his way toward the oblivious couple.

"I can't because . . ." She paused, brushing a hair away from her face as she dropped her gaze to the ground. "Because I . . ."

"Because she's joining me this evening."

Abby spun on her heel, her eyes wide with surprise. "Colin!"

Once again, his expectations were off the mark. Rather than greeting him with a rebuke, she threw herself at him.

He opened his arms and she was in them, her soft fingers locking at the back of his neck, the expression on her face all the thanks he needed for intervening in her interaction with Flynn.

Holding her close as he did, it seemed only natural to dip his head, to capture her mouth with his as he had so many times in his dreams. Her lips, so soft as they brushed against his, sent a reverberation of familiarity zinging through him, like a sip of his favorite whisky after a long, hard ride. The feeling persisted even as the kiss broke.

"What are you doing here?" She made no move to back away, her eyes staring up into his, a thousand questions brimming in them.

He'd come for her. To keep her from harm. To demand the truth of why she'd brought him here. To insist she return him to his own time. So many reasons had brought him to her side.

But this was neither the time nor the company in which to confront her with any of them. That was a conversation for after they'd rid themselves of this overzealous intruder who thought erroneously to spend his evening in her company.

From what he'd seen and overheard, providing her an excuse to get away from Flynn seemed the obvious course of action.

"Yer late, Abby. I grew tired of waiting for you at the pub." She had said she was on her way to the pub. That should satisfy the pushy man.

She nodded her head up and down, her eyes reflecting her understanding before she turned away.

"Colin, this is my employer, Jonathan Flynn. Jonathan, this is Colin, my . . . my boyfriend."

Boyfriend. An odd word, not one he'd heard before,

but the meaning seemed clear enough from Flynn's look of shock. He could be that for now if it was what she needed of him. Her *boyfriend*.

"I was unaware you had any social attachments, Abigail." The chide in Flynn's voice was unmistakable as he extended a hand to Colin. "A pleasure to meet you, Mr. . . ." Flynn left the word hanging, waiting, the question clear.

"MacAlister. Though there's no a need for formalities between us, sir. No with my Abby being in yer employ." Colin smiled broadly, possessively snaking one arm around Abby's waist as he accepted Flynn's hand.

Nuadian!

The knowledge spread over him in a jolt of recognition. Only the years of discipline spent as a warrior allowed Colin to maintain his outward show of calm and friendliness. The man whose hand he held was Fae. Full-blood. Without a doubt Nuadian.

And without a doubt, the source of danger to Abby.

"The pleasure is all mine. Shall we go, Abby?" With a nod of farewell, he steered her away from Flynn and down the cobbled street toward the center of the village. Behind him, he could swear he felt the Fae's anger seething.

Abby was silent until they were well away from Flynn's hearing. "How did you know where to find me? And why? Why did you find me? What are you doing here?"

"Finding you was easy enough. You'd told me you were coming to Scotland this summer." That would hopefully satisfy her for the moment. Somehow he didn't think she'd react well to learning she'd had people watching her every move for months. "And as to what I'm doing here, I'm taking you to eat, am I no?"

The sounds of music and laughter spilled from a doorway just ahead of them, along with an enticing smell that set Colin's stomach rumbling.

He held open the door, allowing her to enter first, and followed her to a small table in one corner of the crowded room.

She was quiet again until after the serving woman handed them a sheet of paper printed with the pub's fare. "No, I mean, why did you come looking for me at all?"

He absolutely intended to tell her everything. This very night. Just not yet. For now he simply wanted to enjoy the feel of being in her company again.

"Is being yer *boyfriend* no reason enough to come to call on you?"

Her cheeks colored a delightful pink and her eyes danced away from his for a moment.

"Okay. I totally deserved that. I do appreciate your not giving me away when I introduced you to Jonathan. I suppose you're going to want an explanation for that now."

"Only as much as yer willing to tell."

"Have you decided then, dearies?" The serving woman had returned, a pencil and pad in her hand, an expectant smile on her face. "We've a special on the haggis tonight. Comes with tatties and neeps, fresh from my own garden."

"I think I'll give that a try." Abby returned the woman's smile before turning her attention to him. "Classic Scottish fare, probably sounds like regular home cooking to you."

"So you might think." In truth, he'd found the food in this time both challenging and absolutely fascinating. There was so much variety to it, in so many combinations, and all of it with special names and ingredients he'd never tasted before. In those first two weeks, he'd paid little attention to the foods his cousin had served him, and certainly the foods he'd eaten in Wyddecol were nothing like here in the Mortal world. "I'll have the same, thank you."

"As to the whole boyfriend excuse, there's not really much to tell." Abby picked up the thread of their conversation as soon as they were alone, launching into a litany of praise that sounded more memorized than from the heart. "Jonathan is a great guy and a dedicated researcher. He's given me the chance of a lifetime by allowing me to participate in his archaeological dig. This experience, and the paper he's chosen me to write summarizing the findings from the expedition, will help me considerably in working toward my graduate degrees and, depending on what we find here, maybe even in my career beyond school."

"But?" Obviously, in spite of the halfhearted positives she mouthed, there had been some reason she had so desperately wanted to leave Flynn behind.

"But," she repeated with finality. She smiled and paused to take a sip from the mug of beer the serving woman had delivered to their table as if trying to decide how much to say. "I'm a little uncomfortable that Jonathan sort of seems to think our relationship might have the potential to be more personal than professional."

"And does it?" Based on her earlier actions, he

thought he knew the answer but he wanted to hear her say the words.

"Absolutely not." She shook her head emphatically, setting the long tail of curls swaying back and forth in a tantalizing dance at her shoulders. "I mean, don't get me wrong; like I said, he's a great guy. I'm just not, you know, into him." She shrugged one shoulder and looked down at her beer.

Her admission was a relief to hear, though he told himself it was only because he didn't want to see her involved with a Nuadian. After all, his priority was returning to his own time and he needed her safe and healthy in order to send him home.

"Okay, so I came clean. Now it's your turn. Why are you really here? I assume your showing up tonight isn't some random accident, so why did you come looking for me?"

The serving woman's return with their food bought him a few minutes to gather himself, but not nearly long enough now that he actually faced telling her what he needed to.

"I need yer help."

Of course he did.

Abby continued to chew the bite she'd forked into her mouth, though what had started out as truly delicious had quickly taken on the feel of just so much mush. Disappointment roiled in her stomach. What had she expected? That his one night with her had sent him scurrying across the Atlantic hunting for her? That maybe he dreamed of her every single, wretched night, just as she dreamed of him? That sort of thinking obviously would be the epitome of stupid, now, wouldn't it?

She flickered her gaze in his direction, darting her eyes away just as quickly when she found him staring at her.

Stupid of her, yes, but you'd think a great-looking guy like Colin MacAlister would have more than enough experience with women to at least lead her on for a bit. Appeal to her vanity, maybe. Lull her into thinking he had a thing for her. To, at the very least, try to make her feel like he actually had some tiny bit of interest in seeing her for, well, for her. But no, he was here because he needed something from her, and he wasn't making the slightest effort to hide the fact.

Was it she who'd always claimed she valued honesty in a man? She might have to reconsider that particular "virtue." A little white lie to soothe her wounded ego wouldn't have been so awful.

"Perfect," she muttered before she reached for her mug and downed a deep swallow, waiting for the dark liquid to wash over her throat. If they liked her, she didn't like them. If she liked them, they wanted something from her. "All right, fine, I'll bite. What exactly do you want from me?" Must be a doozy of a request considering he'd gone to all the trouble to hunt her down.

"I want to go home."

"Pardon me?" *Home?* She looked up in surprise, meeting his gaze this time. "What do you mean, you want to go home? Go. I'm not stopping you. I didn't make you come here in the first place."

"But that's exactly what you did. You and yer wishing."

"That's ridiculous," she denied, even as the warmth of guilt heated her neck and face. How could he possibly know she suffered from some massively stupid infatuation over him? That he'd haunted her dreams since the day they'd met?

"It's no ridiculous at all. It's the Magic."

Magic? Her heart pounded so hard she thought everyone in the noisy bar must be hearing it by now. Was this his way of telling her he'd come to find her because he felt the same bizarre attraction she did?

"So what does that mean? Magic. That you like me? Is that why you hunted me down? Because you like me?"

He sat back in his seat, his expression what she might expect from someone who'd just discovered his dining partner had an extra foot growing out the side of her head, toes wiggling.

"I like you well enough, lass, but that's neither here nor there. We've a need to discuss why you summoned me and, more important, how yer to send me home."

Again with sending him home. Abby carefully placed her fork across her plate and slowly steepled her hands in front of her, struggling to find some appropriately clever and witty retort. She had nothing.

"I haven't the slightest idea what you're talking about."

When Colin leaned forward, his eyes glinted with something that looked remarkably like anger. Abby fought down the urge to back away from him.

"No? So what yer telling me is that you've no idea that you used the Faerie Magic to wish me here, to yer time. Seven hundred years into the future you drag me. And though I've no way back to my own time but to fulfill some purpose of yers that brought me here, you willna even disclose to me what that purpose is so that I might complete yer blighted task and get back to my own life. It's no even of any consequence to you that the lives of my kinsmen depend on my returning. That's what yer saying, is it?"

"Seven hundred . . ." Abby paused, staring at the man sitting across from her. He was kidding, right? He had to be kidding.

But no, there was nothing in his expression, nothing in his serious blue eyes, that said anything even close to *kidding*. This man believed the giant, steaming pile of BS he was spewing.

"Okay. That's it. Done." She stood, catching up her handbag and slinging its strap across her chest. "Don't bother to ask me to dinner again, okay? And you know what else? Since you ruined my meal, thank you very much, you can just pay for it. And make sure you leave Mrs. Duncan a good tip while you're at it, too. I am out of here."

She didn't bother to wait for his response, pushing her way past the men lined up at the bar. The air in here had grown too thin, the walls somehow moving in closer to one another, making her feel trapped and just a bit woozy.

Outside, breathing in the clear evening air, she stopped, looking first toward the bed-and-breakfast and then to her right, off toward the empty tree-lined road that led outside the village and beyond.

She needed some time to think. Some time to regroup. Some time to decide whether she wanted to scream in anger or cry with disappointment.

At the B and B she could escape to the relative privacy

of her room to deal with all this, but more than likely Jonathan waited there, and of all the things she was in no mood for, he was at the top of the list.

No, he'd just dropped to number two on the list.

Besides, number one on the list might very well come hunting her with more of his send-me-home drivel, and if he did, the B and B would be the most logical place for him to look.

That made the decision easy enough.

Turning to her right, she adjusted her purse strap high up on her shoulder and headed out, her pace picking up as she approached the edge of the village limits.

Damn it! Of all the times she'd imagined seeing Colin MacAlister again, of all the times she'd dreamed of him, not one of them had turned out even remotely like the last few minutes. *Damn it all to hell!*

At what point had she made the fateful leap that had sent her hurtling into bizarro world? Instead of simply picking guys to like who didn't like her back, now she was picking men who apparently needed heavy medication simply to function in normal society.

Medication that Colin apparently had been skipping lately.

For the past few months she'd allowed her imagination free rein, skipping along blindly without a protest as she'd almost convinced herself the hunky Highlander was actually The One, for no better reasons than because he'd haunted her dreams and got her totally hot just thinking about him.

And look what she'd gotten out of indulging in that little fantasy.

The man of her dreams, literally, was a total loon, babbling on about needing to be sent to his home seven-freaking-hundred years ago.

"Stark raving lunatic," she growled, walking even faster.

She wanted to kick something. Or hit something. Or simply stomp her feet up and down while screaming at the top of her lungs.

Worse, worse, way worse than his being a loon, was what all this meant about her. She was an idiot of gobsmacking proportions. Because, loon or not, just thinking of him, of his perfectly sculpted features, of the scent that filled her nose when he was close, of the way his hands felt on her skin, or the way his voice soothed her soul—all of it made her want nothing so much as to be with him.

If what she experienced wasn't crushing in a major way, she couldn't even begin to imagine what it could be.

Other than serious mental illness, maybe. Perhaps Colin MacAlister wasn't the only one in need of medication.

Slowing to a stop, she stared off into the distance, listening to the sound of her own racing heart.

She'd left the outskirts of the village behind and reached an area where the road narrowed. Steep rock walls as high as her waist hemmed in both sides of the lane out here, stretching off into the distance.

It was quiet here. Lonely. The perfect place to confront herself.

"I am way too smart to be this stupid."

The affirmation, intended to bolster her confidence, echoed back at her off the rocks in a mocking parody.

Now that she'd stopped moving, Abby realized the bottoms of her feet burned like crazy and she considered for the first time her poor choice of footwear. Flip-flops were hardly intelligent stomping-off-in-a-huff shoes and were even less practical should she need to scramble over one of these rock walls to avoid any vehicle careening down the narrow lane. Not to mention, now that she thought of it, how noisy they were, flapping against her feet when she walked.

"And total gravel magnets," she grumbled under her breath as she braced a hand against the rock wall to balance on one foot in order to remove the tiny, irritating pieces of gravel lodged between her feet and the soles of her shoes.

Everything about her life at this very minute was so ridiculously stupid, from her obsession with a crazy man right up to storming down the road like she had somewhere to go. And she had no one to blame for any of it but herself.

She might not be able to do anything about the way she felt, but she could be sensible for a change and head back to Swan House. Granted, with the sun staying up until almost ten o'clock, she'd have another hour or so before she'd have to worry about being caught out in the dark. But realistically, what could she possibly hope to accomplish from this little jaunt? Blisters, most likely, because peace of mind sure didn't seem to be hanging out anywhere along this path.

Switching hands, she shifted her balance and lifted her other foot, slipping off the second flip-flop to dust away the offending gravel.

"Running away will do neither of us any good, now will it, Abby?"

Colin's voice, coming from mere inches behind her, sent a shock of panic resounding through her. Her breath escaped in a bizarre gagged-sounding squeal, even as her body tried to respond by twirling around to face him. The one-footed maneuver sent her pitching forward, with nothing but Colin to prevent her from landing face-first in the middle of the road.

"What the hell's wrong with you?" she gasped, clutching at the arms that tightened around her as she tried to regain her balance. "You scared me half to death." She'd never heard a single noise to indicate anyone was within a mile of her, let alone right at her shoulder. "You can't just go sneaking up on people like that."

"I had no need to sneak. You looked as if yer thoughts had taken you far away from this place."

Not far enough.

"You know what? Leave me alone. Just turn around and walk away, okay?" Abby forced herself to push out of Colin's arms, refusing to meet his eyes. One look there and she knew she'd be lost. "It's been a long day and, frankly, I'm just not up to listening to any more of your seven-hundred-years-ago crap."

"Then we'll no speak on it again this night. Allow me to see you safely back to the inn where yer staying." He reached out, clasping her hand in his.

She should say no. She should step away from him, jerk her hand from his grasp, and tell him to get lost. So many things she *should* do.

Instead, her hand warmly ensconced in his, she fell into step beside him, allowing him to lead her back toward Swan House. Not a word passed between them the entire way and yet it felt entirely comfortable and natural, as if they'd done this a million times before.

At the gate to Swan House he stopped, pulling her closer, staring down into her eyes with a gaze that sent her heart racing.

"I've handled this all very badly and for that, I apologize. You asked at the pub why I came looking for you. I came because of this." He held out his hand for her inspection, palm up.

There, in the center of his hand, a cut, a twin to the mark on her palm, more healed, but still an identical wound.

"I don't understand."

"I ken how confused you must be. I'll come to you on the morrow when yer rested, and we'll work it out, aye?"

Not tomorrow, now. Explain it now.

Her brain supplied all the proper things to say; her mouth simply refused to cooperate.

Instead she nodded, leaning in as he dipped his mouth to cover hers. He pulled her close and she was lost, wavering somewhere between reality and the dream world where they'd shared this moment so many times before.

"Keep yer distance from Flynn," he whispered when he broke the kiss, his lips still so close his breath feathered over her heated face. "Dinna think to trust the man. He's no what you believe him to be. He's dangerous. Promise me you'll no allow yerself to be alone with him."

"I don't . . ." She paused, refusing to even think about what he'd said. His words now made no more sense than anything else he'd said all evening. At this moment, she had no desire to talk and certainly none to argue. Not with him so close she could practically taste him. "Hush."

As if he were an addiction, she stretched up on tiptoe and pressed her body against his, reestablishing the kiss.

She felt as much as heard his groan against her lips, and a shiver ran down her spine, lodging low in her stomach, agitating the pool of need already growing there.

He dropped her hand and grasped her shoulders, gently pushing away from her, a crooked smile on his lips.

"You should go inside now. Straight to yer bedchamber with you. And lock yer door. I'll see you on the morrow." He bent his head once more to kiss her forehead. "Dinna forget what I told you."

Abby stared after him, trying her best to rein in her stampeding emotions. What she felt when she was close to that man made no more sense than the words that came out of his mouth.

No more sense than the knowledge that, had he not walked away, she would have led him directly up to her room.

And not just to sleep in her bed this time.

He thought Jonathan Flynn was dangerous?

"You're the dangerous one," she whispered to the empty space where he'd been moments ago. Whether he was saying things that sounded crazy or touching her in a way that made her feel crazy, she couldn't decide which was worse.

Abby turned and pushed open the gate, her mind filled with the memory of Colin as he'd been that first morning, gloriously naked in her bed with nothing but a thin bedcover draped across his hard physique.

Two steps down the walk, a prickle of unease colored the lovely image and she snapped her head up to find herself squarely in the intense scrutiny of her employer, Jonathan Flynn. Like some disapproving parent waiting for his only daughter to return from a first date, he stepped from the shadows of the ivy-covered porch, his arms crossed in front of him, an unusual frown creasing his face.

"I was worried about you."

Was that accusation she heard in his voice? She walked closer, stopping at the bottom step. "You didn't need to be."

"Mackenzie seemed to think you and . . ."—he nodded his head in the direction of the road—"*that* one had some sort of argument. She mentioned some concerns that you were upset when you left the pub and that he followed after you."

So what if they had? Abby gritted her teeth against the irritation she felt. What went on between her and Colin was none of Mackenzie's business and certainly none of Jonathan's.

"After speaking to her," Jonathan continued, "when you didn't return, I quite naturally had concerns, too. I don't like those feelings, Abigail. I don't like having to worry over your safety."

Abby took in a deep, sweet breath, holding it for a second before releasing it and, hopefully, all her irritation with it.

No such luck.

It didn't matter, she told herself, stepping up onto the porch next to him. None of this mattered. No reason to let it annoy her. But it did.

"I'm sorry about how you felt, Jonathan. Your worry wasn't necessary. Next time, you and Mackenzie both might try remembering I'm a big girl and you're not my parents."

As she stepped forward to push past him, he snagged her upper arm, drawing her up sharply, his fingers digging into the soft flesh of her arm as he pulled her to within inches of him.

"Let me assure you, Abigail, of all the feelings I do have for you, not one of them is the least bit paternal."

His eyes glittered with the same barely controlled emotion she'd seen that day at the dig. An emotion Abby wasn't sure she wanted to understand.

The hair on her arms seemed to stand on end and it felt like a thousand tiny bugs were crawling over her skin. Her breath caught in her lungs and, for just an instant, she could have sworn Jonathan was going to kiss her, but not in a good way. Not like Colin had.

And then the instant passed and he dropped his hand from her arm, brushing past her without another word to stalk out through the garden and into the woods beyond.

Holy shit!

Rubbing at the spots where Jonathan's fingers had

dug into her arm, she hurried into the house and up the stairs, not slowing until she was behind her locked door.

Keep yer distance from Flynn. He's dangerous.

Colin's cryptic warning hammered at the inside of her head as she reached a shaking hand toward her toothbrush.

Well, if that wasn't just the perfect ending to a perfectly bizarre evening, she didn't know what was.

Fourteen

❦

None of this was going at all as he'd planned!

Flynn slammed his fist into a large rowan tree, jerking back in surprise as pain flared through his fingers. The dark red stain oozing from the torn skin of his knuckles served as evidence of what he should have remembered.

He'd taken her blood only days before. Magic-tainted blood that negated the natural state of nothingness he'd endured since he was cast out of Wyddecol. For untold centuries all full-blood Fae, including him, had existed in the Mortal world, stripped of their Magic, cursed to neither commit nor experience violence. Such an act of anger or intent would result in their bodies turning to mist.

Until Adira, courtesan to his master, had discovered the effects of ingesting blood, that is. Blood brought them the power to be whole again. And if that blood came from one of the half-Mortal Fae descendants, it also carried Magic.

Bloodlust, it had been called in the ancient tome Adira had found, a designation he'd never understood until recently. He'd tried to fight the addiction and he'd lost. But now, with the Magic flowing through his veins, he wondered why he'd ever resisted giving himself over fully to the demon Bloodlust.

Abigail Porter belonged to him. He'd gone to too much trouble and expense to find her only to be thwarted by some young stallion she fancied.

He'd hoped to accomplish his goal in a rational, civilized manner, but now that seemed much less important than it had before. He would have Abigail. He would have her blood, with the Magic and power it imparted. For as long as they both lived, she belonged to him.

If that meant taking her by force and eliminating his competition, he was more than prepared to do whatever was necessary. The choice would be theirs, not his. Whatever happened from this point forward was not his fault.

Lifting his injured knuckles to his lips, he brushed his tongue over the blood, the tang of the Magic no more than a faint aftertaste now.

He'd have to act quickly, before the effects of her blood were completely gone from his system. That, or he'd need a fresh infusion.

A chuckle burbled up from his chest, bursting forth in full-throated laughter that seized and shook his entire body.

As if timing mattered. In truth, he would have a fresh infusion no matter what!

Fifteen

What the hell?

Abby twisted her body in front of the full-length mirror, angling her arm for a better view of what she'd just glimpsed.

Bruises! One, two, three . . . she held up her elbow, checking the underside. Sure enough. Five of them. Exactly where Jonathan had grabbed her last night.

"Son of a—" She bit off the expletive, clenching her teeth against her irritation. Temper wouldn't do her any good. She didn't need to get angry; she needed to get smart.

Muttering under her breath, she dragged her T-shirt over her head and tossed it to the bed before digging through one of her drawers, pulling out a long-sleeved silk undershirt. It was thick enough to hide the marks but thin enough to wear without overheating. Thin enough, as a matter of fact, that she'd never think of wearing the wispy white item by itself. A sleeveless water-repellent zip-up vest over it, though, and the problem was solved.

One of the problems, she corrected herself, grabbing up her backpack and slipping out her door. She still had to deal with the whole "Jonathan issue."

At the bottom of the staircase she stopped, mentally preparing herself to step into the normal bustle of activity she'd find just outside the door.

Most of their crew had already climbed into the nearest van. Jonathan stood by the door of the second, motioning her forward the instant their eyes met.

No way. Dealing with something for her meant avoiding it, and that was exactly what she intended to do now, heading for the first van.

"We're full up, Porter. You're in Two today." Mackenzie motioned her head toward the second van without so much as looking up from her ever-present clipboard.

"Is there a way we can shuffle, Mackenzie? I was hoping to have a couple of minutes to get your advice on an area of the paper I'm writing."

Just as Abby had hoped, the other woman's head bobbed up, her eyes widening for an instant, her surprise evident. To her credit, recovery was instantaneous.

"Fine. I do have a few ideas on the direction of the paper I'd wanted to discuss with you anyway. Barton," Mackenzie pointed her clipboard at the closest woman. "Grab your gear. You're in Two."

Abby climbed into the van, pulling the door shut behind her and scrunching down in her seat. So far so good. Sure, she'd have to make up something to ask

Mackenzie's opinion on, but that was no big deal. If she could just manage to arrange things as neatly at the dig site, everything would be fine.

The van pulled out onto the road and she glanced out the window for the first time. Jonathan stared directly at her. Abby averted her gaze, refusing to meet his eyes.

From the beginning she'd felt oddly uncomfortable around him, but she'd chalked that up to nerves over having a rich, influential man interested in her.

But not now.

In the days since their little accident out at the dig site, he'd been at her elbow every time she turned around. She still wasn't sure exactly what had transpired between them that day other than that being alone with him made her feel even more uncomfortable than it had before. What sane man in this day and age touched his mouth to another person's fresh wound? There were a million diseases out there roaming the planet, and he'd been sucking on her hand like a vacuum drawing poison. Too bizarre. And after that little outburst on the front porch last night? Their relationship, such as it was, had been elevated to a place where she was more than uncomfortable. More like totally creeped out.

From here on out she was taking Colin's advice to keep her distance from Jonathan Flynn. Two months remained until the dig was due to end. Until then, she'd simply have to find a way to make sure she didn't end up alone with him, no matter what she had to do.

Eight weeks of fancy footwork. She could do that. Abby squared her shoulders, sitting up straighter in her seat. After all, how hard could something like that be to arrange?

* * *

"Are you sure you'll no be wanting more eggs and toast? It's no a problem, lad. Or more of the black pudding and beans? I've plenty more in the kitchen. A fine braw lad like yerself needs a filling breakfast to start his day." Mrs. MacKee stood over Colin, supervising every bite he put in his mouth. "You need more tea. I'll be right back with another pot."

He smiled as the woman disappeared through the big white door, humming as she went. He'd asked at the pub last night and several people had suggested Mrs. MacKee as having rooms to let. When he'd arrived on her steps, he'd found the woman perched precariously on a stepladder, attempting to change a bulb in her front hallway.

Considering she looked to him to be easily ninety-five if she was a day, he'd insisted on changing it for her, which quickly enough led to a variety of other little tasks. The result had been one of the best breakfasts he'd ever had, though his admittedly prodigious ability to eat was being tested by the little woman and her seemingly endless supply of food.

She'd started him off with an enormous bowl of sweet, creamy oats followed by a plate she'd referred to as a traditional Scottish breakfast. It followed no tradition he'd ever known, but it was certainly one he could fully support. Eggs, ham, tomatoes, beans, and black pudding had filled the plate from edge to edge, accompanied by a rack of light brown toast and heavenly sweet jam.

A glance out the window told him the morning was getting away from him. Heavy, mist-filled clouds were already rolling in with the heat of the waning morning. If he hoped to catch Abby to make amends for his behavior the evening before, he'd better push himself away from the bounty Mrs. MacKee seemed determined to provide him.

The thought of seeing Abby again this morning brought a twinge of excitement along with it.

Her response to him last night had been all the proof he'd needed that none of this was her fault. At least not intentionally. Oh, he didn't doubt it was she who had brought him here. The Earth Mother's visit in the RoundHouse had been quite clear on that point.

It was just that he honestly believed Abby had absolutely no idea about any of this.

Mrs. MacKee's return with another little metal pot of tea was interrupted by a knock at her door, and she bustled away to see to it.

Colin finished off the last of his food, lifted his backpack from under the table, and left the dining room, saying his good-byes to Mrs. MacKee as he passed her in the parlor, where she was busily checking in a new guest.

He passed through the profusion of flowers that grew on the grounds of MacKee house in a riot of color and scents to let himself out through the gate and onto the quiet lane. The gate itself drew his attention for a moment, an elaborate wooden affair that arched over the walk like a doorway. Above his head the wood creaked and groaned and the roses twining there dropped petals on his shoulders as he let the gate click shut.

All of this would make for a pleasant memory when he returned to his own time. No one in the villages decorated their homes in this manner. Any gardening they might do would be plants that provided food. Only the very wealthy could afford to devote large plots of land and time to that which did nothing more than please the senses. These were things he would miss.

And hot showers. He'd developed quite a fondness for standing under the hot, stinging spray of a shower.

But home was where he belonged, where he was needed. If all went well today, if he could convince Abby of the truth of his situation, he might end this day, which had already begun so well, in the place where he could actually do some good. Perhaps before another sunset he would find himself returned to his own time, where he at least stood a chance to save his kinsmen and his king.

Hoisting his backpack on his shoulder, he made quick work of crossing through the small village, arriving at Swan House only to learn that Abby and her coworkers had left quite some time earlier for the dig site where they'd spend their day.

Damnation. He'd known he should have refused that second plate of food, but he'd allowed the lure of the decadent shower and his stomach to overrule his good sense.

Not willing to waste another entire day waiting for Abby's return, he headed toward to pub to arrange transportation out to the dig site.

Sixteen

❦

A knife! The metal, likely iron, was separated from what had to be the handle. Just a bit more dirt and then she could call to the others to bring the camera to photograph her find before she moved it from its resting place.

She'd known what she'd find the instant Jonathan had brought her to this spot. Separated from the main dig site by a copse of trees, she initially voiced a concern as to whether it was included in their permissions for the dig, but that was, of course, Jonathan's area of expertise, not hers, as he'd quickly reminded her.

There had also been the matter of leaving the comfort of the others to accompany Jonathan to this spot, but she rationalized her actions in that she was well within screaming distance.

Besides, Jonathan had been a perfect gentleman this morning. Maybe he felt guilty for his behavior the night before, as well he should. Whatever the reason, his focus today clearly centered on the work. His excitement had spilled over in his voice as he'd followed the coordinates on his handheld GPS device to lead her here. Based on his latest research he was positive, he'd confided, that this would have been the spot where the peoples he sought would have staged a camp.

He simply wanted some concrete proof before he shifted the whole operation to this spot. Proof she'd known she could give him the instant she allowed her feelings to spread out in search of what might lie underground. Artifacts! Bits of history calling out to her to free them from the layers of dirt within which they lay hidden.

"If we can find one of their campsites, I'm certain we'll find their ceremonial stones," he'd told her, his eyes glittering with excitement. "And once we've found that, all my theories will be confirmed."

No stones such as he sought were in this area, she was sure of that, but she didn't say anything to him. There was no way to explain how she knew it with such certainty and, anyway, there were plenty of bits and pieces left behind by the people who had passed through here. More than enough to justify her working this area today.

And now she'd found this lovely piece. The handle looked as if it had some sort of intricate carving, but it would be difficult to say for sure until she could free it completely.

The fine mist of rain that had begun at some point while she'd been engrossed in freeing this artifact complicated her work, but she didn't want to stop now. She was too close to leave this little treasure exposed to the open elements.

The sound of a car motor in the distance jolted her from her concentration, and she sat back on her heels, realizing as she did that she'd once again spent much too long in one position.

Even as the first sound faded, a second started up and rapidly faded away, too.

What the heck?

She tipped her head, listening intently for any sound coming from the direction of the main dig activity. Why would someone take the vans and leave everyone stranded out here in the middle of the afternoon? Especially with the rain picking up again.

Closing her eyes, she concentrated to catch any sounds. The mist hitting the leaves of the trees and brush around her was all she could hear.

That made absolutely no sense at all. There was always some type of noise with a group the size of theirs. Unless the group was gone.

What a ridiculous thought. They wouldn't leave without her. Even if no one else remembered her, Mackenzie's ever-present clipboard would have prevented anyone's being left behind.

She pulled off her vest and staged it across the ribbon surrounding her hole in an attempt to protect her find and then rose to her feet. Her legs tingled with lack of use and the blood rushed to her head in a dizzying whoosh, forcing her to pause for a moment before starting off.

Pushing through the trees toward the main site, she moved as quietly as possible, listening for the normal noise she'd expect from the group.

Nothing. Not a single sound.

"Mackenzie?" She waited in uncomfortable silence for a response, picking up her speed when none came. "Anybody?"

Even before she'd made it all the way through the trees, she could see what her mind didn't want to accept.

The site was empty. No vans, no people, nothing but rain peppering down on the canvas covers they'd left behind.

A lurch of disbelief tracked like a shot of nausea through her stomach. Disbelief and hunger. She'd skipped breakfast to avoid bumping into Jonathan, and she'd been so involved in following the vision in her head to the artifact underground, she'd completely forgotten lunch.

"I don't freaking believe this." Propping her hands on her hips, she scanned the area again for any sign of her group.

They'd abandoned her. Wet, dirty, hungry, "And pissed," she announced emphatically to the empty site. "Totally pissed as hell!"

Just wait until she got her hands on Mackenzie and that piece of crap clipboard of hers.

"There you are."

Abby barely avoided a full-scale scream when Jonathan emerged from the trees behind her.

"What the hell, Jonathan? Where did everyone go?" And, more to the point, why did they go without her?

"When the rain started to pick up, I sent them on ahead. I'd just checked on you and saw that you were immersed in your work so I thought you'd prefer having the extra time and riding back with me. Besides, we've barely had a moment alone together for the past week. My car is parked only a short walk down the road."

Damn straight they hadn't had a moment alone. She'd had to put a lot of effort into arranging it that way, too. All that careful maneuvering for nothing. No avoiding him now. Best laid plans and all that rubbish.

"Why don't we secure your site before we go? I take it you found something? I saw you'd left your vest there."

He raked a hand over his mouth and chin, his eyes fastening much lower than her face.

Oh, damn.

Only now did it occur to Abby what she must look like. A quick glance down confirmed the worst. The rain that had turned her hair to a thick soggy mat had rendered her silk shirt almost invisible. She might as well be standing here in nothing but her bra.

Leaving her vest to protect the artifact she'd found seemed a pretty stupid idea in retrospect.

Her face heated to the point she expected steam to begin rising any second as she headed into the trees. Jonathan was instantly at her side, pushing back branches to assist her, his free hand lingering at her lower back guiding her forward.

When they stepped into the little clearing where she'd been working, he hurried ahead, snatching up her vest and reaching down to run a finger over her find.

"A magnificent treasure, to be sure," he said, his eyes

fastened on her. "Come, tell me, what do you think these markings might mean?"

Reluctantly eying the vest he'd tossed out of her reach, she dropped to her knees beside him, once again studying what appeared to be a design carved into the ancient wooden handle.

"I can't be sure until we have it out and cleaned, but I'm thinking it might be some type of overlapping circles."

Her thoughts were cut short with a gasp as Jonathan trailed a hand up her spine, his fingers tightening around the base of her neck, firmly urging her face toward his.

This wasn't happening.

On reflex she jerked her arms up between them, pushing against his chest. "Look, Jonathan—"

"I have looked," he interrupted, "and I very much like what I see, Abigail. I like it and I want it for my very own."

To her surprise, he dragged her forward, crushing his mouth over hers, roughly catching up her bottom lip with his teeth as his free hand covered her breast.

"No!" she grunted, and shoved against his chest with all her strength, pushing away and scrambling backward across the muddy earth.

His hand was so quick, she hardly saw the movement, but his fingers caught her wrist and tightened in a viselike grip. She pulled against his hold in quick, useless jerky movements, as he drew her inexorably closer to him, dragging her to her feet as he stood.

"I'd hoped to do this the easy way, Abigail, but you thwart me at every turn. You're leaving me no choice, love."

He'd flipped out. Total off-the-wall bonkers. And she hadn't a clue what he intended or what she should do. Except get away. She knew she had to get away.

She grasped at straws. "No, no . . . you have choices. There are lots of choices, Jonathan. We always have choices," she babbled, her voice little more than a squeak in her desperation to escape him.

"We'll see," he answered, tightening his grip on her wrist as he reached his other hand into his pocket, pulling out his gold knife.

That couldn't be good. "What? What do you think you're doing? Jonathan? You're frightening me. Let go of me right now."

He drew her hand to his lips for a kiss, overpowering her struggles as if she were a child. Lowering the hand, he chuckled, a wicked light in his eyes as he sliced into the tip of her index finger with his knife.

Seventeen

~~~~

As if the Fates themselves had intervened in his life this day, absolutely nothing had gone as Colin had planned. He felt as though he'd been blocked at every turn, from his arrival at Swan House only to learn Abby had already gone, right down to the lorry driver sitting beside him now.

Having missed Abby, he'd gone to the pub to ask after transportation out to the dig site. Though the village had no official taxi service, one of the older gents in the pub had offered to drive him. Though the walk to the man's home was short in distance, it was far enough for Colin to realize the elderly man had already had far too much of the fine Scots whisky to be operating a vehicle of any sort. He could barely walk without stumbling.

He left the man at his front door, thanking him profusely for his offer but refusing, and headed back to the pub only to be stopped by Mrs. MacKee.

The memory of the feisty, white-haired woman perched on the top step of a tall ladder still had him shaking his head in disbelief. After he'd left her home this morning, she'd decided to take it upon herself to repair the top of her garden gate. The woman was an accident waiting to happen. Had he not chanced upon her when he did, he had no doubt she'd be in bed with broken bones at this very moment.

He'd had no choice but to offer his assistance. How could he not? One simply did not leave an elderly woman to fend for herself. At least not where he came from.

Four hours and a lovely lunch later—she'd insisted and would not take no for an answer—he was finally free to go find Abby.

Mrs. MacKee arranged for him to catch a ride with the lorry driver who'd stopped to deliver a package to her neighbor, and as he'd waved his farewell, he'd once again felt in control of his day. Until, that is, Big Mike had told him he could take him only part of the way to where he wanted to go.

"Here's the crossroads, lad. You'll but need to head down that wee lane a few kilometers to find yer friend. It's sorry I am to be dropping you off in this weather, but it's the rain itself that's left it too muddy for me to risk taking this big lorry down there. It's a heavy load I'm hauling today, and I dinna care to be calling my supervisor to report meself stuck."

"Of course. My thanks to you again, Big Mike."

Colin climbed down from the lorry and began his trek on the muddy lane as the old vehicle's gears ground out a noisy farewell.

The silence had barely settled around him before his thoughts turned to Abby and how anxious he was to reach her. Perhaps the overriding anxiety he experienced was only natural now that he'd located her. Seeing her yesterday had confirmed for him how real his dreams of her had been. It was as if he'd seen her, touched her, every single day since they'd first met.

And yet he must remember that those encounters were only dreams.

She hadn't really spent every night in his bed, in his arms. She didn't feel the sense of intimacy he imagined existed between them. In fact, what had happened when he'd finally spoken to her outside the dreams? He'd wasted the moment by promptly driving her away.

Not a waste, he corrected himself. A learning experience. When he reached her this time, he'd use some self-restraint. He could do that. He'd successfully exercised a remarkable amount of self-restraint just last night at their parting. Instead of sweeping her into his arms and carrying her to the nearest bed, he'd sent her to her rest at the inn. When he found her today, he'd draw once again on that same self-restraint. He'd explain the situation slowly, rationally, allowing her time to adjust to him and to the truth of what had happened.

Such an encounter would have to be easier than pushing her away had been last night.

His only regret was that he couldn't remain in this time long enough to get to know her better in reality rather than in dreams. But she was not his fate. He'd recognized from the first time he'd seen her that she'd already met the man fate intended for her, her Soulmate.

As for him, he was meant to return to his own time to save his friends. And his only connection to Abby was that she was meant to return him there.

The sound of an approaching vehicle interrupted his thoughts, and he stepped back from the lane to wait for the oncoming car to round the curve and pass him.

Not one vehicle but two appeared, both white, mud-splattered vans approaching slowly. The first passed him by, a few of the occupants lifting a hand in greeting to a stranger as they went. The second, wheels sliding on the slick lane, pulled to a stop and a young woman rolled down her window. The same young woman he'd noticed watching him after Abby had stormed out of the pub last night.

"You're Abby Porter's friend, aren't you? Did you come out here looking for her?"

"I am," he responded, moving closer to the van. "Is she in there with you?"

"No." Her voice wavered as if she was reluctant to answer. "But you're welcome to hop in here with us and ride back to town."

Not likely. He'd come for Abby and he intended to see her. "Where is Abby?"

The woman tapped a clipboard she held against the window frame, her brow furrowed as she came to some sort of a decision. "Look, from what I saw in the pub last night, I don't get the impression Abby's all that anxious to see you again, sport."

"She's back at the site," someone yelled from inside the van. "About half a mile. Let it go, Mac. Abby's personal life is none of your business."

"You left her alone out there?" He made no attempt to hide the accusation in his voice. These people were supposed to be Abby's friends.

"She's not alone," Mac snapped back. "Jonathan's with her."

Whatever else the woman might have had to say, he hadn't the time nor the inclination to listen. Nor did he bother with the slow pace of his earlier travels, instead breaking into a steady run to cover the remaining ground as quickly as possible. With each footstep, one thought reverberated through his mind: Those people had done far worse than strand Abby alone in the forest. They'd left her in the company of the Nuadian.

Finding her now was no problem. He could feel her not far ahead, her soul shining like a beacon in the dark. As he expected, she wasn't alone. The soul with hers was dark and fouled whereas hers shone a pure, bright gold.

They did not belong together.

The relief brought on by that realization was short-lived, shattered into painful shards by a scream piercing the forest.

Abby's scream.

Eighteen

———

Fighting him was an exercise in futility. Abby had never once imagined anyone could have such physical strength.

Even as that knowledge sparked through her consciousness, ratcheting up her fear, she struggled to free her wrists from Jonathan's grip, clawing at his face with the hand he held close while he continued to suck on her index finger.

"Let me go!" she screamed at him, resorting to kicking his shins when all else failed.

"I feel it," he laughed, lowering her hand from his mouth but pulling her body closer, crushing her to him. His eyes glittered with a terrifying mania. "I feel it all and I want more!"

He dropped his head to the crook of her neck, roughly scraping his teeth across her tender skin. The trail of his tongue over the spot stung and she kicked again, connecting so hard that she feared for an instant she might have broken her toe.

"Again," he demanded, laughing as he backed her up against a large tree trunk. "Do your worst, my love. I want to feel more!"

Through the haze of her desperation, her mind only faintly registered the bark digging into her back, the wet silk she wore no protection at all.

Helpless. She was absolutely helpless against him. Nothing she did made the slightest difference. She should have taken those self-defense classes last year. Should have stayed in bed this morning. Should have given up archaeology and learned to serve a wicked cup of coffee. Should have done anything that would have kept her from this terrifying moment.

Though there was no one to hear, she screamed again, this time as much in anger and frustration as in fear. He had no right to do this. She had no way to stop him.

He crushed his lips over hers, jamming his tongue in her mouth, muffling her cry.

There was no one to come to her rescue. No one to hear her. No one to help. If she had any chance of getting out of this, she had only her own wits as weapons.

Now if she could only gather those wits. Or even find them to gather.

"Move away from the woman, Nuadian!"

Colin?

He stepped from behind a tree, perhaps ten feet away from where they stood. Though the gap between them felt like a gulf, he was here!

"Nuadian, is it?" Jonathan angled his body toward Colin's, shoving her to the ground as he faced off against the newcomer. "Is it a Guardian I face, then? Am I to believe this to be mere coincidence?"

Abby scrambled back, digging her heels into the mud as she pushed herself onto her knees.

"I don't give a damn what you believe, Nuadian. I only want you gone from this place."

Abby froze, the steely menace in Colin's voice sending a shiver up her spine.

"Ah, but you see, Guardian, what you want is of no importance to me. Only what I want matters." From inside his jacket, Jonathan produced a gun, aiming the weapon directly at Colin. "And what I want is the woman."

This wouldn't do. Not at all. She had to do something. Colin might be crazy, spouting all that crap about being from the past, but he hadn't hesitated to jump to her defense in an attempt to rescue her. She could do no less for him.

Desperately scanning the ground for a rock or a stick or anything at all she could use for defense, Abby's eyes lit on the little gold knife Jonathan had dropped.

Slowly, Abby snaked her hand forward until her fingers touched the handle of the small knife. She kept her eyes glued on the two men who glared at each other across the open ground.

Got it! As her hand closed around the handle, she realized she had no idea what to do next. The knife wasn't large enough to do any real damage. It was really only good enough for one thing. Distraction.

Pushing up onto her haunches, she lifted her arm in preparation.

"Getting out of here with Abigail is no problem." Jonathan babbled on as if thinking aloud. "But what am I to do with you, Guardian? I can't very well leave you behind to alert everyone to what I've done, and I've certainly no desire to take you along with us. Seems to me that leaves only one—"

Whatever dark ending he envisioned for Colin was lost in a blood-curdling scream as Abby slammed the blade of the knife deep into the back of his thigh, driving the little weapon in and down with all her strength.

He dropped the gun, clawing at the back of his leg, and she threw her weight against him. Off balance, he fell to the ground while she scrambled away, racing to Colin and past.

"Come on." She tugged at his arm, ignoring the look on his face. "Come *on!*" Whether he was amazed or horrified by what she'd just done, she didn't have time to discuss it now.

She ran for all she was worth, the sound of Jonathan's screams fading as the distance between them grew.

After several minutes, Colin latched on to her arm, pulling her to a stop.

"Where are you leading us?"

"According to the locals," she managed between gasps, "there are caves up ahead."

Surely one of them would be large enough that she could force herself to go inside. They could hide there until she could think of what they'd need to do next. Maybe even until someone came looking for them. She only hoped that the *someone* would be a rescuer and not the homicidal maniac they'd left behind them.

"Good enough," Colin grunted, sounding not the

least bit winded. "Though I dinna understand how you were able to injure the Nuadian unless . . ."

They didn't have time for this nonsense. Stabbing Jonathan didn't mean she was a bad person. It had been an absolute necessity. In doing it, she'd probably saved Colin's life, for God's sake. She'd certainly saved him from getting shot.

"I had to. I had no choice." The excuse sounded hollow, especially in light of her having rejected Jonathan's use of the same words.

"Has he taken yer blood, Abby?"

"*What?*" Their conversation had slipped totally into the surreal right along with everything else that was happening. Not just surreal. Bizarre. Nightmarish. Enough so that she half-expected to awaken from this horrible dream at any moment.

Colin grabbed her shoulders, giving her a little shake. "Did he ingest any of yer blood? Answer me!"

The thought of Jonathan sucking on her finger after slicing it open floated through her mind. "I guess he did."

In response, Colin merely nodded, whatever emotion her answer elicited hidden behind the expressionless mask he wore. He slid his hand from her shoulder and entangled his fingers with hers to pull her along after him in the direction she'd indicated, moving them much more quickly than the pace she'd initially set.

The locals who'd spoken of the caves had said they were small, some no more than a large indentation. Those wouldn't work. They'd require one of the larger ones to hide in. Right now what she wanted was the largest, deepest, darkest cave in the entire mountain range.

Pulling against Colin's hold, she slowed her steps once again.

"What's wrong?"

"Just give me a second." She bent over, hand at her waist, buying time. Concentrating, she watched the tendrils in her mind's eye fanning out over the mountainside until one began to glow.

"The largest of the caves is this way."

She straightened and pointed in the direction she'd seen in her mind, and they were off. Halfway up the rocky slope, she slowed again, checking to make sure they were still headed toward the largest cave. She didn't have to feign needing a breather this time, not with the pace Colin had set for them.

"We have to keep moving to stay ahead of Flynn," Colin cautioned, his eyes scanning the area behind them.

"I know." Except that the farther removed she got from what had happened, the more she wanted to believe it was over, like some horrible aberration of reality. Maybe Jonathan had given up. That knife in his leg had to be powerfully painful. Maybe the pain had brought him back to his senses.

"I bet he's gone back to town. I don't think he'd stay out here with that wound. I can't imagine that he's still following us."

The sound of her last words hadn't yet died on her lips when a sharp metallic *pop* rang out, followed by a *crack* that sent chips flying off the rocks less than a foot from where she stood.

"Move!" Colin ordered, dragging her after him. "Stay low to the brush until we're in the trees again."

"Was that . . ." She couldn't finish the thought aloud, not and continue to gasp for air as they ran. It had sounded like a firecracker.

"Bullet," Colin hissed over his shoulder. "Yer imagination must be rusty."

Back in the trees, she tugged at his hand, pointing in the direction they needed to go until, at last, they reached the little opening.

"This is somebody's idea of a cave?" It looked like little more than an opening between some rocks.

"Animal den. Get in and move to the back," Colin ordered, shoving her to the ground as another *pop* sounded somewhere behind them.

She closed her eyes and forced herself to scramble into the dark opening, shoving back against the cold rocks to make room for Colin.

Only Colin wasn't crawling in behind her.

"What are you doing?" she hissed, afraid to raise her voice but equally frightened of being left alone as his legs disappeared down the trail past her hiding spot.

Moments later his body reappeared in the opening, the light from outside almost completely blocked as he crawled in backward, tucking a bushy limb in the opening behind him.

"Misdirection," he explained, scooting in next to her and looping his arm around her shoulders. "It will slow him down, but it willna do more than buy us a bit of time at best. We must leave this place, Abby. It's the only way."

The eerily familiar words rattled her. As if she didn't know already that they needed to get out of here.

"You have any bright ideas on how we're to do that with him out there shooting at us? Because I'm fresh out."

Which was probably just as well since her whole hide-in-a-cave thing had pretty much bombed. Instead she was holed up in some bear cave with the man of her dreams, but instead of having a romantic tryst, they were waiting to be shot or eaten.

Though, in truth, as small as this place was, it would have to be a pretty small bear, so maybe *eaten* was a slight exaggeration. If they even had bears in Scotland.

And to think Colin had doubted the might of her imagination.

As if a crazed gunman and bear or lack of them weren't enough for her imagination to practice on, there was also the fact that they were crammed into a hole in the ground. The weight of the mountain could simply collapse the whole thing on them at any moment, burying them alive.

"There's only one thing to do." Colin's urgent whisper broke her line of thought. "Wish us out of here. Send me back to my own time."

Not again. Not here. Not now. She simply couldn't take being cooped up in this dark little tomb with Colin flipping out again. "You are *not* going to start up on that Faerie Magic, time travel crap again. We're in a lot of trouble here, Colin. Try to hold it together for me."

Because if he didn't, she wasn't sure she could.

"Listen to me, Abby Porter. Dinna you say a single word until I've finished, do you hear? I ken the absurdity of what I say, but it's the truth, every word of it. Yer a descendant of the Fae. You've the power of their Magic and you used it to bring me to yer side that morning in Denver. I dinna ken the reason why but that's of no importance now. That man out there is a Nuadian Fae. He took yer blood to share in yer Magic. He willna give up and he willna go away until he finds us. We must leave this place, Abby. It's the only way."

His last words rang in her mind, a duplicate of what he'd said to her in her dreams.

Her body began to tremble uncontrollably and he tightened his arm around her, whispering into her ear.

"You've the power, Abby. Wish us out of here."

"How the hell—"

His large hand clamped over her mouth and he held her close. Only as she heard the footsteps directly outside did she realize he'd stopped her in time to keep her from giving away their hiding spot.

"I know you're close," Jonathan's voice called from somewhere outside. "I'll find you. It's only a matter of time, you know. Make it easy on yourselves and give up now."

Whoever had first said you weren't really scared while something was actually happening, but only after it was over, should have his butt kicked seven ways to Sunday. Because whatever this mess was that she was in, it was happening right at this moment and Abby could confirm for a fact that she'd never been so frightened in her entire life.

Crazy guy in here demanding she *wish* them out of trouble; crazy guy out there taking potshots at them with a gun.

"How?" she whispered when Colin moved his hand.

"Wish it. Concentrate on sending me back to my own time. Wish us safely in our homes and say the words aloud."

Insanity. But no more insane than sitting in a hole in the ground waiting to be murdered or eaten or crushed to death.

"I wish we weren't here." Though the words were more truthful than any she'd ever said aloud, nothing happened.

Not that she'd really expected it to.

"No," he breathed into her ear. "You must wish for the places where we are to be. For the places we need to be. We'll concentrate together. See it in yer mind. See us there in yer mind."

How did he expect her to see a place she'd never been?

She closed her eyes while he held her close, snuggling her forehead against his chin as she formed a picture of the two of them together in her mind's eye. "I wish for us to be in a safe place. In whatever place you would most like us to be. I wish to be in your home, in your time." There. That should make him happy.

She tried to imagine the place she felt most safe, with walls firmly separating them and the maniac searching for them. Walls, hell, she wanted Jonathan in a whole different place from them.

Try as she might, the only vision she could bring into focus was the one from her dreams, she and Colin in that huge bed, the room around them lit only by the dancing flames of a fireplace.

A thought flickered through her mind, allowing her

to wonder if, when Colin concentrated, he saw them as she did, naked, limbs entangled in the great bed from her dreams.

"Wait." His hands tightened on her shoulders. "What words did you say?"

She had no time to think about Colin's question, as the ground around them began to shake. Her eyes flew open as he tightened his hold on her.

"Oh, shit," she breathed. This was it. The mountain really was coming down on them.

Her view was mostly obscured by her position in Colin's arms, but from what she could see, she'd almost swear they were being attacked by a swarm of bees. Fast-flying, multicolored bees dived all around them, sounding as if they pinged off the walls on every side of them.

She waited, expecting to feel the sting of attack any moment. Instead, it suddenly felt as if the ground had given way beneath them, the sensation one of falling a great distance.

Only the knowledge that Colin held her, his arms tightening around her yet again, gave her any measure of security as the black void closed in and reality slipped away.

Either the mountain had given way or all this had, in fact, been no more than a bad dream after all.

Nineteen

Find her, find her, find her . . .

The words echoed inside Flynn's head, pounding at his mind even as the pain seared through his thigh in a hideous, utterly foreign sensation. Somewhere in the deep recesses of his old self, he recognized that it was the Bloodlust that had taken him. The Bloodlust that tinged his vision as though he viewed the world through a red prism.

Even knowing, he was powerless against it. He had become the Bloodlust.

He scrambled higher up the rocky hillside, his feet slipping on the loose gravel and twigs. A flash of white brushed his peripheral vision and he lifted his weapon, firing a shot blindly in that general direction.

No! Too dangerous. Can't risk killing her.

All would be lost if that happened.

Must find her. Reason with her. Convince her to come with him.

"I know you're close." He called out in his desperation, hoping against hope they'd give their position away. "I'll find you. It's only a matter of time, you know. Make it easy on yourselves and give up now."

Not far now. He could all but feel her. Could almost feel her heart beating in time with his own.

Must be systematic. Slow down.

He retraced his steps, stopping where the path curved into the trees.

Find her, find her, find her . . .

No longer able to ignore the throbbing in his thigh, he dropped to his knees, struggling to breathe through the pain.

It was then he saw it, dancing in the corner of his vision. A green light that seemed to glow from the misshapen branches to his right. Branches oddly growing from the rock face.

He stuffed the gun into the pocket of his jacket before he reached out to clasp his hand around the rough bark, intending to pull himself to it for a closer inspection. But the wood gave way, revealing an opening in the rock.

What had appeared as a mere glow through the branches burst from the opening in a shaft of brilliant emerald light, knocking him flat even as it bathed him in a flood of frenzied sparkles.

From this vantage, he could see beyond the opening, into the interior of the shallow cave. There, in the very heart of the light, the woman he sought, cradled in the interloper's arms!

He would have called out, would have dragged himself forward to claim what was rightfully his, but the world turned upside down and sucked him soundlessly into a vast, black void.

Twenty

❦

Colin awoke in the dark, aware only that he was no longer in the cave. The Magic had worked, and though he sensed no immediate danger, where the Magic had taken him—or when—he had no idea.

Where or when it had taken *them*.

Abby lay in his arms, her legs entangled with his. Warm, soft, and invitingly naked, her skin caressed his, seriously impairing his ability to concentrate on their surroundings.

When her hand slid up his chest to his face, tenderly guiding his mouth down to meet hers, what little sense he had deserted him completely. He ran his tongue across her lower lip before dipping inside. Just as he remembered, she tasted sweet, like a marvelous mix of mint and honey.

She anchored her hand behind his neck and pressed

her body against his. He tightened his arms around her, deepening the kiss, losing himself in the moment. She moaned against him, a soft mewling, needy sound that drove him wild with desire.

Rolling her to her back, he fit himself into the warm cradle between her legs, eliciting another of those little noises as she locked her ankles behind his back. He rocked against her once, twice, his need growing until he thought he might burst.

She met each of his moves with one of her own, and on the third he found his mark, inching slowly inside her tight heat.

Like coming home to a place created just for him, in this moment, he feared he'd never find its equal again in this life.

Her hips lifted, grinding against his pelvis, and he dropped his hands to those lovely hips, holding them still while he prayed he could last long enough to satisfy them both.

Slowly, very slowly, he eased himself almost all the way out before slowly sliding back in again.

By the Fates! Swiving had never felt like this before.

"Yes. Oh yes," Abby breathed the words into his ear, urging him on with the movement of her hips against his. "Yes . . . *No!*" Her hands swept from his neck to his chest, pushing against him. "Oh my God! This is real. It's not the dream at all. This is actually happening. You have to stop. You have to stop this right now!"

Stop? What was this stop *she spoke of?*

His mind blanked and his entire body shuddered as he ceased all motion, still buried just inside her warm sheath.

"We can't do this. We *cannot* be doing this! Get off me!"

Abby wiggled beneath him and he tightened his grip on her hips, pinning her to the bed below him. Much more of that from her and it would be too late to stop.

"Be still, woman," he ordered, his breath coming in short, desperate pants. "I'll do as you ask, but dinna you move again. Give me but a moment to collect myself."

He rested his head against her breast, fighting to regain command of himself as he listened to her heart beat a furious tattoo under his ear. At last, his control somewhat returned, he withdrew, rolling off her and onto his back. Eyes closed, he concentrated on an intricate series of sword work patterns he'd learned in Wyddecol and the footwork involved in each thrust and parry.

Thrust. He groaned and tried once again to clear his mind.

"I know this place." Abby's voice came from just above him in a breathless whisper. "I've seen it a hundred times in my dreams. Where are we? How did we get here?"

When he opened his eyes, a dull gray light filtered through the room, emanating from the early morning sun shining through a crack in the wooden shutters high up on the wall. He knew the place as well.

"This is my own bedchamber."

As soon as he could move again, he'd have to deal with all this. Dun Ard was not where the Magic was supposed to take them, though why he should have expected the Magic to do as he wanted this time was beyond him. His intent had been that she should be sent to the safety of her own home even as he should have found himself in the woods near Methven. He had certainly not planned on bringing Abby back through time with him, no more than he'd planned on bedding her.

So much for his plans.

He'd feared there could be a problem when he'd realized the words she'd said aloud, but by then, it was too late. The Magic had already been invoked.

"You've sent us to my home, Abby. To Dun Ard."

"As if. Don't you even try that line on me. I know for a fact that Dun Ard is not your home. I was there. I went there looking for you. Those people had never even heard of you." Abby sat next to him, her face determinedly turned away from him, a woolen coverlet pulled up to her chin. "How did we get here?" she demanded again, twitching nervously at the cover. "And what the hell did you do with my clothes?"

"What did *I* do?" He pushed himself up to sit, shaking his head at how wrong everything had gone. "It's as I told you. It's you what did the wishing, lass. You who said the words to send us here. I should be asking what *you* did with *my* clothes. Again."

It was her words that had directed the Magic to put them here, together, so very far from where they both needed to be, but the fault was all his. He should have realized the danger and told her exactly what to say.

Rising from the bed, he made his way to the fireplace and squatted beside it. The fire had been laid at the ready as it always was. All he had to do was strike the tender and start the flames to bring some warmth to the chamber.

"Right. Like you expect me to believe I could simply wish us out of that cave? That's about as truthful as Dun Ard being your home."

Flames licked up over the wood and he rose to his feet, facing the bed.

"First, if you canna accept that it's yer wishing that sent us here, then how *do* you explain it? And, for the record, Dun Ard *is* my home. Here. Now. In 1306, no in yer time." Assuming the blasted Magic had at least transported them to the proper time. He resented her implication that he'd lied about his home, though as he thought about it, he did find some satisfaction in the idea that she'd gone there in her own time searching for him. "You looked for me there, did you?"

"Wait. Let's just back this up for a second. Did you say 1306? That's crazy. It's not possible." She turned to face him, immediately dropping her eyes to her lap. "Could you please put something on? I can't think with *that*," she waved her hand in his general direction, "when it's like that."

He looked down to where she'd pointed and frowned. His swollen manhood was only now beginning to return to normal.

She waited in silence as he strode to the chest at the foot of his bed and pulled out first a shirt and then a plaid, which he deftly wound around himself.

"Better?"

Abby nodded, her eyes glassy when she looked up. "What's happening here, Colin?"

"It's as I told you. You've the blood of the Fae in you and the power of their Magic at yer disposal. You saved us from that filthy Nuadian by sending us here."

Though he could have spent the rest of his day simply watching her, he had to get moving. If the Fae had sent them to the wrong location, there was no telling what date they'd chosen. He could only pray he wasn't too late to save his friends.

For now, he needed to find his cousin Blane, the MacKiernan laird, and his brother Caden to tell them both what had happened. He also needed to find someone to help ease Abby into life here until they could figure out how to send her home.

His stomach knotted at the thought of her leaving but he pushed the foolish emotion from his mind and walked to the door. Of course she had to leave. She should never have been here to begin with.

"What do you think you're doing now? You're going to leave me here? Alone?"

She'd risen from the bed when he turned, the coverlet clutched to her breasts. The look of desperation on her lovely face drew him back to her side.

He enfolded her in his embrace and she leaned into him. "Don't leave me here, Colin. I don't think I can wrap my head around this. I'm scared."

With a kiss to her forehead, he pushed her away. "I'll only be downstairs, Abby. You've no a need to fash yerself. Yer safe here. Climb back into bed and I'll send my mother with clothing for you."

"You'll send your *mother*? Oh, Lord, Colin. Your mother's going to come in here and find me bare-ass naked in your bed? That's just perfect. Thank you so much for making things all better for me."

A twinge of guilt held him in place. A guilt that

forced him to confront what they had done earlier, a task made all the more difficult by his own confusion.

"About what passed between us, Abby. I'm sorry for . . ." He paused, suddenly unsure of exactly what he wanted to say. It would be a lie to say he was sorry it had happened. He wasn't. If anything, he was sorry they hadn't finished what they'd started.

She saved him from having to finish. "Forget it. It was as much my fault as yours. I'm sorry it all went so badly and left you, you know, so uncomfortable and all."

Yes, for that he could honestly say he was sorry as well.

Again he kissed her forehead and turned away, saying at last what was really in his thoughts. "Perhaps next time will go more smoothly, aye?"

Her strangled "Next time?" brought a smile to his lips as he closed the door behind him.

Twenty-one

‿‿‿

Colin did not enjoy being made to feel as if he were but a bairn again, called up in front of his mother and the laird to answer for some new misdeed.

"So you drag the lass seven hundred years into her past and then you abandon her? You leave her sitting on yer bed all by herself. And naked at that, if I'm no mistaken, aye?" Caden shook his head and exchanged a look with their laird and cousin, Blane MacKiernan, as if he couldn't believe his younger brother's stupidity. "What were you thinking, Col? Have you no good sense about women at all?"

"It was she who did the dragging," Colin muttered in his own defense.

In hindsight, perhaps he should have waited for a private moment with his mother to mention Abby's need for clothing rather than to have asked within

Caden's hearing. His prudish older brother would be hammering away at this one for quite some time, he had no doubt.

"And as to what I was thinking, my mind was set upon ending up at the camp in Methven in time to see to the safety of Dair and Simeon. I'd no intended to bring Abby here."

"Then I suppose we should be thanking the Fates the lass dinna end up unclothed in the middle of our king's army encampment." The lady Rosalyn spoke wearing her best no-nonsense expression.

"I'd intended that the Magic send her to her own home, in her own time."

His mother opened her mouth as if to speak, but held back, her mouth drawn into a tight, disapproving line. He suspected she had quite a bit more she wanted to say, but she yielded to Blane with a stiff nod of her head.

"Intent or no, Cousin, the lass is here, seven hundred years from where she belongs, and it falls to you to deal with what's to become of her." Blane peered over steepled fingers held against his face.

"I canna." Colin shook his head emphatically as if by his action alone he could abdicate his responsibility. "I dinna have time for any female hysterics. Even if I leave at first light and ride my horse into the ground, I may still be too late to reach Methven before the battle that is to come. At best, I can only hope Dair and Simeon survive long enough for me to reach them."

Not that he'd ever actually found Abby to be hysterical, not even when hiding in that cave.

"You never change, little brother." Caden pushed back his chair and stood, shaking his head in disgust.

"Always so sure only you have the answers. How quickly you seem to have forgotten all the worldly advice you poured in my ears regarding Ellie. Can you no see yer responsibilities lie not in battle but with this woman you've brought to our time?"

"What passed between you and Ellie was an entirely different situation!" The Fae had sent Ellie from the future to this time specifically because she was Caden's Soulmate. His older brother had simply been too blindly stubborn to see it without trickery on the part of the entire family to force his hand. "Abby's being here is an accident, no the plan of the Fae. As I explained to you before, it was only a slip of her words that brought her here with me rather than sending her to her own home."

Caden threw up his hands and stalked to the door. "I've no the patience to argue this with you now, Colin. I go to send my Ellie to the woman in yer bedchamber. If anyone can help her accept what's happening to her, my Ellie's the one."

"My thanks, Brother," Colin offered stiffly, but his words were lost in the slamming of the door.

Just as well. With Caden gone, perhaps he could get on with making his arrangements to set out for Methven. Surely his laird could see beyond all this bickering to recognize the urgency of his mission.

"With yer permission, my laird, I'll be off for Methven at first light on the morrow. With luck, I'll find our king and advise him of the treachery awaiting his army, hopefully in time to save Dair and Simeon."

To his surprise, it was his mother who spoke up first. "I'm no so sure our laird should agree to that plan."

Blane nodded thoughtfully, his long fingers stroking his chin as he spoke. "I would hear your reasoning, Aunt."

"Our family heritage has long presented us with uncommon abilities and challenges. Those carry with them a heavy burden of responsibility, as well. Yer own father, Colin, fashed himself over what harm we could bring this world if we used the Faerie Magic for our own gain. I dinna believe it wise for you to act based on what you learned of our future while you were in that other time. Yer cousin Mairi told me herself the Fae forbade the changing of history."

Always it came back to the damn Fae.

"And who am I to follow the rules of the Fae after all the harm they've brought down on our family? Because of the Fae, our lives have been disrupted time and time again. Two of your own children suffered at their hands and almost died, or did you forget that, my lady mother?" Not to mention his own suffering thanks to the Faerie Queen.

"I've forgotten nothing, Colin MacAlister. It's quick you are to point out the bad. But can you no give equal consideration to the good? Would either of yer brothers be happily wed today if not for the Magic of the Fae? And what of yer sister, Sallie? Had she not gone through such as she did, things might have turned out very differently for her as well."

Colin ground his teeth but refused to argue any further with his mother. Rosalyn was obviously blinded by the happiness she desired for her children. He, meanwhile, was talking about the fate of the entire country. The knowledge of the future he possessed could make a difference in obtaining freedom for all of Scotland.

"No to even mention all the problems you could cause in the future," Rosalyn continued. "There are too many unknown disasters you could bring down on the heads of our own descendants with one careless slip in the here and now. There's a reason you're no to tinker with the way things are meant to be."

Blane nodded and steepled his fingers again. "I'll take yer words into consideration, Aunt. And as for you, Colin, I'll have my answer to yer request by the time we sit down for the evening meal."

A moment of doubt assailed Colin, but he firmly pushed it away. It made no difference that he'd not had the chance to read any further in the wondrous book he'd found in Mairi's library. He knew as much as he needed. Certainly enough to prevent King Robert's army from complete destruction at the hands of the MacDougalls after Methven. That was all that mattered.

Colin stood respectfully as his mother and his laird left the room. For now, there was no further discussion to be had. But that didn't change anything.

At first light on the morrow, he would be on his way to Perthshire to find his king. With or without his laird's blessing.

Twenty-two

❧

*I*t was the stick prodding at his chest that awoke him. A stick wielded by an oddly costumed young woman.

"You alive?" Another poke accompanied her heavily accented words.

"Of course I'm alive, you silly twit." Flynn slapped away the offending implement to roll to his side and push himself up to sit. "I'm fine. Where the bloody hell . . ."

He lay in an alleyway, tucked between two low, dirt-covered walls. Taking in his surroundings, the sights, the smells, robbed him of his ability to speak. He recognized this place. Rather, he recognized a thousand sordid places such as this one. *Where* was no longer his concern, so much as *when*.

"You dinna look to be so fine, to me." The woman stepped closer, tossing her long, red braid over one shoulder before prodding once again.

A fiery trail of pain shot through his leg as the tip of her stick pressed against the wound on his thigh. He grabbed the stick and jerked, dragging the young woman to the ground next to him as he wrenched the implement from her hands.

Before she could draw breath to scream, he captured her gaze and forced his will into her softly yielding mind. The fear coloring her expression a moment before gave way to the blank, emotionless stare of the Compulsion's entrancement.

"Where am I?" he demanded.

"The village of Dunkiernan."

It had the sound of Scotland as it rolled from her tongue. The style of dress screamed Middle Ages.

But how could he have traveled through time?

Faerie Magic was the only possibility. Abigail's Magic? He'd had no earthly idea she had this ability. He'd never felt even a touch of something like this in her blood.

"Take me to your home. I need care."

Wordlessly, she helped him to his feet and led him out behind the buildings, across a field, and into the nearby woods.

With a backward glance at the village behind him, any lingering doubts as to *when* he might be evaporated. No one who'd ever lived through this bedeviled time could possibly forget it.

Beyond the tiny village, the land rose. In the distance, a castle perched atop the highest point.

"Who lives up there?" he asked, pointing behind them.

The young woman paused to turn her head, her dull eyes following the direction he indicated.

"The MacKiernan. Our laird." Question answered, she continued forward, still taking part of his weight as he leaned on her shoulder.

MacKiernan. He might have heard the name before, but as to what he'd heard, he had no memory. He'd traveled these lands, but it had been such a very long time ago.

How is this possible?

The question battered against his consciousness over and over like some heathen warrior's drumbeat.

When he stopped suddenly, the woman stumbled but caught her balance before falling.

If Abigail's Magic had sent him to this hellhole, it was Abigail's Magic that could take him back. He'd researched her too carefully not to know she didn't belong in this time any more than he did.

She didn't, but perhaps that so-called boyfriend of hers might?

"Where can I find Colin MacAlister?"

Again the woman's footsteps faltered and she paused to turn, lifting her arm to point up toward the castle in the distance.

If MacAlister was there, Flynn's ticket home would be there, too. He'd survived this cesspool of history once. He had absolutely no intention of living through it a second time.

Twenty-three

~~~~

Abby lay in the big bed just as she had so often in her dreams, her body throbbing with disappointment and need, her mind reeling with confusion.

When she'd first awakened, she'd been so sure it was simply the dream. So sure, until Colin's lovemaking had moved far beyond anything she'd ever experienced in the dream. Only then had she realized it was actually happening.

Even then it had taken all her willpower to call a halt.

None of this made any sense. Simply *wishing* for something couldn't make it happen. It wasn't possible. It wasn't rational.

And yet . . .

Something had definitely happened. One minute she was in a cave with a homicidal maniac hunting them and the next she was in Colin's bed, with him making love to her.

"Explain that one if you can, Miss Faeries-Don't-Exist," she said aloud, sitting up as she did so.

She couldn't explain it. The harder she tried to come up with something, the more Casey's words echoed through her mind.

I'm telling you, it's that wish we made. I don't know how, but it has to be.

When she was little, her dad had spoken of magic often, attributing all sorts of things to the mysterious force. Like her ability to find things. But that was just a story meant to soothe a child, wasn't it? Could any of this be true?

No, no, no. She pressed her knuckles against her eyes, rubbing as if her surroundings might be different when she opened them once again.

Accepting any portion of this bizarre business would mean she'd have to accept the whole of it. And there was no way on earth she was accepting the idea that she was sitting in a lumpy bed in medieval Scotland.

She snorted her disbelief, bolstering her confidence, and pushed herself out of bed, pulling the woolen coverlet along with her and wrapping it around her body.

Besides, given time, surely she could come up with some plausible explanation for how she could pass out in one place and wake up somewhere else.

"That could happen." She again spoke out loud, comforted by the sound of her own voice reflecting off the stone walls. "Easily." There had to be all sorts of nonmagic and certainly non-Faerie explanations for such a thing. There'd been an earthquake, she remembered that much. And afterward, Colin must have carried her somewhere, though what had happened to Jonathan Flynn she had no idea at the moment.

That explanation made sense. Sort of.

But wishing something into existence? No. Faerie Magic? No. Time travel?

"Oh, hell no!"

There. She felt better already.

She padded over to the fireplace and turned back to survey the room. First thing she needed to do was get out of here. While this place would certainly pass muster as a first-class reproduction of a medieval bedchamber, outside these four walls she would surely find evidence of where she really was.

Though, if there actually were other people downstairs as Colin had said, she'd really prefer not to be traipsing around in nothing more than a blanket.

A knock on the door caught her off guard. It wasn't likely Colin would bother to knock. He had, after all, claimed this was his bedroom.

"Bedchamber," she corrected under her breath, as she went to open the door a crack to peek outside.

"Hi!"

The woman standing in the hallway was stunning. Her long, black hair was pulled back in a tie and hung over her shoulder in a soft, dark swath. She smiled over a huge armful of cloth she carried.

Abby's first thought centered on hoping that bundle was clothing. Her second hit with a little more shock. Could this possibly be the woman Colin had said he was sending?

"Please don't even try to tell me you're Colin's mother." She couldn't be more than mid- to late twenties at most.

The woman laughed as she pushed past Abby and into the room, a hearty, happy sound trailing after her much like the scruffy little dog at her feet.

"No, I'm not Rosalyn. I'm Colin's sister-in-law, Ellie. And this is Missy." She pointed to the dog who had already made herself very much at home in front of the fire. "I hope you don't mind dogs, do you? They're with me so often, I sometimes forget that some people are bothered by them."

"No problem." Abby shook her head, tightening her hold on the coverlet she wore.

"Great!" Ellie smiled and dumped her fluffy load on the bed, busily sorting things out into piles. "When Caden—that's my husband. He's Colin's older brother. Anyway, when he asked me to come up and help get you oriented, I just grabbed up an armload of stuff from a bunch of us. I figured somewhere in the mix, we'd find something to fit you until we can get the sewing ladies to do their thing."

Abby's stomach sank at the thought of a whole houseful of people knowing she was hiding out in Colin's bedroom, sans a single stitch of clothing. Humiliation might have had a chance to really get its claws in if something else hadn't distracted her.

"Do their thing?" How not medieval was that? "It's kind of hard to swallow Colin's line about this being 1306 when your speech patterns sound pretty much like mine. Well, except for the whole southern thing you've got going on there."

Ellie plopped down on the bed next to the piles she'd

laid out. "Texas drawl. I don't think it ever goes away." She shook her head, a soft smile curving her lips. "But don't let that fool you, Abby. It is Abby, right?" When Abby nodded, she continued, "This is most definitely 1306. Believe you me, two years ago when those damn Faeries dropped my butt here in a bolt of their green lightning, I didn't believe it either, so I completely understand your hesitation. Nevertheless, it's a fact. You've just made yourself a trip to medieval Scotland."

Abby took a step back, sitting rather suddenly with a definite thud on the stool by the fireplace. Next to her, the little dog readjusted its position, scooting closer to her foot as if to comfort her.

"Okay then, how? How does it all work? Convince me this really happened. I have an open mind. I'm a scientist. An archaeologist. At least, I will be when I finish up my graduate work." She shook her head, irritated that she couldn't even rant properly without correcting herself. "But I won't be easily fooled. I've had history classes up the wazoo. If this is truly medieval Scotland, tell me how you communicate with these people. They sure as heck didn't speak our version of English. Don't speak. Whatever. How do you explain that one?"

Ellie shrugged one shoulder, lifting what looked like a thin nightgown and shaking it out. "I'm not sure I can. To be honest, Abby, I don't put much thought into it anymore. It's all tied up in the Faerie Magic. It brought me here to where I belonged. Because of it, I understand them, they understand me, and I've never been happier. So, what say we just let all that go and find something in this mess that fits you so we can take you downstairs and introduce you to the family. How's that sound?"

It sounded like distraction to Abby, and she wasn't having any part of it.

"Magic. Faeries are responsible for whisking me through time. You honestly expect me to believe that line of bullcrap?"

Ellie stood and walked over to where Abby sat, holding out the garment in her hand. "I don't expect anything from you, Abby. You can deal with all of this however you need to. This is fact. Whether you like it or not, there really are Faeries in the world. There really is Magic. Just like in all the stories we heard as little girls. But the thing you need to understand is, it's not the Fae who are responsible for your being here. *You* are responsible for your being here. You obviously have Faerie ancestry, because you wished yourself here and here you are. Now, let's try this one on you. I think it looks about the right length."

That *wishing* crap again.

Abby stood and accepted the gown, lifting it to drop over her head, but Ellie stopped her, running her forefinger over the dark bruises on Abby's upper arm.

"Lady Rosalyn has some herbs that might help that. And the scrape on your neck."

"Thanks." Abby darted her eyes away from the other woman's, hiding her ridiculous embarrassment by sliding into the gown. She thrust her arms into the long sleeves and allowed the yards of material to float down around her. There was no reason for her to feel like this. It wasn't her fault she'd been attacked.

Too much. There was just too much happening to allow her to think straight. All this sensory overload had cluttered her mind and kept her from thinking rationally. She just needed to look at the situation from a scientific, logical perspective.

Not that it felt like there was anything either scientific or logical going on here as her reality tumbled away from her.

"It's okay," she murmured to herself. "Even Einstein said that reality is merely illusion."

"I'm sorry?" A little frown furrowed Ellie's brow as she lifted her head from digging through the piles on the bed.

"Nothing."

So, if logic had failed her, maybe she should forget reality and work with what she had. If she accepted what both Colin and Ellie said, if all it really took was a wish . . .

"Just for the sake of argument, Ellie, let's say everything you're telling me is the truth. If I wished myself here, then I should be able to wish myself home again, to my own time, right? Whenever I want to." She fumbled with the lacing at her neck, finally managing a small bow before looking up at her companion.

Ellie's face clearly reflected an internal battle over the words she chose. "It certainly seems like it *should* work that way, doesn't it?" With a shrug, she picked up another item from the bundle and headed around the bed to where Abby waited. "By all means, you can try wishing yourself back any time you want, but I wouldn't hold my breath expecting it to work."

"Wait." Abby caught Ellie's hand with her own as the other woman held out another garment to her. "What do you mean it won't work?"

Again Ellie shrugged. "I'm not saying it absolutely won't. I'm only saying it didn't for me. The real version of Faerie Magic isn't at all like the fairy tales you and I grew up on. You can't just rub a lamp and get three wishes. See, the thing is, the Faerie Magic works for its own purpose. It's almost like the Fae are only loaning you their Magic to get you to do something they want done. If they granted your wish, they had a reason. They want something to happen. Whether it's some lesson you have to learn or some task that needs to be performed, until that particular thing is done, no matter what you want, you're stuck here. At least, that's how it worked for me."

If all this was real, how completely awful for this poor woman to be stranded here, so far away from her own time.

"Couldn't you ever figure out your task? Is that why you're still here?"

"Oh, no," Ellie chuckled. "I'm here because this is where Caden is. And I was meant to be with Caden."

"In fourteenth-century Scotland," Abby countered, fully aware of the sarcasm in her voice. "With no cars and no cell phones, and not even any freaking toilet paper."

Ellie's responding giggle was infectious. "Oh, honey, believe me, there are things that are so much more important than any of that stuff. I wouldn't trade my life with Caden MacAlister for all the toilet paper in the entire twenty-first century. You wait and see. You'll get used to it here."

"Used to it? Oh, I don't think so. I can't even begin to imagine wanting to live in the fourteenth century. If I really am out of my own time, you can bet I'm going to do whatever it takes to get myself back to where I belong."

Ellie shrugged. "But until you manage that, since you're an archaeologist and all, maybe you can think of this as a hands-on learning experience. You know, like an up close and personal chance to study the things you normally only see after they've rotted in the ground for centuries." She leaned back over the bed, digging through the piles of clothing while she spoke as if she were discussing nothing more important than the weather. "Well, darn. I guess I didn't grab those little slippers after all. You wait right here, and I'll be right back."

With that, she hurried out the door, pulling it softly shut behind her.

Abby brushed her hands down the long overdress she'd slipped over her head, absently smoothing the soft fabric as her mind worked frantically to process all she'd been told.

Just because wishing didn't work for Ellie didn't mean it wouldn't work for her. Assuming it had ever worked at all.

One way to find out.

"I wish to be back to my own time." She stood very still, eyes closed, waiting.

Nothing.

Maybe the Faeries were simply concerned with her well-being and didn't want to send her back into danger.

"Okay, then. I can respect that. I wish I were safely back in my own home, in Denver, in my own time." Again she waited, watching for any tiny sign that might indicate it was working.

Where was the green lightning Ellie had spoken of? Or the green bubble of light she'd seen in the cave?

Or even—oh, my God!—the green glow she'd seen the night in the bar when she'd wished to find the one man for her?

Maybe it was true. Maybe it was all true. But if it was, why wasn't it working now?

The little dog at her feet let out a growly moan and laid her chin on Abby's bare foot, her big brown eyes actually looking sorrowful.

"Sucks, doesn't it, dog?" Abby reached down to scratch the little furball at her feet. "I'm doing the wishing thing, just like everybody keeps swearing is true, but I'm sure not seeing anything."

"Missy's real sorry it didn't work for you."

Abby jumped, thinking for a moment the dog had spoken, since she hadn't heard Ellie's silent entrance.

"I'm sorry, too." Ellie handed over a pair of soft leather slippers. "But I can't say I'm surprised. Like I said before, Faerie Magic works on its own mysterious timetable, only when *it's* good and ready. You know, it's likely that, since the Fae sent you along with Colin, he's part of whatever it is they want from you. One thing I've learned: there are no coincidences when it comes to Faerie Magic. Everything that happens, happens for a reason. I'm guessing that whatever you have to do to get home, you have to do it *with* Colin."

Colin was the missing piece of her return-home equation? In that case, wherever Colin was, that was where she intended to be.

"He's downstairs?"

Ellie nodded. "As far as I know he is. The midday meal is the largest one of the day. One thing I should mention, though. We don't really talk openly about the

Magic in front of everyone. Though the whole clan has heard the Faerie stories, they don't all have firsthand knowledge of their truth. We try to keep that limited to just the immediate family."

Abby nodded her understanding. She could see how that might tend to be the sort of thing that could scare off the hired help.

"So." Ellie smiled brightly and looped her arm through Abby's. "Speaking of the family, you ready to meet them?"

"As ready as I'll ever be." What she was really ready for was to find Colin MacAlister and give that wishing thing another go.

Twenty-four

———

"Colin?"

His back stiffened and he sat straighter in his chair at the long table in the Great Hall.

He hated it when his mother began by using his name in that particular tone of voice. It was the one she reserved for determining which of her boys had broken into her dried fruits or which of them had trampled through her herb garden when they were young. To this day it immediately put him on the defensive.

"I met yer Abby at midday meal. She's a lovely young woman, though I believe she was distressed you dinna join us."

He felt the rebuke of her statement but couldn't bring himself to explain his absence. It wasn't as if he were actually avoiding Abby. There had been arrangements to be made for his travels on the morrow.

"She's no my Abby."

"Oh?" Rosalyn smiled up at the serving girl who filled her cup, waiting until the girl moved on. "There's a thing which has troubled my thoughts since our talk this morn. Would you mind if we discussed it before yer Abby joins us?"

With resignation, he nodded his acquiescence. There was obviously no deterring his mother once she set her course.

"Once I sat down to my mending, I began to wonder, Colin, if the Magic sent this lovely young woman, this Abby of yers, into yer bed without a single stitch of clothing, would I be correct in my assumption that you also were in that bed? And that you also were unclothed as she was?"

"I'll admit, Cousin, the same has crossed my mind," Blane added from Rosalyn's left.

"And mine, as well," Caden chimed in.

Perfect. The whole of the clan seemed intent on joining in this discussion of his and Abby's state of undress.

He started to answer but paused, considering where his mother was leading this conversation. As if the room were closing in on him from all sides, he quickly realized there was no answer he could give that wouldn't bring looks of disapproval to every face at the table. For a brief instant he considered lying but discarded that idea even as it formed. It wasn't just that the telling of untruths violated his sense of honor. He also doubted it would help, since he'd spent the better part of his childhood half-convinced that his mother had the uncanny ability to read his thoughts.

The truth it was, then.

"Aye."

The admission was made more uncomfortable by his inability to follow up by telling them it had all been perfectly innocent and platonic. It had, in fact, been anything but. And truth be told, he knew in his heart that were he to find himself in a similar situation, he'd do the exact same again.

"I see."

The arch in his mother's brow should have warned him of what was to come, but he chose to ignore it, hoping he was wrong.

"And what do you propose to do to rectify having dishonored this young woman?" Blane asked, clearly speaking in his capacity as Laird of the MacKiernan rather than concerned older cousin.

"Dishonored?" This was not a conversation he had any desire to pursue.

"Aye," his cousin answered. "You've taken the lass to yer bed, with full knowledge of yer entire clan. She is a lady, without protection of kith or kin. If she's unable to return to her own home, what will you do to make this right for her?"

"What would you have of me?" Surely his cousin couldn't be suggesting a marriage. The fate of two of their clansmen, as well as the whole of their king's army, hung in the balance and these people were fashing themselves over the reputation of one woman?

"I would have you do the right thing, Cousin. I would have you wed this Abby of yers."

"Hold on a minute. Let's not anybody get carried away here."

Somewhere during the back-and-forth with his

family, he'd missed Abby's entrance. She stood behind him with Caden's wife, Ellie, who even now pulled out the chair next to him for Abby to sit.

Abby seated herself and clasped her hands in front of her before looking up with what could only be irritation on her lovely face. "Pardon me for jumping in, but I must have misunderstood what I just heard. Colin and I aren't getting married. I am not marrying him, he's not marrying me. There's no marrying of any sort going to happen. Just so we all get that straight. I'm only here for a little while."

"Thank the Fates someone here has some sense," Colin muttered, ignoring the twinge of uncomfortable emotion her immediate rejection of him brought with it. Ridiculous, that. He felt exactly the same way she did. "On the morrow I leave for Methven. Once I've found—"

"Excuse me," Abby interrupted, laying a hand on his forearm. "You meant to say *we're* leaving for Methven, right? Because you're not going anywhere without me."

"I go to save the lives of my clansmen. I go to warn my king of the treachery awaiting him." Surely she could see the higher cause here. "It's no a place for a lass such as yerself."

"Yeah. See, that's not going to work for me." Abby paused as the serving girl set a trencher between them. "It appears that the only way I can get home is with your assistance. So, whither thou goest, and all that stuff."

Perhaps he'd credited the woman with good sense far too quickly.

"You canna mean to accompany me on this journey, Abby. I head toward battle, my purpose too important to risk on having to fash myself over yer safety. I ken you have no experience with the ways of our world, but I assure you, where I go is no a place for a woman such as yerself."

An uncharacteristic silence filled the room as his entire family watched and waited for Abby's response.

"You said you were going to save people, not to fight them." Abby shook her head stubbornly, picking at the meat in front of them. "I may not have actual experience in your world, Colin, but I'm not ignorant of its ways. I'm not waiting here while you traipse off and get yourself killed leaving me trapped here in this time. You aren't going anywhere without me. Where you go, I go. Simple as that."

This was not a disagreement he relished having under the avid view of his family, but he would not back down. As far as he was concerned, there was nothing left to discuss. "Yer staying here and that's my final word on the matter. It's as simple as *that*." He could have sworn he heard his brother chuckle behind him.

"Oh, really?" She turned to meet his gaze, her eyes narrowing. "Well how about this for simple?" She leaned in close, lowering her voice and forcing him to lean toward her. "How about I just wish us both back to my time right now? How about that? If my wishes are so damn powerful and you're so damn set on saving these friends of yours, then I'd strongly recommend you reconsider taking me with you or the only place you're going is the twenty-first century."

"You canna mean that. My clansmen face death if I'm no allowed to go to them. My king faces defeat." Aloud, he denied her threat, but from her expression, he feared she meant every word she uttered. "You wouldna do such as that."

"No? Try me."

Colin sat back in his chair, waiting for a wave of anger and frustration to pass over him. If anyone was trapped anywhere, it was him. He couldn't risk being tossed back through time. Not before he'd had a chance to warn his king of what was to come.

"I've changed my mind," he announced in a loud voice. "When I leave on the morrow for Methven, Abby will accompany me."

"Damn straight," she murmured beside him.

"As yer laird, I canna allow that." Blane spoke up for the first time. "As yer own mother has just reminded me, an unmarried lass canna travel unaccompanied with a man who is not of her family. It's no a proper thing to do and we've none to spare to send along with the two of you."

"I'm not the least bit concerned with what's proper," Abby rejected.

"But we are," Rosalyn added from her spot at Colin's elbow. "Now, if you were to wed, there would be no cause for concern."

Colin jerked his head around to glare at his mother. What was wrong with the woman, sitting there smiling like some brainsick banshee? Was it not bad enough he was being forced to drag Abby into danger? His mother of all people should be using her considerable intelligence and charm to convince Abby to stay at Dun Ard. He opened his mouth to remind her of that very fact but Abby's next words interrupted his protestations.

"Marriage has nothing to with any of this. It isn't even a consideration."

Perhaps his mother was doing exactly that. This could be the escape route he'd earlier thought cut off from him! Abby had made it clear from the beginning of this conversation that she had no desire to wed him. All he needed do was to join ranks with his family, insist on marriage as a precursor to her accompanying him, and he was free to leave Dun Ard without her.

"I fear my hands are tied, Abby." Colin reached for the tankard in front of him, relaxing back into his seat for the first time since he'd entered the room. "It's my laird's decree and I must obey. In order for you to accompany me, we must wed. But it's clear that's an option you reject. As it stands, through no fault of my own, you'll need to remain here. I've no choice in the matter. Without a marriage, I'm no free to take you with me."

Colin drank deeply of the dark, spicy wine. With all this nonsense of Abby's insistence on accompanying him out of the way, he could relax and enjoy his evening with his family.

"Like marriage makes any more sense to you than it does to me? That's ridiculous." Abby lifted her cup but immediately set it back down again, untouched. "You're only grabbing onto that excuse because you know there's no way we have time to marry before you go. You're determined to head out first thing in the morning and that doesn't leave any time for a wedding."

"That's not exactly true," Ellie piped up. "A formal church wedding would take longer, true, but technically, all you have to do is declare your intent to be husband and wife in the present tense in front of witnesses and that's it, you're married. It's not like back in your—" She bit off the rest of what she was about to say, glancing around the room guiltily. "It's not like where you come from."

Colin glared at his sister-in-law. The woman had the uncanny ability to endlessly irritate him.

Abby tapped her fingernails rapidly against the wood of the table before lifting her head to glare at him. "You are not leaving me behind when you ride out of here tomorrow. So, if that's what it takes, fine. It's not like it means anything, anyway, right? What do I care?" Abby pushed back her chair, rose to her feet, and called out in a loud, clear voice, "I, Abigail Gwendolyn Porter, take this man, Colin MacAlister, as my husband. Right here, right now, right in front of all of you guys as our witnesses. Your turn."

The shock of her words sent wine surging upward rather than down his throat, burning the sensitive pathway into his nose and forcing him into a fit of coughing.

The woman was absolutely without sense of any kind.

"By the Fates! What do you think yer doing?" he at last managed to ask when he'd caught his breath.

"Getting married so I can go with you. Your turn. Go ahead. Do your little speech thing or I do my little wish thing."

She was serious. The witless woman was absolutely serious. Rather than saving himself with his earlier comments, he'd trapped himself like a greedy fish in a net. Any refusal on his part, especially after that earlier performance with which he'd been so pleased, would bring down the wrath of his entire family and likely send him reeling back through time.

"If I do this, do I have yer oath no to wish us back before I've done what I need to do here?"

Her lips pressed together in a thin, straight line, even as her eyes narrowed. "Yes. I promise."

There was only one thing he could do now.

"I take this woman to be my wife."

"*As,*" Ellie corrected, a grin splitting her face as she looked from him to her husband, Caden, and back again. "As my wife. *To be* is future tense and doesn't work for this."

"I take this woman *as* my wife," he corrected, fighting the urge to grind his teeth.

Clearly, none of the women in this family had the good sense they were born with.

"It is done," Blane announced, pushing back his own chair and lifting his tankard. "To our kinsman's marriage. To the new husband and wife."

"Okay, then. Good. Done." Abby spoke quietly as if even she was a bit shocked. Her hands busily worried at the carving on the back of her chair and she nodded her head repeatedly. "Okay. I guess I'd better go get all my things ready for our little trip."

With that, his new wife made her exit as his family continued to toast his marriage.

Wife. Just thinking the word made him grateful he was seated, so sure he felt at the moment his legs would not support him. What had he done?

He'd long ago given up any idea of ever marrying after the Faerie Queen had told him he'd not find his Soulmate in this lifetime, so it wasn't as if he sacrificed some future chance at happiness by wedding Abby. And it certainly wasn't that marriage to a woman like her would be a burden. Far from it. She was beautiful, intelligent, and, as he could attest from personal experience, exceptionally desirable. For a fact, he could imagine no one he'd rather be married to, and therein lay his problem.

How could he allow any woman he cared for that much to embark on the dangerous journey he envisioned for himself?

He had to think of some way to convince her not to go with him.

"Perhaps I can persuade her to return to her own time alone," he muttered into his cup, fervently wishing it was filled with the Faerie Nectar he'd heard so much about during his stay in Wyddecol.

"And why, in the name of all that's holy, would you think to do such a foolish thing?"

His mother's question startled him. Surely even she could see the reason behind his words.

"Because it is for the best for everyone."

Instead of acknowledging what he saw as the truth, she rolled her eyes and sighed in the way only his mother could do.

"She's yer wife now, Colin. The woman yer to spend yer life with. Why would you want to send her away?"

"You ken as well as I, my lady mother, the marriage you just witnessed is a sham. Traveling with me on the morrow only puts Abby's life in danger. Besides, she disna belong in this time and she certainly disna want to be here. The Fae made a grave error in sending her with me."

Rosalyn stared up at the ceiling, and for a moment he wondered what fascinated her so. Until she turned back to him, eyes blazing. It was not interest in the architecture but a pause to gather her wits and control her tongue. He'd used the same type of pause often enough himself. He should have recognized the signs.

"You question the actions of the Fae as if you've never been witness to their work before. I've simply no the patience to guide another of my sons down this path, Colin. I'm too old and weary for it. I'd ask you to use yer own wits, lad. Dinna be so thick-skulled. You've seen the work of the Faerie Magic too many times no to recognize what's happening here."

"What are you saying?"

"They've made it as plain as the hand on yer arm, lad. They've all but rubbed yer nose in it. All of us can see it well enough. You said yerself when you were swept through time to the future, it was to this woman. Did you never stop to question why? Did our troubles with Caden and Ellie teach you nothing at all? Abby is the one who's meant for you, son. She's yer Soulmate and the Magic has shown you this not once, but twice. Dinna be such a fool as to turn yer back on what's gifted to you by the Magic."

His Soulmate? Impossible. "I canna accept that as truth, mother. The Faerie Queen herself warned me I'd no find my own Soulmate in this lifetime."

In this lifetime . . .

The words had barely cleared his lips before the implication of their meaning hit him. Was it possible that Abby had changed the Faerie Queen's decree by wishing him into her time?

His vision in the RoundHouse came back to him then, his own question from that day echoing in his mind. *Why?* Why had Abby needed him? Why had she summoned him to her time? He'd demanded the information from the Earth Mother and she'd laughed at him, as if the answer should be so clear he should have no need to ask.

Perhaps it was that clear. Perhaps it had been there staring him in the face the whole time. Perhaps he'd simply been too dense to see it.

Abby had wished for her Soulmate, and the Magic, responding to its highest calling, had drawn him seven hundred years into the future. Into another lifetime.

A lifetime where his Soulmate *did* exist.

It might be possible. But if it was true, that made it even more important that he not take her with him to Methven. There was no way he would risk the safety of his Soulmate.

"If you believe this to be fact, how could you encourage Abby to ride out with me on the morrow? You have to be aware of the danger. Sending her back to her own time is the only way to keep her safe."

His mother nodded, her expression sober. "I ken what you say, my son. But you canna turn yer back on what the Magic would have you do. There's a reason she's to go with you as much as there's a reason she was sent here in the first place."

"Besides." Ellie had risen from her seat and stood behind him, her hand lighting on his shoulder. "From the marks I saw on that girl, I don't see how she'd be any safer in her own time. At least here she has you to look after her."

"What marks?" She'd said nary a word to him of injuries.

"Bruises on her arm, scrapes on her neck. God only knows what else." Ellie shrugged and headed for the door, following the direction Abby had taken earlier.

The memory of the scene in the glen, Flynn forcing himself on Abby, colored Colin's thoughts red with fury.

Flynn. He'd all but forgotten the Fae.

Too bad the Nuadian pig wasn't here in his time. He'd be more than happy to show him how they dealt with his kind in this century.

Twenty-five

❦

I'm married.

Abby dropped a hand to her midsection as she made her way up the narrow stairs, hoping to calm her nervous stomach.

Say a few words and *poof*, married.

Not that there was any need to stress over or second-guess what she'd just done. After all, it wasn't like it was a real marriage or anything. Just some words she'd said so she could make sure she didn't lose contact with the only person who could get her home again. Besides, a marriage didn't really count if she hadn't even been born yet.

Unless she ended up stuck here. Trapped in medieval Scotland *and* married.

Not that having Colin for a husband would be such a horrible fate. If she allowed herself to be totally honest, which wasn't the most comfortable thing to be right now, she could think of only one thing that kept him from being a pretty decent candidate for husband material: he lived in the wrong century. And worse? This was where he wanted to be. Where she'd promised to stay with him until he'd completed his quest to save his friends.

Her step slowed at the thought and she stumbled, grabbing onto the cold stone wall to keep from slipping on the topmost stair.

She really had to let all that go. She couldn't think about it right now. Accepting time travel and Faerie Magic would mean accepting other things that shook her whole world. Things like her being some Faerie half-breed. Things like finding The One only to learn they could never be together because they existed seven hundred years apart. The whole of it was simply too bizarre, too depressing, for her mind to comprehend without some gigantic cry fest at the end, and truly there was no time for wallowing in self-pity.

Only one thing needed to be important right now: getting back to her own time. And since the only way it seemed she had any chance of making that happen required Colin's presence, her main goal at the moment was to make sure she didn't let her new husband out of her sight.

A shiver ran up her spine as she thought of him in that fashion—*her new husband*.

Whatever it was that made Colin MacAlister so attractive to her, it certainly was powerful. Powerful as in he really might be The One. It would explain everything.

"No," she rejected. "Nothing more than stupid pheromones." She pushed open the door to the bedchamber, her eye drawn immediately to the bed that seemed to loom large in the room.

Their bed now.

Not that it hadn't been their bed before that ridiculous excuse for a marriage she'd just gone through. It was, after all, the same bed in which she'd awakened this very morning, wrapped in Colin's incredible arms.

Stop it! She wanted to shout the words out loud and stomp her feet to drive the image away. That had to be strictly off-limits mental territory. She wouldn't even think about getting into a bed with him again because, obviously, in bed with him, thinking was all but beyond her abilities. Just being close to that man wrapped her in a sensory cloud of hormonal overload.

She put a hand to her heated cheek, reminding herself that she'd come up here to pack.

"I need to pack. But pack what?" she asked the empty room.

How did she even begin to prepare for this journey she'd insisted on making? Setting out with Colin tomorrow was like some backwoods road trip gone horribly wrong. And yet, she felt certain to the bottom of her soul she had no choice but to go with him if she ever wanted to get home again.

The quiet knock on her door came as a welcome relief, and she hurried to answer it before whoever was there disappeared and left her alone again with her own miserable thoughts.

"Hey." Ellie smiled at her as she pushed past her

into the room. "I brought you some things I think you should take with you tomorrow."

Thank goodness someone had some ideas about what she'd need.

"I don't suppose you have a pair of jeans in that bundle?" Days spent on horseback wearing a dress was not at all what she'd choose if she actually had a choice.

"Don't I wish," Ellie chuckled. "I do miss my jeans some days, but you'll get used to it after a while and the dress won't seem so cumbersome."

Maybe. If she were going to be here that long. Which she wasn't. Absolutely. Was. Not.

"I do have the next-best thing, though." Ellie held up what looked like a pair of narrow-legged pants, made from the same material as the shift she wore. "I made these for myself for riding. They're not standard issue for the time period, but they make being on horseback a relatively more pleasant experience."

Abby took the soft garment gratefully, wondering what her new friend would pull out of her cloth bag next.

"Now these, they're not so comfortable but, trust me, you could end up finding them to be much more important to you than those bloomers."

Ellie walked over to the bed and pushed the pile of clothing out of her way to roll out a bundle of cloth. Inside were two belts and two daggers.

"Weapons?" Abby stepped back, surprised to see Ellie holding two very different-looking knives.

"Exactly." Ellie nodded, her expression completely devoid of any trace of the humor she'd expressed only a moment before. "Based on everything the family says,

Colin is very likely the best warrior this clan has ever produced, so you've got that going for you. But believe me, Abby, wandering around the countryside in this day and age isn't like a stroll in your old neighborhood. In our time we complain about the occasional man who thinks he has the right to do whatever he wants to any woman. That man is more the norm than the exception in this world. You can't put your safety entirely in Colin's hands. You need to be prepared to take care of yourself, too."

Abby accepted both the daggers along with their protective wrapping, taking a closer look at the smaller of the two. With its fancy scrollwork and tiny jewels, it reminded her of something decorative she might expect to see adorning a Halloween costume. "This is beautiful."

"It's practical," Ellie corrected. "You wear that *beautiful* one around your waist, on the outside of your clothing. If you find yourself in trouble, any bad guy is simply going to take it away from you because chances are good you won't be able to stop him. But this—" She pointed to the longer, thinner dagger lying next to its daintier companion. "This one you strap around your thigh, under your dress. No one but you knows it's there until you need it. Colin's sister taught me this trick. She gave me this set to match one she owns. I'll feel a lot better knowing you have them with you."

Abby might have been tempted to discount the whole idea if it hadn't been for her experience back at the dig site. If it hadn't been for that little gold knife of Jonathan's, she and Colin might not have escaped without one of them getting shot.

"Thank you. For this and for everything else you've done for me today. I really do appreciate you and everyone else down there supporting my demand to go with Colin. I sort of expected everyone to side with him and insist I stay behind."

"Well, now that you mention it." Ellie sat down on the stool by the hearth, reaching up to clasp Abby's hand. "There is a reason we were in favor of your going along with him. I have something I need to ask of you. I can't overstate how important this is and how really difficult it's likely to be."

Wonderful. Like she didn't already have enough next-to-impossible tasks on her plate just trying to get back to her own time. Still, she could hardly refuse when she hadn't even heard what Ellie wanted from her.

Abby sat on the rug next to Ellie, waiting to hear what her new friend had to say.

"We need your help, Abby. With Colin."

"With Colin?" What help could Colin possibly need from her?

Ellie nodded, letting out a deep breath before she began. "He's learned just enough about the future to be a danger. He's set his mind on warning the king about a surprise attack the English will make on our sovereign and his men so he can prevent Robert's army from being decimated and scattered. You have to stop him from doing that."

"Hold on a second," Abby held up a hand, her mind racing to keep up with the conversation. "King Robert? You're saying Colin plans to go find Robert the Bruce?" It was one thing to accept the bizarre situation she found herself in while she sat in some isolated castle, but to try to wrap her head around meeting the people she'd studied about? *Mind-boggling* didn't even come close. "Wow. When you suggested I consider this a personal learning experience, you weren't kidding. An opportunity to actually speak to someone like—"

"No!" Ellie leaned forward, staring into her eyes. "The point is, you can't let him do that. Think about what I just said. He wants to change what's already happened in your time. He wants to warn the king that the English are waiting for him. If he does, they'll be prepared for that battle instead of walking into an ambush."

"The war for Scottish Independence goes on for years and years." You didn't need a minor in history to know that: you only had to watch movies or read a few romance books. "One skirmish isn't going to change the outcome of that war."

"How did you make it into graduate school without developing a single shred of critical thinking ability?" Ellie clicked her tongue, obviously exasperated. "Think! We're not talking about changing the history of the war. We're talking about changing the very threads of the future. If those men go into that battle forewarned, people who would have died will likely live. More important to our discussion, people who would have lived will likely die."

Abby nodded, a glimmer of Ellie's point starting to crystallize for her.

"What if one of those English soldiers who's supposed to live but doesn't is named Washington, or Jefferson, or Lincoln, just to pick out a random few? We don't know whose ancestors are there. They could be yours or mine. We don't know whose ancestors are at risk and we can't take a chance, because we don't know what would happen to that future if we plucked some entire family line out of existence."

A wave of weakness hit Abby, making her glad she was sitting. The possibilities were horrifying.

"We have to convince Colin not to go through with his plan. I know he has to go after Alasdair and Simeon, they're family. But he can't take his warning to the king. You have to stop him."

"I have to stop him," Abby repeated, the importance of Ellie's request settling over her. "I'll do my best."

"Good, then. Your best is all we ask." Ellie rose to her feet and crossed over to the door. "I'll check with the kitchens to make sure they have everything ready for you to take along with you tomorrow. Good night."

"Good night," Abby echoed, but the door was already shut behind Ellie.

For several minutes, she sat on the floor, the potentially catastrophic possibilities racing through her thoughts, each scenario she imagined worse than the one before it.

Earlier today, Ellie had mentioned something about the Faeries whose Magic had sent her here having some reason of their own for having sent her. Could this be it? Could it be that she was meant to prevent Colin from ripping apart the fabric of space and time by altering history?

Talk about biting off more than she could chew. Abby rubbed her fingertips over her temples, wishing she had a few physics classes under her belt rather than the micro-mini understanding of the subject she possessed from watching the Discovery Channel. Maybe knowledge of that kind would allay some of her fears.

More likely it would just give her more to worry about.

"Just enough knowledge to make us both dangerous," she muttered, pushing up from the floor to stand.

Something would come to her. It had to. She'd think of a way. No task was impossible if she simply broke it down into its smallest parts. How hard could it be? Keep Colin from totally screwing up the future and then get herself back home, leaving the man she was falling in love with here, seven hundred years away from her.

"Not love," she denied aloud, balling her hands into fists. Lust. Pure and simple. What she felt was only lust. It had to be. She wasn't sure she could survive the pain of leaving him if it were anything more.

Across the room, the door opened and Colin walked in, filling the whole room with his presence, completely blurring for her any difference between love and lust.

Twenty-six

———

The sight of Abby standing by his bed took Colin's breath away.

Suddenly unsure of what to do or say, he simply stood drinking in the sight of her. The candlelight flickering in the room shone around her like some mystical halo. Her long, brown hair cascaded over one shoulder, exposing her soft, slender neck and the raw, red mark that marred it.

She'd suffered enough.

How could he ever have considered risking her life by taking her with him tomorrow? Whether through reason or trickery, she must not go with him. If nothing else, he'd convince her to wish herself home. Anything that would keep her safe. Even if it meant losing her forever.

And yet now, as their eyes locked, all schemes flitted

away like tiny midges at sunset. He could think of nothing more than pulling on the ribbon hanging loosely at her neck, releasing the fluffy gown that concealed her lovely body. In his mind, it already floated to the floor in a whisper of cloth, revealing the treasures beneath.

He could almost feel her soft skin against his as he'd lower her to the bed and cover her body with his.

"We should probably talk."

Not at all the words he'd heard from her in his momentary fantasy. Though, in truth, there had been no words at all, only those tiny little moans of pleasure he knew she would make.

"Indeed we should." He strode to the darkened fireplace, turning his back to her, hoping she'd not noticed the evidence of his earlier imaginings that even now pressed out against his plaid.

Damnation, but the woman had a powerful effect on him. More evidence to support his mother's claim that she was his Soulmate.

"I must ask you again to reconsider your decision to come with me. You would be safe here with my family." Straightforward, to the point, was always his first choice, though with Abby, he had little hope it would work.

As he expected, it didn't.

"No way. That discussion is closed. I'm going with you. I mean, we got married and everything just so that your whole family would agree to it. Why waste a good marriage, right?"

They had indeed married. The mere idea sent a wave of disbelief coursing through him. It was done. She was his wife now. If his mother was to be believed, he was married to his Soulmate. He should be the happiest man alive. But happy was about as far from what he felt as he could imagine.

Instead, he'd only added to his burden of responsibility and worry. Now it wasn't just the lives of his clansmen and the fate of his king resting on his shoulders. The life of his Soulmate lay in his hands as well.

His options to protect her were dwindling.

As he'd expected, straightforward hadn't worked. He already knew she was too stubborn to give in to any arguing he might try again, and he certainly wasn't willing to risk her whisking them both back to the future in a pique of anger. Not before he'd had the chance to find his kinsmen and warn his king.

If only he could get her to relax, to let down her suspicious guard, maybe then he could reason with her.

"As you say, wife, why waste a good marriage?" He turned to face her, sending his best smile her direction as he strode to the chest at the foot of his bed and lifted the lid. Digging under his spare shirts, he pulled out a drying cloth and tucked it under his arm. "I've a lovely idea for our last evening of civilization. Will you accompany me?"

He held out a hand in invitation and waited.

Indecision danced over her face as she wrapped the ribbon holding her gown closed around and around her finger until he feared she might cut off the flow of blood to the digit.

"Like this?" she asked at last, her hand sweeping down the front of her nightdress.

Modesty? The woman amazed him. In her own time she walked about in broad daylight wearing less than half the covering she wore now.

"What you have on is fine. It's late. Most of Dun Ard's people have taken to their bedchambers. If it makes you feel better"—he paused to open the chest again, pulling out one of his plaids—"take this. Wrap it about yer shoulders."

Abby did as he suggested and then accepted the hand he offered, following along with him down the stairs and through the castle, out into the gardens and to the low building beyond.

"A bathhouse?" Abby stood in the doorway, her widened eyes reflecting the flames from the massive stone fireplace.

"It's no as good as a hot shower, granted, but it's pleasant enough." And too bad it was they had no shower. A mental image of Abby standing under the flowing waters, her head flung back, her soft throat waiting for his tongue to forge a trail downward . . .

He roughly pushed the idyllic fantasy from his mind. He was here for a purpose, not a dalliance.

"No, I think it's great." She smiled up at him before moving farther into the room. "I just didn't expect it, that's all. My studies had led me to believe bathhouses were only common in areas settled by Viking peoples."

"So much for yer modern-day studies, aye?" Colin returned her smile, placing a hand at the small of her back to direct her toward the far side of the room.

A half wall, not quite as high as the top of his head, separated two bathing areas. A large, carved tub sat on either side of the wall, waiting to be filled from the enormous iron kettles hanging in the fireplace.

"Yer welcome to take the tub on the far side, and I'll stand outside to act as yer guard. No one will enter, you have my word."

He headed to the fireplace and filled a bucket from the nearest kettle. When he turned, he found her rooted to the spot where he'd left her, her face a picture of discomfort.

"Is there something wrong? I thought you'd enjoy a good soak before we set out on the morrow. It'll be a long time before you'll find such as this again."

She shook her head and her hands fisted in the cloth of the plaid she wore around her shoulders. "You're going to wait outside?"

"I would consider nothing else." He only hoped he'd managed to sound offended enough to put her concerns to rest.

She followed him to the kettles on his next trip, picking up another bucket and helping him to fill the tub.

"We have soaps here on the shelf. My mother makes them herself and takes great pride in the variety of smelly things she can do with them." He chose one of the bars and handed it to Abby as he passed by her on his way out.

Once through the door, he leaned against the wall, knowing from here he'd never hear the whisper of falling cloth on her side of the partition or even the small splashing sound she'd make when she stepped into the tub.

Again the visions assaulted him, the soft gown sliding down over her curves and fluttering to the ground at her feet. He slid down to sit, back against the wall, and dropped his head into his hands, fighting to push the vision from his mind.

He still had work to do this night.

Raising his voice, he called out to her. "Yer water is warm enough?"

"It's perfect." Her answer floated to him. "And I love your mom's soap. I don't know what she's used, but it smells just like my favorite lemon candles."

Candles! How could he have forgotten?

"Aye, it's no so very different from the great steaming tub out back of yer own home, though we've no so many candles for you to light."

Enough chatter. Time to address his purpose tonight. After another minute of silence, he sent the first volley of reason her direction.

"Yer accustomed to days on a horse, are you? It can be discomforting to a new rider." Give her something to think on.

"I'm comfortable with horses. Granted, I rode for fun, not for transportation, but I'll be able to keep up with you, if that's what you're worried about."

"I dinna recall saying I was worried. I'm only thinking of yer comfort." And of convincing her to stay behind. "We'll have need to ride hard to cover as much ground as we can each day. You ken we'll be sleeping in the open as well, do you? There'll be no luxuries to comfort you. No bathhouses, no garderobes for yer convenience."

"Convenience? Ha!" The water splashed loudly as if she had sat up suddenly or moved about. "Garderobe? That smelly stone bench with a hole is hardly what I'd call a convenience. I'm not even sure that qualifies as a whole step up from peeing behind a bush. Trust me, Colin, I'm fine with bushes. I've been training for archaeology field work for years. I can handle whatever you throw at me."

Not at all the response he'd hoped for. She was likely the most stubborn woman he had ever encountered! Even his younger sister, Sallie, on her worst days had never been so set in her ways.

Neither his demands nor his arguments had worked, and now even reasoning had failed to budge her from her insistence on accompanying him.

Perhaps a more subtle form of persuasion would work.

If she was indeed his Soulmate, she should feel the pull of attraction every bit as deeply as he did. Taking advantage of that might be akin to dishonesty, but a little dishonesty seemed a small price to pay for his Soulmate's safety.

"Not much longer," she called. "I'm almost ready to go."

It was the signal he'd waited for.

Pushing up to his feet, he turned back inside the building, picking up the plaid she'd dropped on the bench as he approached her. She bent from the waist, vigorously rubbing her hair with the end of the drying cloth she'd wrapped around herself.

Her eyes widened when she straightened and noticed him standing there.

"You'll need this for the walk back." He held out the plaid as he again started toward her.

A few more steps and she was within reach, the outline of her enticing curves just visible through the cloth. He wrapped his arms around her to drape the plaid over her head and shoulders, drawing her close within the confines of the soft material.

Too late he realized his inability to control his own attraction to her. Not even the plaid that separated them could disguise his quickly hardening shaft.

"Oh!" She looked up at him, her eyes large with surprise.

There was little he could say. His traitorous body spoke loudly on its own.

"He"—Colin glanced quickly down and back to her face again—"is, I fear, beyond my ability to control. While I canna prevent his appearance, I can see to it that he behaves himself while he's here."

She continued to stare up at him, the corner of her mouth twitching until she broke out in a peal of laughter.

"Honest to God, Colin." She pulled the corners of the plaid from his hands and hugged them close before moving around him to collect her nightdress. "Men and their penises totally crack me up. I'm frankly surprised you haven't given it a name."

Struggling to regain both his composure and the upper hand he felt he might have lost in that exchange, he followed her out of the bathhouse. There was a slight chance he should be offended by her laughter and her comments, but the sight of her perfectly rounded arse swaying back and forth in front of him as they made their way back to their room occupied too much of his imagination to let him dwell on any slight or insult.

Though all of his other attempts to dissuade her from going with him had failed, he wasn't yet ready to admit defeat. The tactic on which he had just embarked, wooing her into agreement, would, if nothing else, be a most enjoyable way to spend his evening.

The only problem with his current plan was that he'd have to use great care not find himself ending up the wooed party.

Was it just this afternoon she'd been wishing she'd taken more physics classes in pursuit of her degree? She'd been way off on that call. It was definitely more biology classes she should have taken.

Specifically, she desperately needed one that covered how to control her raging hormonal impulses in the presence of this certifiable Holy-Shit-Hot-Guy.

Abby pushed open the door of their bedchamber and entered, all too aware of Colin so close behind her. When the door clicked shut, she nearly jumped.

Skittish much? Oh yeah. Skittish very much.

"I don't suppose you'd consider waiting in the hall while I change into my nightgown?" The smirk he wore answered before he did.

"No, wife, I dinna think I'll be doing that. But I will turn my back if you like."

"Yes, I'd like that. And you don't have to keep calling me your . . ."

The words died in her mouth as he turned his back, pulling his shirt up and over his head as he did so.

A noise escaped from her, something primal rising up out of her throat. Something between a whimper and a squeak over which she had no more control than Colin had had over his erection out in the bathhouse.

A pretty impressive erection, too, now that she thought about it. Easily as impressive as the muscular back he was now presenting to her.

The man's body clearly belonged on a piece of Michelangelo's marble. It was, without a doubt, the best she'd ever seen. Not that she'd seen a lot so up close and personal. But of the ones she had seen, his was definitely the best.

Letting out a shaky breath, she grabbed up her nightdress and dropped it down over her head, letting the drying towel drop only after the gown had fallen into place. For the first time since she'd seen the clothing selection Ellie had presented, she was actually grateful there was so much material in what she'd be wearing through the night.

"Okay. I'm done."

"Then it's time for bed," he announced, crossing the room to poke at the fire until the flames died down.

One look at Colin's expression as he approached and Abby knew it was time for immediate action. She pulled the coverlet from the top of the bed and quickly wadded it into a roll, plopping it on top of the nearest pillow and pushing the entire bundle toward him.

"There. Do you think that will be enough bedding for you? I mean, you are planning on sleeping on the floor, right?" Because he wasn't sleeping in the bed. Not with her. She remembered all too well how she'd behaved the last time she'd been horizontal next to Colin.

"I've enough of the hard ground in my future. It's my own bed I'll be sleeping in this night."

"Okay." She pulled the bundle back toward her and picked it up in her arms. "You're right. It is your bed. I'll take the floor."

The hearth looked a likely spot. There was already a rug there to soften the stone floor a bit. She skirted around the bed, but made it only a few steps before Colin's big hand clamped down on her arm.

"No." He pulled her to him until their faces were mere inches apart. "You'll have yer own fill of the hard ground in a day's time."

And then he was kissing her.

She somehow missed the start of it. One minute she was staring into the deep pools of his Caribbean blue eyes and the next thing she knew, her tongue was buried in his mouth, her fingers tangled in his hair, and her body thrumming with need.

He broke the kiss, his warm lips trailing across her cheek and to her neck as she fought to catch her breath in quick, desperate little huffs.

Damn, but he was dangerous. And not just because of the way he looked. Or the way he kissed. It was the soft-guy interior packaged in a tough-guy wrapper. It was the kind and gentle way he touched her, the sweet things he did for her.

It was everything about him.

"A shame it is. Hard, rocky ground under yer lovely soft body," he whispered. "Every night, stones and twigs digging into yer flesh. Unless you'll but agree to stay here and wait for me to return to you."

Okay. Not everything about him. His unrelenting stubbornness wasn't all that attractive.

"No."

He buried his face in her neck, holding her so close she could feel his heartbeat pounding against her breast.

"Then wish yerself home now. I'd have you lost to me rather than risk yer safety by taking you with me."

He was nothing if not honest with her. She owed him no less. It was time to confess.

"It won't work. I already tried. You're my only way home, Colin. I don't understand all that much about Faerie Magic, but I do know I can't go back without you at my side. I'd be happy to wish us both back, if that's what you want." In a heartbeat.

"I canna. And I've yer oath you'll no try it without my consent." He drew his head up from her, pain evident in his face. "Can you no understand that I couldna live with myself if I thought I'd let my kinsmen die without even trying to save them?"

"I do." Her oath was all that kept her from saying the words to send them home right now. "Can't you understand my need to be at your side?"

"I do," he answered in an echo of her own words, sweeping an arm under her legs and lifting her off her feet like a small child. "Truce, then. We'll share the bed this night, me to my side and you to yers, aye? I swear to you that I'll make him-with-no-name behave himself."

When he gave her that almost smile of his, she had to force herself not to drag his face down for another kiss. How could she not agree to his offer? Even in his annoying efforts to leave her behind, she knew his goal was to keep her safe. He'd hidden nothing from her.

"Truce, then," she agreed, rolling onto her side to blow out the candle next to the bed.

Candles. Her eyes fluttered open, the word niggling at some uncomfortable spot in the back of her mind. What was it about . . .

It's no so very different from the great steaming tub out back of yer own home, though we've no so many candles for you to light.

"How did you know about my hot tub? You didn't go into my backyard when you were there."

The pause before he answered seemed to last an eternity.

"I returned later. I saw you there, with yer candles lit all about you."

"You spied on me? You hid out in the bushes and spied on me? Why would you do that?"

"I needed to see for myself that you were . . ." Another pause, as if he had changed his mind about what to say and was hunting for new words. "I wanted to see you were safe."

Perhaps she'd been too quick to conclude he hid nothing. Too quick to assume his honesty.

"And you never thought to tell me about that?"

"I thought it for the best."

The finality in his tone told her their conversation was at an end.

Her thoughts, on the other hand, raced. If he had kept something like that from her, what else might he be capable of in pursuit of what he thought best?

A truce, he'd offered, a truce she'd accepted. But that didn't mean ignoring her common sense.

Truce, but no trust.

She lay very still on her side of the big bed, waiting until his breathing slowed and deepened before climbing out of the bed to find her clothes and dress. The little knives were too much of a hassle in the limited light of the dying fire, so she compromised by sticking the smaller of the two into the bust of her gown.

Once ready, she retrieved the bundle of bedding from the floor and carried it to her side of the bed, slipping it under her covers. She tiptoed to the door and quietly let herself out into the hallway.

Dropping to her knees, she propped her back against the doorway and stretched her legs across the opening.

Truce but no trust.

In the last twenty-four hours, Colin had tried every tactic she could imagine to avoid taking her with him tomorrow. Only sneaking out without her was left.

After seeing the sincerity and pain in his eyes tonight, she had little doubt but that he'd try that one, too.

And when he did? He'd find her waiting.

Truce but no trust.

Twenty-seven

Why did she have to be so damned stubborn?

Colin tightened his hold on his reins and cast another stealthy glance Abby's direction. She sat her horse well enough, though her back slumped a bit more than it had in the first hours of their ride. Her face showed the strain of their long day in the saddle but she rode on, refusing to admit a need to stop and rest.

"There's a place no too far ahead where we'll set up camp for the night."

Relief flashed across her face, but she quickly suppressed any evidence of the emotion, giving him a solemn nod to show her agreement.

"You don't have to stop for me. We've still got daylight ahead of us. I can keep going as long as we need to."

Stubborn woman. Brazen and demanding. In all

fairness, he had to give her credit, too, for her wit and intelligence as well.

Far too intelligent for her own good, perhaps.

Charitable and forgiving, too, though it galled him to admit these last qualities. Admitting them forced him to face his own shortcomings.

He'd awakened early, even before the first rays of the sun had made their appearance. Using great care to avoid waking Abby, he'd dressed and silently gathered his things.

Nothing he'd tried the night before had worked to convince her to stay behind, so all that was left to him was to go while she slept. Once it was done, there would be nothing she could do about it.

Quietly, ever so quietly, he'd opened the door to their bedchamber and attempted to slip away, only to stumble over her legs and land beside her on the hard stone floor.

"I knew you'd try that," she'd said, her disappointment in him palpable.

He'd made one last desperate appeal to her and the whole of his family, all to no avail. As if in a great conspiracy against common sense, they all agreed she should accompany him.

And accompany him she did. Without a single reference to his deceit and trickery. Without a single word of rebuke. In truth, with almost no words at all. She'd simply sat on her horse the whole of the long day, never once complaining.

Not even now.

"I've no a doubt you could carry on endlessly, wife, but the horses grow weary after such a long day."

Her eyes cut to him and away, as they did each time he called her by that appellation. He found he rather enjoyed it, both the sound of the word itself and her reaction to it. He hid his unexpected need to smile in explanation.

"We have more light than we ken what to do with in our summers. The light outlasts the stamina of our mounts. They need rest in order to carry us tomorrow."

A little farther on, he directed them from the road through the trees and to a sheltered spot by a fast-flowing stream. There he dismounted and led his horse to a grassy area, looping the animal's reins around a branch within reach of the water, all the while keeping a close watch on Abby.

She was slow to dismount, stumbling when her feet hit the ground.

"Do you need help?" he called, knowing before he asked she'd refuse.

She didn't disappoint.

"You just worry about yourself. I'm fine." With a hand at her lower back, she stiffly led her mount over to join his.

"I'll gather kindling and start the fire if you want to carry our foodstuffs and blankets over to that flat area by the rocks."

She nodded, her fingers already fumbling with the ties on her pack. "Fire? We're not cooking, are we? Why do we need a fire this early?"

"It's later than you realize, Abby. And after the hours we've spent traveling today, sleep will likely overtake us as soon as we finish our meal. The fire will burn down, but the rocks I'll place around it will give off heat during the night. Dinna fear, wife, we'll have plenty of cold dark nights ahead of us on this journey, but for now, there's no a need to forgo a fire."

Wordlessly, she returned to unlacing the pack on her mount's back and taking it to the area he'd indicated. She returned to fetch his as he headed into the trees.

It was a dry year in the Highlands, bad for the sheep and the shepherds, but welcome for his needs at the moment. Dry underbrush and twigs meant he could easily gather the fuel he needed for their fire without having to lose sight of Abby.

Not that he actually expected any trouble here. He could easily feel that they were alone in this remote area. When he let down his barriers, Abby's was the only soul he felt for miles. He concentrated and allowed his senses to expand. Like a bird in flight, his mind flew through a foreign landscape of colors, ignoring the tortured calls of the souls he bypassed. Farther on he explored, following the two familiar patterns that glowed like a beacon on the horizon.

Alasdair and Simeon both lived, their lonely, broken souls shining as brightly as ever.

He prayed that they might stay that way until he could reach them. Even without Abby to slow his progress, time was against him, conspiring to keep him from reaching his kinsmen until after the battle at Methven. Too late for that perhaps, but not too late to warn his king of what was to come, no matter what his family had said.

Arms full, he rejoined Abby, settling in to the work of building their fire in silence. The flames were just beginning to lick hungrily around the dry tinder when she stood.

"I'll be back in a minute."

He was on his feet before she finished pushing away the first branches. "Where do you think yer going?" he demanded of her retreating back.

"To do my girl thing in the bushes."

He didn't care for the idea of having her out of his sight. "Would you like me to come stand guard as you—"

"Absolutely not!" she interrupted, her eyes widening in shock. "Relax. I'll scream real loud if I need you. I promise."

Of that he had no doubt. His Abby was not one to go down without a fight. Besides, he'd scanned the area and knew there wasn't a single person close enough to cause her any harm.

He'd barely had time to sit before another worry replaced the last. No people, perhaps, but there could well be animals. He was back on his feet, moving in the direction she'd disappeared in, when he heard her returning.

They'd need to work on her ability to move more stealthily if they planned to go undetected once they reached more populated areas.

Night had firmly settled her cloak over the land by the time they'd finished their meal of bread, cheese, and meat.

Abby spread out her blanket close to the fire and sat down, rubbing her hands up and down her arms. "You were right. It does get a lot cooler when it gets dark. I'm glad you built the fire rather than listen to me."

As if he would have allowed her to talk him into something so foolish.

He untied the strings on his blanket and crossed to her side of the fire, rolling out his bedding and laying it next to hers.

"What are you doing? I don't need you to sleep next to me. I'm not afraid of the dark, you know."

"The cold," he patiently explained. "We'll be more comfortable sleeping closer together as the temperature continues to drop." Not to mention, he'd be more comfortable having her well within his reach throughout the night.

"Okay. I can accept that." She rolled over, presenting her back to him, and pulled her blanket up over her ear, leaving only the top of her head peeking out.

He settled down next to her, contenting himself with listening to the gentle, lulling cadence of her breathing. He pushed back the accusing finger of guilt that prodded at his chest with each new sign of exhaustion Abby displayed. He could have led them in a more westerly track so that they would have spent their first night at the home of his sister and her husband. It would have meant the loss of a day's travel time, but there would have been a warm bed at the end of their journey.

He'd avoided it on purpose. He didn't have a day to spare. Not even for her comfort.

"How will you know where to find your friends?" Her voice was muffled by the blanket she'd pulled around her. "I mean, if the battle is over by the time we reach them, how will you know if they're still alive? And if they are and they've moved on, how will you know where to look for them?"

He considered ignoring her, pretending to sleep, but his gut told him he'd tried deceit on Abby too often as it was.

"I'm cursed," he said simply. "The only positive aspect of my curse is that it will allow me to track Dair and Sim no matter where they go, as long as they are alive." And if they'd died because he was too slow, he'd know that, too.

"Cursed, huh?" She rolled over to face him, her head propped up on her arm. "I want to hear about that. Cursed, how? Tell me the whole story. How did you end up cursed?"

And so he told her. Everything. Every facet of his fateful encounter with the Faerie Queen. He described to her what he'd seen, what he'd heard, even what he'd felt that day, details he'd shared with no one else in all these years. Why he told her, he couldn't say, other than that she had asked and he had found himself with no desire to deny her.

At one point she'd closed her eyes and he thought she might have fallen asleep, but when he stopped talking, she urged him to continue.

"I can almost see it in my imagination when I listen to your descriptions," she said, and he found himself trying harder to find the perfect words to describe every detail.

"And what of you, wife?" he asked at last. "What are the gifts carried in yer Faerie blood?"

"I don't really have any gifts." She rolled to her back and cushioned her head with her arms. "I'd tell you I didn't have any Faerie blood, either, but then I'd be at a total loss to explain how the heck I ended up here, wouldn't I?"

The fire's dying embers cast a glowing backdrop for her profile, encouraging him to drink in the sight of her lying there with her eyes closed. He searched for something to ask, anything that might set her to talking so he could soak in the sound of her voice.

"How is it you came to be digging in the earth for worn-out trinkets in the Highlands of Scotland?"

Her lips curved into a smile that beckoned him. Only with great restraint was he able to resist reaching out and pulling her to him when she pushed herself up to sit.

"A dream called me. Sounds crazy, right? From the time I was a kid, I loved old things. My grandmother's yellowed teacups, antiques stores, museums, you name it. The older, the better. By the time I hit middle school, I figured I must be meant to be an archaeologist. Always in my dreams there was one special ancient treasure calling out to me, waiting just for me to come to Scotland to find it. So when I got the chance, I jumped at it." She yawned, her jaw stretching wide, followed by a relaxed little sigh. "If I have any gift, I guess it's finding stuff. When I look for things, it's as if I can hear them calling to me, tempting me with their stories and their histories. Things, mind you. Not people. Send me after any *thing* and I can find it."

They'd talked late into the night. Time that should have been spent in sleep. Still, he'd not trade those moments with her. Not even for a well-rested tomorrow.

"We should get some rest now," he assured her while lifting her blanket for her to lie back down.

Instead she leaned forward, placing the lightest of kisses on his cheek. "Thank you," she whispered. "For letting me inside those walls of yours."

The blanket fell unnoticed as he pulled her close, his lips covering hers. He hadn't intended anything of the sort, but in the moment, he had no choice.

Far from protesting, her hands slid into his hair and she pressed against him even as he lowered her to her back, covering her body with his.

The kiss deepened and he shoved at the yards of cloth she wore, urging her skirts up and out of his way. Her legs parted and he fit himself into the cradle she formed, pressing against her welcoming heat.

His fingers tightened on the blighted undergarment she wore. One sharp tug and he'd be home.

"Shit!" she squealed, her hands shoving at his chest even as she squirmed her way out from under him. "Holy shit!"

His breath came in great sharp gulps as he pushed up to his knees, guilt and anger warring at his own lack of control, battering him with each beat of his heart.

"I'm sorry," he gasped, unable to meet her gaze until she pounded her fist into his chest.

"There!" she squeaked, "in the trees. He's in the trees."

Colin was on his feet, sword drawn, before she managed her next words.

"It was Jonathan. I swear to God, Colin, I saw Jonathan watching us."

Twenty-eight

〜⌒〜

Come on now, up with you. We've miles to cover this day."

Abby stretched, each of the pebbles and sticks on the hard ground beneath her making its irritating presence known.

"I finally feel sorry for that princess with the pea in her mattress," she muttered, rolling to her knees.

"What's that you say?"

Colin appeared to have been up for a while. He'd packed up their campsite and laid out a small square of cloth beside her, with a hunk of bread and some dried fruits arranged on it.

At the moment, she'd give her right arm to see a cup of coffee there in the mix.

"Nothing."

Colin had to feel worse than her. The last time she'd

checked before falling asleep, he'd still been wide awake. Her whole hallucination about seeing Jonathan Flynn in the shadows had pretty much ruined any decent sleep for either of them

He bent to pick up her blankets, shaking them out before rolling them into a neat little bundle. "We need to put some speed under us this day."

"I'm up for it."

Assuming her head didn't explode from caffeine deprivation. Of course, that was something she was going to have to get over if she ended up stuck in this time.

"Not going there," she muttered to herself as she leaned down to splash cold water on her face.

Biting back a groan, she made her way over to her mount and climbed up on his back. She'd ridden horses all her life and thoroughly enjoyed the experience. But there was a big difference between a couple hours on horseback for fun and a full day on horseback for transportation.

"I've a sister who lives no too far from here. Maybe half a day's ride. I'm thinking it best we take you there."

Colin spoke without looking at her as if he half-hoped by not making eye contact she'd be more likely to fall for his line of crap.

"You said yourself we're already in a race with time to reach your friends. Besides, if I didn't choose to stay behind with people who at least knew where I came from, what makes you think I'd stay with this sister of yours?"

He shrugged, looking back before he spoke this time. "A day in the saddle. A night on the ground. It's no so pleasant. There are dangers out here to be sure, wife."

She'd love to tell him where he could put his dangers and that *wife* stuff, if only she had the energy. As it was, she hadn't any to spare.

"Forget it. If this is because of what I thought I saw last night, you don't need to worry about me. I was just exhausted and imagining things. We go on together." The stiff back he presented her told her more than any words could. "So which way does your Spidey sense tell us to head this morning?"

"My what?"

His look of confusion was almost adorable enough to make her forget how miserable she felt. Almost, but not quite.

"Never mind. Which way to your friends this morning?"

"You've decided, then?"

She nodded her answer. "Hey, even if he really had been out there, I can't imagine any place I'd feel safer than with you."

He'd been quite formidable as he'd gone into warrior mode last night.

On his horse now, Colin stilled, his eyes searching hers before he closed them. A light seemed to radiate up from his face, flowing out in all directions before focusing like a laser and streaming directly ahead of them.

"This way," he said, leading his horse off in front of her.

She tried to blank her mind, to lull herself into some sort of automatic pilot that would allow the hours to pass quickly.

Good Lord, this was only Day Two.

She should have gone right to sleep last night instead of gabbing for hours, but she'd really wanted to know how they were going to find these friends of Colin's. And then when he'd opened up and began to tell her about his encounter with the Faerie Queen, there had been no way she was going to stop the conversation and just go to sleep.

Colin wasn't much of a talker, and he didn't strike her as someone who easily shared personal details of his life. That he'd decided to share some of those with her had made her feel closer to him. For a little while there, it had almost lulled her into believing he really cared about her.

Of course he'd gone and ruined it all this morning by trying to convince her to let him abandon her at his sister's house. Though, thinking about it now, his attempt had seemed almost halfhearted.

"Yer no much of a morning person, are you?"

How long they'd been on the road when Colin at last slowed enough to ask his question, she had no idea. What she did know was that between the heat and the pounding she was taking on the horse, she was in no mood for any attempt at light conversation.

"I'm a great morning person when my morning is anything even remotely resembling civilized. Anyway, I think we left morning quite a ways behind us." The rumble of her stomach as much as the sun in the sky assured her she was correct.

"We can stop for a short rest and a cold meal if you need to."

She briefly considered refusing just so she could show him that she could keep going as long as he could, but her growling stomach won out.

"Good. Let's do that."

She pulled up on her reins and slid off her horse. The earth greeted her feet much sooner and much more forcefully than she expected, buckling her knees. Only her grip on the side of her saddle kept her from landing on her butt.

Though staying on her feet would probably be smarter, she found herself a fallen log and sat down on it, amazed at how comfortable it could feel to sit without having to straddle something.

Colin handed her more of the bread, cheese, and dried fruit they'd brought along with them and she settled back, munching quietly, deciding that she was quickly developing an aversion to all three foods.

Thunder rolled in the distance and she glanced toward the sound, noticing for the first time the dark clouds that filled the southern sky.

"Think we'll get rained on?" Soggy was what she'd come to expect from Scotland. At least it had been back in her time, though, come to think of it, she hadn't seen a single drop since she'd been here.

Colin shrugged and finished off the last of his meal. "It would be a welcome rain. The summer has been hot and much drier than most. The sheep are suffering for it."

"Are we headed in that direction, do you think? Toward the storm?" She wasn't particularly fond of traveling into those lightning strikes.

"That we are." Colin stood and held out a hand to help her to her feet. "Mayhaps we'll get lucky with a shower today."

Right. Lucky. The only thing she could imagine

that would be more uncomfortable than a day spent on horseback would be a day spent on horseback soaked to the skin.

"No rain. Hear that, whoever controls this stuff? No rain."

Her poor, tired leg felt like an anchor when she lifted her foot into the stirrup, enough so that she didn't make a sound of protest when Colin fastened his hands around her waist and boosted her up onto her mount. She even managed a mumbled "Thanks."

It didn't take long to realize he'd been right. They were on a direct course to intersect with the storm.

Colin allowed his horse to drop back next to hers for long enough to point out what passed for rain gear in this century. "You've a woolen there under yer pack. If we do hit the rains, wrap it over yer shoulders and head. It'll keep you dry for the better part."

They hadn't ridden much farther before the ground shook with the next peal of thunder, almost at the same time as the sky lit up around them.

"Hey," she called, urging her horse to pull even with Colin's. "That was really close. We need to get away from these trees. It's a very bad place for us to be in a storm like this. Trees and lightning are not a good mix."

The look of irritation he cast her way was well deserved, she'd admit. She realized there was little he could do but to keep moving them forward. Still, that didn't mean that she wasn't going to point out the obvious when she felt it needed pointing out.

Another crack of thunder rumbled so close by, she could swear she felt the hairs on her arm stand on end.

"This is so not a smart place to be," she called out.

"Isn't there a house or a castle or a . . . a something around here we can go to? Isn't there at least a—"

She bit off her words as just ahead of her he pulled his horse to a sharp stop, holding up his hand as if to silence her.

"Do you smell that?" He'd pushed up in his saddle, his head pivoting to scan the horizon in all directions.

She breathed in deeply, noticing for the first time that both their horses were testing the breeze as well.

"Smoke? Is that smoke?"

"Fire," he confirmed, pointing behind them toward the haze gathering in the direction from which they'd come. "I'd hazard a guess the lightning has struck dry tinder back there."

A wildfire?

"What do we do? Are there any people we should warn?" Now that she was aware of the fire, the smell of smoke seemed much stronger than it had only seconds before.

"We ride. Stay close to me and keep up. The river crossing is no too much farther ahead. Once we make it across, we'll be safe."

"We might be safe, but what about the people who live around here?" Surely they needed to be warned.

"There are no people around here, Abby. We're in the middle of miles of nothing but blessed nature. Now quiet yer blethering and concentrate on keeping up with me."

Almost before she could think, he was two lengths ahead of her.

"Ride, woman, ride!" His words floated back to her, their urgency unmistakable.

Her horse pawed the ground and jerked at his reins,

not the least bit pleased with her delay. She urged him forward, leaning low over his neck as he raced to catch up with Colin. The trees slipped past much faster than she found comfortable, but the scent of the fire was stronger now than ever and she gave her mount his head, allowing him to go as fast as he wanted.

Colin led them on until they reached the water's edge, a river too wide and too deep to be crossed. They followed the river downstream, maintaining the fastest pace the land would allow.

Abby fought down the panic building in the back of her throat. The smell of burning wood surrounded them, stinging her eyes and nose even as a dull roar behind them increased in volume. A glance over her shoulder showed billows of smoke rising into the air.

She took it all back. There was nothing she wanted to see more than rain. Nothing except maybe the river crossing Colin had promised.

Colin's *not too much farther* seemed to take forever to reach but there ahead of them, at last, was the place he'd sought.

"We can cross here. Stay with me and allow yer horse to find his way. He'll follow me. You hold on tight and you'll be fine, aye?"

She nodded, at a loss for words as she looked out across the swirling waters.

The river separated into narrow fingers around small islands of land angled through the whole of it. The islands broke the flow of the water, slowing it a bit.

Abby could only trust that Colin knew what he was doing, because none of her past experience riding through meadows or on back trails in Colorado had done anything to prepare her for something like this.

Her horse wasted no time in wading in, matching his pace to that of Colin's mount. Near the middle of the largest open stretch, the water rose well above her knees, almost to her mount's shoulders, and she allowed her mind to flirt uncomfortably with the idea that the large animal might actually be swimming rather than touching the bottom.

As long as he seemed calm, she reassured herself, things must be going well enough. Now if she could only convince herself that there was no need to panic.

Ahead of her, Colin slowed his horse, waiting for her to come abreast of him. "Yer doing fine, Abby. We're almost across. Yer mount is a good one. Trust him."

She tried to smile at him, to show him she was handling this all like an experienced outdoorswoman, but for some reason her lips simply refused to cooperate, and she knew without a doubt that if she opened her mouth to speak, she was just as likely as not to end up a whimpering mess.

He reached over and plucked up the slack in her reins, maintaining a hold on it until they reached the far bank.

Somehow, that small move reassured her more than anything up to that point had. She found herself relaxing her own death grip on the reins just a bit, as if sharing that strip of leather with him allowed some of his confidence to leach into her.

When they at last reached the other side, she wanted nothing more than to slide off her horse and kiss the solid ground, but considering she strongly suspected her legs would give way and humiliate her, she stayed in the saddle.

"Look there."

She turned her head to follow the direction Colin pointed in, and her heart pounded in her chest as she realized those were flames licking against the trees they'd ridden through not ten minutes ago.

"I think that's just about the scariest thing I've ever seen in my whole life."

Colin nodded, his attention already fixed on scanning the area behind them. "We canna afford to delay here."

Now that the immediate danger seemed past, Abby began to notice the little discomforts left behind. For one thing, her shift and overdress were soaked up to her thighs and felt as though they carried an extra fifty pounds of water. She very much doubted anything in the cloth bag tied to her horse's back had fared the river crossing in much better shape.

While Colin seemed to work through some internal debate about the direction they would travel from here, she got down to practical matters. Grabbing up the hem of her skirt, she began to wring water out of it, section by section.

"Look at you." Colin had returned to her side, a reluctant grin breaking over his face. He caught up one of her freshly wrung out sections and touched it to her face. "Now we've a great problem. It seems I've uncovered a clean spot."

"What are you talking about?" She glanced to his

face as he dragged a finger across his forehead leaving a lighter trail in a smudge of dirt. "Soot?"

If she looked anything like he did, which she was sure she must, simply wringing out her skirt wasn't going to accomplish much in the way of making her look presentable.

"There's a small village, maybe an hour's ride ahead. We should be able to make it there before dark settles. I know a man who lives nearby and like as no, he'll give us shelter for the night. You'll be able to freshen yerself there."

He ducked his head, not waiting for her answer, and started off down the trail again.

So he knew a man in a village, did he? A place he could stay that didn't involve a long cold night on the hard ground. Interesting he hadn't mentioned that before. In fact, he'd been pretty specific about the whole journey's lacking in accommodations. If she were the suspicious type, she might be tempted to suspect he had wanted her to believe every night would be like their last one just so she would stay behind with his family rather than tagging along with him.

If she were the suspicious type.

"Which I definitely am," she muttered defiantly, kneeing her horse to keep pace with Colin.

Twenty-nine

❦

Flynn bent low over his horse's neck, kicking the animal's sides, demanding more speed. Not that the terrified animal wasn't already giving all she had.

Behind him, the screams ceased abruptly, leaving only the roar of the encroaching flames. Like the beating of hooves, the sound reverberated against his eardrums, as if Hades' own chariot chased him.

Once he made it out of this mess, he'd need to find himself some new weak-minded mortal to enthrall. He'd warned the fool to ride faster. Pity he'd lost their supplies as well.

The fire raged around him, leaping from tree to tree, consuming everything in its path. The dry timbers exploded with the fury of the inferno, showering burning shrapnel down on him that stung his face and hands.

His frenzied mount burst free from the tree line at

last and plunged into the river without breaking stride. Possessed of the same madness as the horse, the same fear-crazed need to survive, Flynn made no attempt to slow the animal until they approached the opposite bank.

Only then did he regain himself, sparing but a single thought to how much he hated the mortality bestowed on him in taking blood. The pure, pitiful weakness that was Mortal.

Still, without Abby's magic flowing in his veins, he would never have been able to find the crossing in time.

He dismounted, stooping to the ground to scan the tracks around him.

It was the odd huffing noise that caused him to turn in time to witness his horse's legs buckling. Her great weight dropped to the ground with a *thud*, signaling yet another impediment to his quest.

Her entire hindquarter had been charred black, her big brown eyes wild with fear and pain. The Glock tucked into his waistband crossed his thoughts. It shouldn't take more than one bullet to put her out of her misery.

But that one bullet could well be one he'd need in order to get his hands on Abigail and make his way out of this time.

It appeared he'd be walking for a little while.

No matter. They weren't so very far ahead of him. Their trail was easy enough to follow. He'd find another horse.

And then he'd track them. Following along, waiting for the perfect moment to strike.

It was only a matter of time until he'd have Abigail and return to his own time, where he belonged.

Thirty

I'll give you time to have a proper soak before I return, so dinna dawdle and expect me to linger about the hallway waiting for you to finish."

With those words of warning, Colin stepped through the doorway and closed it firmly behind him, leaving Abby to wonder how long a "proper soak" lasted in Colin's mind.

The friend he'd spoken of had turned out to be the laird of a clan friendly to his own. Instead of a small hut as she'd imagined, they were spending the night in a castle at least as large as Dun Ard, though it appeared to have seen better days. The laird himself, a man named Roderick, had seemed pleased to see Colin and even more pleased to see him accompanied by a wife.

Soon after their arrival they'd been shuffled into this large bedchamber, and a parade of boys and young girls had traipsed back and forth, filling the large wooden tub that now sat steaming in front of the fireplace.

Abby could hardly wait to climb inside and sink down under the hot water.

She untied the knife from her waist and dropped it to the floor, followed by the smaller knife she'd hidden in her bodice. Then she pulled off her sleeve covers and her overdress, tossing them both in a pile on the floor. Cold bumps covered her body as the breeze slipped in around the two high, shuttered windows, and her tired muscles shivered. If she could muster the energy, she might try to wash her clothing out in the tub after she finished her bath. Her shift followed next, along with the long pants Ellie had given her.

The cold air made her anticipation of the hot water all that much sweeter. She stepped into the tub, planning a slow, decadent inch-by-inch descent into the steaming water.

Until the door opened.

She dropped to her knees like a rock, sending water splashing over both sides of the big wooden tub.

It was Colin who leaned in the door. He tossed something in her direction, and as a reflex she managed to block it, knocking it into the water with a splash.

"I almost forgot that. Lady Rosalyn sent it along for you once she heard you liked it. It's balm she uses, by the way."

"Balm?" What on earth was he going on about this time?

"Balm," he confirmed confidently. "And mint."

As quickly as he'd shown up, he was gone again.

Abby felt around in the tub, at last locating the object

that had joined her in her bath. Rosalyn's handmade soap.

A little thrill tingled through her heart, bringing with it a smile to Abby's lips.

Lemon balm and mint, though in this day and age, it was called only balm. Those were the herbs Colin's mother combined to get that lovely smell.

He'd remembered how much she'd liked it and that she'd wondered what herbs his mother used. He'd remembered that little detail about her, and then he'd bothered to ask his mother what she put in her soap to make it smell the way it did. That he'd cared enough to take the extra time to ask made her happy. That he'd taken the time the morning of their departure to do so—even in the midst of his ranting to every living soul at Dun Ard in an attempt to find someone to support his position that she should remain there when he left—made it even more special.

The smile his action had put on her face wasn't going anywhere for quite some time.

Abby ducked her head back in the water, making sudsy the ends of her hair with the lovely little soap, hoping to banish the smell of charcoaled forest.

The hot water lapping around her sore muscles felt almost good enough to make her forget that she'd always favored showers over soaking in her own filth.

"When in Rome," she murmured in an attempt to silence her annoyingly active inner critic.

All things considered, what she experienced at this moment was like living in the lap of luxury. If your lap happened to be located in the Highlands of Scotland, circa 1306, that is.

The water had begun to cool to an uncomfortable level by the time she finally managed to drag herself out of the tub, and she shook out the bundle of drying cloth the maids had left for her use.

No wonder terry cloth towels had caught on so well. Would catch on, she amended. These things were like trying to dry yourself off with big linen sheets.

A quick look around reminded her that the big linen sheet she was disparaging was all she had to wear for the moment, since the clothing she'd taken off was soot-covered and soggy and Colin had sent all their other things off with one of the maids to be dried in the kitchens.

Seeing no alternative, she wrapped herself up, toga-style, pulling the end of the cloth up and over her shoulder and tucking it into the tight wrap around her breasts.

Once she felt herself securely covered, she gathered up her dirty things and dropped to her knees, shoving her pile of dirty clothes into the tub. It might not be the best washing they'd ever get, but it had to be an improvement over what they'd been through in the last five or six hours.

She'd just started to wring out the long pants when the door opened and Colin entered carrying a tray laden with food and a large jug.

"Good," he said as he set the tray on a small, round table in the corner closest to the fire. "Yer out of yer bath. Come up from there and join me for a bit of supper."

Abby grabbed on to the side of the big tub to push herself up to stand, every single one of her muscles screaming in protest at the move.

As if he read her mind, Colin was at her side in an instant, his hands under her elbows taking the full force of her weight to lift her to her feet.

"Thanks." She smiled up at him and might have said more if not for the chill of his hands on her arms. "Your hands are like ice. What have you been doing?"

"You had the tub, so I used the loch. Was no so warm as yer own fine bath, my lady."

No wonder his shirt and plaid clung wetly to his body.

"Here." She walked to the bed and scooped up the second drying sheet that had been left for them. "You should probably get out of those wet things. You can drop them in the tub with mine and I'll wash them out after we eat."

A look of surprise danced over his face. "Is that what you were doing there on yer hands and knees? Washing yer things? Roderick has maids to do that for you, wife. You've no need to do it yerself."

"Those girls that were in here before?" She handed him the drying sheet and turned her back to wait while he changed. "I don't think so. They were just kids, and besides, I'm guessing they're all in bed by now."

Behind her she heard the slap of heavy wet cloth hitting the stone floor.

That would be his plaid.

Followed by another wet plop.

His shirt.

Abby bit the inside of her bottom lip, struggling to wipe from her mind the image of him standing behind her completely naked. In the buff. Gloriously buffed in fact, she knew from experience. She'd seen him that way one too many times not to have the image engraved on the back side of her retina.

"Do you think you might lend me a hand with this?" he called. "I canna seem to manage the fastening as you have with yers."

Her mind blanked for a second when she turned, the vision of him wrapped in the drying cloth, his damp hair curling at his shoulders, filling every available brain cell.

She crossed to where he waited and reached out to take the cloth's end from him, only vaguely embarrassed by the way her hand shook as she looped it over his shoulder.

"There you go." She tucked the end behind the material wrapped at his chest, patting it for good measure.

Or perhaps simply as an excuse to touch the hard expanse of his chest.

Had she been thinking of Rome such a short time ago? It should have been Greece, because here she was, standing in front of her own personal Greek god. Maybe Aries. He looked pretty warlike. Did the Greeks even have a male God of Gorgeous? Because Colin could definitely be him right this minute, whatever his name might be. If she'd only paid more attention in those classes, but she'd been so much more interested in Celtic than Roman and Greek mythology.

"Are we to stand here, then, staring at each other, or shall we have our food?"

Abby blinked and then blinked again, slowly dragging her thoughts back from the expanse of linen-covered chest spread out in front of her as all the fantasies it had sent her off pursuing faded away.

"Sorry. I guess I'm more tired than I thought."

Tired. Right. It wasn't *tired* that was knotting itself around her organs. It was desire. Hot, desperate need.

She took a seat across from him, face flaming, and waited as he poured from the jug into the two cups on the table.

"It's a fair honey ale Roderick's people make," he said as he passed the cup to her. "No so good as the one we put by at Dun Ard, but this'll do in a pinch."

She sniffed the brew before taking a sip. *Not bad.* Not at all bitter, but it did leave a heavy aftertaste, similar to that of a dark beer.

"How do they keep it from being warmer than this?" There certainly wasn't a refrigerator in the back room.

"I'd imagine they store it underground. That's what we do at Dun Ard."

She emptied her cup and pushed it forward for a refill. Not quite a true cold brew, but cool enough to hit the spot after such a long day. The wooden tray held meat shavings, bread, cheese, and dried fruit, the same as every other meal she'd had in this century with the exception of the large midday meal when she'd first arrived. They'd served a thick soup along with everything else at that meal.

If she was this tired of the food after only three days, mealtimes for the next week or so were looking pretty grim.

"You know what sounds good to me? A big old salad. With ranch dressing and bacon bits and every kind of green leafy thing you can imagine. Doesn't that sound good to you?"

She could almost feel the ale humming through her

bloodstream as she emptied her second cup and pushed it toward Colin for another refill.

His eyebrow arched, but to his credit, he didn't question her. He simply refilled her cup and returned it to her before he rose and headed over to the tub.

"There are any number of things that sound good to me, but yer weeds are no one them. Though I will say this: yer time did present a pleasurable abundance of variety at the dinner table." He spoke as he kneeled down to pull the first garment from the tub.

She should tell him not to bother, that she'd take care of those things when she finished her meal. But with each twist of cloth, the muscles in his forearms corded and rippled and she couldn't seem to bring herself to encourage him to stop what he was doing.

Besides, it was such a sweet gesture on his part. No wonder she had fallen in love with him.

"Like!" she blurted out as the candle sitting nearest her sizzled, its wick burned down into the wax. The little flame flickered out, leaving the room a fraction darker than it had been a moment before.

"You like what?" Colin asked, still bent over the tub.

"Nothing," she muttered, pushing the ale away. So maybe she did like him. No big deal. For a fact she lusted after him. But love? No. Absolutely not. She wouldn't allow that to happen.

"We should get some sleep. Morning will come early and we've a long day's ride ahead of us." Colin made his way around the room as he spoke, snuffing out each of the candles in turn until, at last, he stood in front of her with only the light from the fireplace flickering behind him.

He held out a hand and she accepted it, rising to her feet and allowing him to lead her to the bed.

It was a massive, high affair that would require her to hoist herself up into it, the sort of furniture she'd expect to see a step stool sitting next to. Colin lifted her to sit, saving her the problem of clambering inside. She remained where he'd set her, her feet dangling over the edge as he loosed the bed's draperies and let them fall into place before he joined her, climbing through the draperies into his side of the bed. Once he'd made his way inside and the draperies fell shut, no trace of the wavering firelight was visible.

It took only a moment for the apprehension to begin to build.

"It's like a box." A dark little coffin kind of box.

"This is an old keep and the shutters dinna fit so very well. They let in as much of the wind as they keep out, so we can consider ourselves fortunate it's no likely to rain. The bed draperies will add to our comfort."

"If you happen to be comfortable sleeping in a dark little box, maybe." Wrapped up like a mummy in a linen sheet, laid out to be preserved for a thousand years. The whole effect was one she didn't find the least bit comforting.

"Lay back and get yerself some sleep."

The mattress next to her rustled as Colin worked his way under the covers.

With the impenetrable black closing in on her, there was no way she could even begin to think of adding the weight of a layer of blankets on top of her body. It would be like throwing dirt on top of herself.

As if the draperies had sealed them in an airtight

container, she struggled for her next breath. It felt like the dark little box was closing in on her, getting smaller and smaller with each breath she took.

Thinking to distract herself, she rolled to her stomach and flattened her face against the mattress.

That worked no better. If anything, it was worse. The linen cloth tangled in her legs and felt much more like a binding now than the toga she'd imagined earlier.

This was likely all she had to look forward to if she couldn't return to her own time. Night after night in cold, drafty castles, using a stone bench toilet and shutting herself into a dark little tomb to sleep. And that was a best-case scenario.

Moment by moment, the panic built, like fingers tightening around her throat. Her mind filled with images of long-dead bodies wrapped in linen, hidden away in airtight boxes to preserve them.

But she wasn't ready to be preserved.

"I don't think I can do this." She sat up, twisting onto her knees. "I absolutely know I can't do this."

"Do what?"

Any of it. "I can't breathe in here. I need out."

Desperation peaked. Completely disoriented by the dark and the panic, she flailed her arms in search of the drapery opening, stopping only when she smacked into Colin's shoulder.

He was on his knees next to her, holding her, when the trembling began. She collapsed against him, shutting her eyes against the encroaching black void.

"It's this dark little box. It's closing in on me!"

"Calm down," he ordered, his voice low and soothing. "I'll help you."

She heard a *swish* of fabric and swiveled her head in the direction of the noise.

Thank God!

The wavering light of the fireplace shone through the break in the draperies, and she scrambled toward it like a drowning man toward the water's surface. Just like that drowning victim, she gasped for air as her feet hit the floor. Her arms locked around her middle and she bent at the waist, hanging her head forward to take in great gulps of air as if she'd just reached the end of a marathon run.

"You've a problem with enclosed spaces?"

Colin was at her side, his large, warm hand rubbing up and down her back. She could only nod her answer.

"You should have told me. Here." The hand at her back urged her toward the fire and down onto the rug. "Sit. Relax. Yer going to be fine now."

Of course she was. Out here in the open, in this big room, with all this space and all this air, she could feel her heartbeat slowing to normal.

He rejoined her, sitting down at her side and pulling her close to him before he draped a blanket he'd taken from the bed around their shoulders.

"There," he comforted. His arm tightened around her as he pulled her head to rest on his chest and, with only a small shift of his body, he lay back, drawing her down with him. "Try to close yer eyes and get some rest."

Rest? With the adrenaline she'd just pumped through her system in that panic attack? Not hardly. Not for a while. And certainly not with his heart pounding under her cheek and the heat from his chest searing her palm.

Searing her leg, too, now that she laced it over the top of his.

"I don't think I'm sleepy anymore." With her body ensconced in his embrace, she was about as far from sleepy as she could imagine.

Not that her imagination wasn't busy picturing other activities.

"If no sleep, what would help you to relax?"

She bit back the groan that question brought to her lips and shifted against him, trying for something approaching comfort.

"We could talk," he offered. "Would you like that? When my brother Drew and I were but lads, we'd lie in our beds and tell each other stories to see who could put the other to sleep first. We could—"

"Nope," she interrupted.

Talk wasn't at all what she had in mind. Stranded seven hundred years from home in the draftiest, most uncomfortable castle that had likely ever existed, lying in the arms of the sexiest man she'd ever met, she was in no mood for talk.

"I only thought that since it had worked so well for Drew and me, we might—"

"I'm not your brother," she interrupted again, rubbing her toe against his ankle.

"I ken the truth of that well enough," he muttered.

"Good." She lifted her head to watch his eyes as she ran her finger along the top of his linen toga, playing with the flap that ran over his shoulder and tucked into the wrap. "In that case, if you're up for it, I have an idea of what we can do and I'm pretty sure it's not something you and Drew would ever have considered."

With a flip of her finger, she untucked the flap and tossed it over his shoulder, watching his eyes narrow as she waggled her eyebrows up and down.

"If yer suggesting what I think you are, I'm up for it, as you say."

Before she could even begin to try to come up with another double entendre, he had her on her back, his big body looming over hers.

"More than up for it."

The hard bulge pressing against her lower stomach was absolute proof of his claim.

He shifted to his knees and pulled her up into his arms. Their bodies pressed against each other, face-to-face. His mouth captured hers, sending her off on another flight of fancy as his tongue swept her mouth before his lips left hers to travel down her neck.

She lifted her arms to his neck, twining her fingers in his hair. A cold shiver took her body, and she realized her wrap was gone, pooled at her knees. An instant later, it was joined by his, and he pressed his heated body against hers as he lowered her once again to her back.

His mouth traced a path from her neck to her breast and when he suckled, his tongue flickered over her nipple in lightning-quick touches that drove her wild with need. She lifted her legs, locking them at his back, pressing herself against the heated skin of his erection.

He groaned and lifted his head to search her face. Bracing his arms on either side of her, he lifted his weight from her body while his hands slid under her head to cradle her like a living pillow.

This was it. He was in position, his hot flesh pressed against her opening. Any second now, he'd enter her.

The anticipation built by his slow back-and-forth agitation over that opening was driving her mad with need.

"I'd no idea before this moment how badly I wanted this," he whispered, and dropped his head next to hers, nibbling at her earlobe. "Or how much yer commitment would mean to me, wife."

Her brain was fuzzy with excitement. "I totally know. I feel exactly . . ." *Wait. Commitment?* "What commitment?"

"To us," he breathed into her ear. "To the entwining our souls demand. To our lives together."

His hands slid to her waist, clasping her tightly as he drove inside her.

Behind her eyelids, there were sparkles and fireworks. It felt that good. Her entire body trembled, held on edge waiting for that magnificent moment of release. He pulled out and prepared for a second assault.

If only she could let that last comment go and just lose herself in the moment.

"Our lives together?" she panted. "You mean you'll come back to my time with me?"

He hung motionless above her as if frozen in the time she meant to travel through. "I've told you why I canna do that. There's too much for me to accomplish here. Surely you ken the changes I can make that can be made by no other. No, my love, it's you who'll stay at my side, aye?"

No, no, this whole thing was going sideways, right at the worst possible moment.

"I never said I'd stay here. I don't even want to stay here. I can't. You should know that. Just like you can't go around changing history, Colin. You should know that, too. It's wrong."

A tension that was in no way sexual slipped into the stillness between them, and Colin rolled away from her to lie on his back.

"What might be history to you, wife, is but the future to me. A future that has yet to be written."

"Oh, really?" She turned to her side to stare at him. "Well, while you're busy contemplating all those big changes you'd like to write into that future of yours, just keep in mind that with every change you make to my history, you run the risk of making someone I care about blink out of existence. Maybe even me. Pretty damn hard for our souls to entwine if I don't exist, don't you think?"

He pushed up to stand, ignoring her question. "I'm going to bed. Are you coming?"

Abby lay on the floor, her body thrumming with frustration, the spot beside her resonating with its emptiness. He'd walked away. He'd simply gotten up, turned his back, and left her lying here in a pool of her own disappointment.

"You're doing this to get even with me because I was the one who stopped everything last time, aren't you?"

"This has nothing to do with last time. I stopped because yer no willing to give the commitment I seek. You want only a physical coupling with me. Sex, and nothing more."

That wasn't it at all. She wanted commitment as much as the next person, but not if it meant spending the rest of her life in the fourteenth freaking century. And not if it meant risking the world as she knew it.

"So?" she demanded. "What's wrong with just sex? I can't agree to the kind of commitment you're asking. Why's that so difficult for you to understand? You're not willing to commit to the things I see as important."

"It's no at all difficult for me to see what you intend. My intent is something else entirely. Good night, Wife."

He climbed up into the bed, pulling the draperies firmly shut behind him, and in what seemed like a matter of moments, soft snores emanated from the bed where he lay.

Abby, meanwhile, curled on the rug, cocooned in her blanket, thinking dark, spiteful thoughts about life in general and Colin MacAlister in particular.

Fine. He could sleep in his stupid little coffin box of a bed all by himself. There wasn't enough money on the face of the planet to get her back into that dark hole. She had enough crap in her life at this moment without adding another round of suffocating claustrophobia into the mix just to try to appease him.

Who else but she could be unlucky enough to find maybe the one man in the entire world who seemed to fill all the empty holes inside her, only to discover that he was also possibly the only man in the whole world who insisted on commitment before sex?

Worse yet? In spite of all her big talk to the contrary, she was pretty damn sure she'd been stupid enough to let herself fall in love with the guy.

That she'd had to travel seven hundred years into the past to find all this out only added insult to the injury.

Thirty-one

❦

Colin awoke in a foul, gray mood, more than ready to growl at anyone who crossed his path. He shoved back the heavy, dust-laden draperies with much more force than was necessary to greet a morning that was equally as foul and gray as he felt.

The shutters on the high windows had blown fully open during the night and rain sprayed in, soaking the entire room in a fine wet mist.

It would seem the dry spell had ended.

He rounded the bed to check on Abby and found her still asleep, curled up in a tight little ball with only the thin blanket he'd pulled from the bed last night to provide her protection.

And precious little protection it had been. A fine mist beaded on her hair, and as he approached, he could see that her body shivered with each breath.

Little wonder, since the fire had long ago burned itself out.

Some fine protector he was turning out to be.

He had made the fire his first priority, building it back to flaming warmth before he pulled another blanket from their bed to drape over her body, tucking it close. He'd briefly considered carrying her to the bed and slipping in beside her.

But that would have awakened her, and she needed all the rest she could get.

One last tug to cover her properly and then he slipped into his clothing and quietly out the door, pausing in the hallway to gather his thoughts, doing his best to beat back the guilt that washed over him in waves.

If he managed to get her through this journey and back to Dun Ard in one piece, it would truly be a miracle beyond even the power of the Fae.

Or maybe in spite of the Fae.

Halting his steps, he closed his eyes and dropped his guards, reaching out. He pushed away the cries battering his aura from within the castle, stretching out, far out into the countryside, until he found the one soul he sought.

Black, ragged, stained with evil, it pulsed, taunting him with its nearness.

Flynn. The Nuadian was here.

He'd debated whether to tell Abby that it had been no hallucination she'd suffered in the forest, deciding at last it would only give her one more thing to fear in this world. Instead, he'd spent the rest of that night, sword at his side, daring the Fae to step into the light of his campfire.

Somehow, someway, the bastard had managed to follow them here. And now Colin had no doubt that he hunted Abby.

Too bad for the Nuadian that he didn't understand Abby belonged to Colin. She was indeed his Soulmate and as such, no one would ever lay hand on her without going through him.

"And that I promise, you black-hearted bastard, will be no easy task," he vowed aloud.

Emotional walls firmly back in place, Colin stomped downstairs wearing his anger and the unshakable guilt like a heavy moth-ridden cloak, his mood growing darker and fouler by the moment.

With a great shove he threw back the doors to the laird's hall and swept inside to be met by the ancient chatelaine. Her face a mask of anger, she ran the length of the hall to meet him, her keys jangling at her side even as she lifted a finger to her lips, angrily shushing him.

"What?" he demanded as she reached his side.

"I'd thank you to keep yer voice down," she hissed. "Our poor laird's only just managed to nod off and we dinna need you to wake him."

"I'm no sleeping, you old scold," Roderick called from the table where he sat without lifting his head from his folded arms. "Leave my guests alone, woman. Be off with you now and send back some food for my friend."

"What ails you, Roderick?" By the morning's gray light, it was clear something did. His friend's face was drawn and haggard, his hair pushed up on one side of his head as if matted there. This was not the same man he'd seen only the evening before. "You look as if you'd spent the night in yer cups rather than in yer bed."

"Fine observation, MacAlister." His host lifted his tankard, his eyes narrowing in disgust when he found it empty. "They've stolen away my drink again."

Colin sat down next to his old friend, asking him yet again, "What ails you?"

In their youth, this man had ridden with him and Dair. Then Roderick's father and older brother had died and he'd been called home to take over as laird. In short order, he'd married and settled down to the business of running his clan.

"My heart," Roderick confessed, his voice breaking as he pushed back in his chair. "It's my heart, MacAlister. It's broken and will never be right again."

"I dinna understand, old friend. Are you ill? Where's yer wife that she'd let you spend yer time wallowing in self-pity and whisky as you have this past night?"

"That's it exactly!" Roderick slammed his hand down on the table, sending empty cups toppling over as the chatelaine returned with a serving girl and two large trenchers. "I've lost my Karen. She and the wee bairn she carried, both dead, what is it now, Madeline? Six months?" He turned his bloodshot eyes to the old chatelaine as she placed a trencher filled with a thick paste of oats in front of him.

"Aye, yer lairdship, as well you ken. Half a year, today." Madeline patted the man's shoulder, casting a reproachful eye toward Colin.

"I'd no heard of yer terrible loss, Roddy. I'm so sorry." No wonder his friend drank through the night. He remembered the delicate, smiling woman his friend had married. He also remembered the way Roderick's face had softened whenever he'd looked on his wife.

"You ken the worst of it, Col? It's what a poor excuse for a husband I was while my Karen lived." He shook his head, pushing away the comforting hand Madeline offered. "Off with you, woman. Leave me to my misery this day."

"How can you say that? I saw the two of you together with my own eyes. I never heard tell of you lifting a hand to her or even allowing a negative word to pass yer lips where she was concerned." Roddy had always been the model of calm and patience.

"That may well be true, but there's worse a man can do to his wife. It's in the things I dinna do, Col. The things I thought but never said, the things I meant to do and never did. And now it's too late." Roderick dropped his head to his hands.

"I'm sure yer Karen kenned the way you cared for her. How could she not?"

Roddy looked up, his eyes suspiciously glassy. "Because I never said the words. Dinna you make my mistakes with yer own lovely wife. Dinna you wait for the perfect moment to declare yer love. Tell her often. Tell how her laughter brightens yer day or how her touch comforts when you need it most. Dinna you wait as I did. Dinna you let her slip through yer fingers never hearing from yer own lips that which your heart holds most prized. Dinna you waste one precious moment together. It's the lost moments that will burden my heart for the rest of my days."

Meeting his friend's gaze, Colin knew there were no words he could offer to ease the man's pain. Not on this day. No platitudes would lessen the loss for Roddy. Time was the only magic that would help him. Time and perhaps, one day, the love of a good woman.

Abby's face filled his thoughts then, followed by an empty pang of longing to return to her side upstairs. It wasn't just a need to protect her that squeezed his chest. It was a need to see her, to be with her. An unreasonable need to reassure himself, in the face of his friend's overwhelming sorrow, that his own love yet lived.

"I thank you for yer advice, my friend. I will take it to heart."

That seemed enough for Roderick, who pushed back his chair and wobbled unsteadily to his feet. "I'm off to bed, then. It's sorry I am to miss yer departure, MacAlister, but I've no stomach for facing this particular day alone."

By the time he reached the end of the table, two young boys had appeared through the back doors as if they'd been waiting for this moment. One on either side of him, they assisted their laird into the hallway and out of sight.

Colin pushed back from the table and stood, his appetite vanished. Pain such as he'd just witnessed could not easily be forgotten.

At least there would be no fires chasing them today.

Abby wiped the mist from her face and tugged the heavy plaid lower over her head exactly as Colin had shown her to do when he'd helped her to put it on.

She'd labored a good hour to come up with something even vaguely approaching a positive thought for this day's ride, and lack of fire was still the best she could manage. *Miserable* had taken on new proportions on this day when the long-absent rains had returned to the Highlands. The constant precipitation, ranging from heavy drizzle to a fine, face-stinging mist, wore her down. Thank goodness the plaid was more water-repellent than it looked.

"That's two," she muttered. Two positives she'd managed to find in this oppressively gloomy day.

"What's that you say?" Colin pulled his mount closer to hers and tilted his head in her direction.

"Nothing," she countered, maintaining the unspoken battle of wills between them this day.

He might have shaken his head at that; she couldn't be sure, considering the plaid wrapped around him like a cocoon. She liked to think he had, anyway.

With no further word, he pulled his horse ahead of hers again, picking up the pace once more.

It had been this way between them all day long, the tension from last night's unresolved conflict hanging over their journey as heavily as the gray skies above them. Had they said more than twenty words to each other all day? She very much doubted it. But it wouldn't be she who broke down first. Colin was the one who needed to make amends, not her.

Hours passed, one blending into another in the silence of the gray rain. Abby's mind had glazed over, as numb as her bottom by the time Colin dropped back beside her on the trail again.

"We'll leave the road here. No too far through the woods there's a place where we can seek shelter for the night. It's long deserted but with nightfall approaching, it will offer some protection."

Silence returned as they rode forward, weaving their way through forest and underbrush that looked as if it hadn't been disturbed in years. Rain beat down on them, spattering against the woolen draped over Abby's head. Each drop landed with a wet plopping noise that grated on her raw nerves. After what seemed an eternity, she opened her mouth to point out how very different her view of *not too far* must be from Colin's, but stopped when she saw the structures looming in the clearing ahead of them.

Surely those burned-out remains of what had once been someone's home couldn't be their destination, and yet Colin appeared to be slowing his horse.

"That's it?"

She could hardly believe her eyes when he nodded his answer. How in the world did he expect them to stay dry in that place? It was little more than rubble and charred wood. Even the forest they'd ridden through would likely provide better shelter.

"It's no the castle where we'll stay for the night," he called back to her as he dismounted and began to lead his horse forward on foot. "It's the stable beyond that offers shelter."

"Right." Abby drew her own animal to a halt, her dismay multiplying. "I guess that would be the *burned-down* stable?" Did he not see the same thing she saw?

"There's more of the building still standing than you might think."

Through the murky light of dusk and gray drizzle, she finally spotted the area he intended. It looked like little more than a shed left standing, backed up against a large outcrop of rocks. Once she dismounted and approached it, however, she could see that it was, as he had said, larger than it appeared. It likely had been a storage area for the original stable, carved deeply into the earth it backed up against.

She untied her wet bundle from the back of her mount and handed over her reins to Colin to allow him to see to the animal's care. After a day spent in this relentless rain, she wanted only to be out of the wet, even if that meant nothing more than a cold hovel dug into the earth.

Thank goodness half of the front was open. If the whole wall still stood, she doubted she'd be able to remain inside, no matter that it was the only half-dry place around.

A fire pit made out of stacked stones sat near the opening, making it obvious even to her that she and Colin weren't the first travelers to seek shelter here. It was equally obvious that no one had been here in a very long time, so this likely wasn't some slightly off the trail well-known stop.

"This seems rather out of the way. How did you even know this place was here?" she asked as Colin joined her.

He stopped at the entrance to shake the rain droplets from the plaid he'd worn over his head and shoulders before he answered.

"The MacBrydes who lived here had ties to my own clan, the MacKiernans. My mother knew them from her childhood." Colin disappeared into the far, dark corner, returning with an armload of wood and tossing it into the fire pit.

Abby leaned against the opening, peering out to study the remains of the once large castle. Such devastation set her imagination loose trying to picture what could have led to such ruin. There must have been large numbers of people here at one point in the past.

"What happened to them?"

"War, disease, breeding." Colin grunted and coughed, scooting back from the smoke of their newly started fire. "Or lack of breeding, I should say. The last laird of the MacBrydes sired naught but female offspring and when his wife died, he went mad from grief and ended his own life. His only surviving daughter refused to take a husband and instead allowed the castle and its lands to fall into ruin. Gradually their people drifted away, aligning themselves with other clans. Time and any number of battles raging through here have left MacBryde Hall as you see it now."

"I'll give you this much: one thing you Scots never seem to lack for is a tragic story."

" 'Tis all too true," Colin agreed, his eyes unfocused as he stared out into the ever-worsening rain. "Tragedy steals the dreams of even those who dinna deserve it."

Flames licked upward from the fire he'd coaxed to life, like yellow arms wavering in a ghostly dance, spreading their heat with intensity.

Abby backed away, the heat so overwhelming after a couple of minutes, she was sure she could see the steam coming off her plaid. Only feet away from the fire, the chill hit her, seeping through the wet clothing she wore.

She unwound the woolen from her head and shoulders and draped it across the rails at one end of the shed. If she was lucky, it just might dry by morning.

To her surprise, the top of her shift and overdress where the plaid had covered her were only lightly damp, though the skirts of both, along with her riding underpants, were completely soaked up to her thighs.

That little fact gave her some hope for her extra bundle of clothing. She dropped to her knees feeling there was a chance that she might be able to find something dry in the center of the roll. As she worked at the wet, swollen laces holding the bundle tight, her fingers shook, as much from impatience as from the chill.

"Let me do that." Colin placed a hand under her arm, gently pulling her to her feet. "Go and sit by the fire until we can get you out of those wet things."

She considered protesting but decided against it, the lure of the fire too great to be ignored.

In no time at all, he was lifting her things from the unrolled bundle and shaking them out before he draped them over the fencing that separated the storage area from the original stalls in their shelter.

"It's all wet?" She didn't even try to keep the disappointment out of her voice. The prospect of the long, uncomfortable night she faced loomed large in her thoughts.

"Dinna fash yerself over it, wife. I've a dry tunic and plaid in my bundle."

"How?" The rains had fallen on him equally hard as they had on her.

"Because I carry our provisions, I wrapped them first in an oiled leather. Here." He crossed over to where she sat, stopping to scoop up an ivory-colored shirt, which he handed to her. "You can change over there. I promise no to watch if that makes you feel better."

An uncharacteristic grin broke over his face as he teased, causing her heart to beat a little faster than it had a moment before and forcing a smile to her lips in return. As if his seeing her in any state of undress made a difference anymore.

Shirt in hand, she hurried behind the stable wall and worked her way out of her overdress and shift, letting them drop to her feet before slipping his shirt over her head. It hung down past her knees while the sleeves draped several inches past her fingertips.

Last, she wiggled out of the wet linen underpants, balancing on one foot after the other to pull them off. She then located a spot on the rail to hang them to dry before heading back to the fire.

She brushed a hand down the soft linen of the tunic she wore, surprised at the case of nerves that suddenly afflicted her. How stupid was that? She'd never met a man, never met anyone, with whom she felt as comfortable as she felt with Colin. And yet, when she stepped around the fence, she felt her face color with embarrassment as he watched her approach.

After what seemed like the longest minute of her life, she suddenly realized it wasn't her attire at all, but the expression on his face, that elicited her discomfort.

"What?" she asked nervously as she sat down on the blanket he'd spread close to the fire.

He continued to stare at her for a moment longer, as if he had something he wanted to say. A pensive expression he'd worn off and on all day. Then the moment passed as quickly as it had come. He shook his head and turned his back, stirring whatever was in the pot he had placed at the edge of the fire.

"Stay to the middle of those woolens," he cautioned.

"They're from under the horses' saddles, so their edges are quite wet."

So that was where he'd gotten them. She pulled her feet up under her and tucked the big shirt down over her toes, watching Colin as he fussed over the pot, yet again going out of his way to take care of her.

"What is that you're making?"

"Porridge. It's only oats with bits of dried meat, but it will be warm and filling. It needs stirring so it doesn't burn. Would you mind looking after it while I change into something drier?"

"Go." Abby rocked up onto her knees and took the stick Colin was using from his hands. "I've got this under control. Go change." She could handle campfire cooking.

She couldn't help but notice how the wet plaid he wore clung to his body. When he bent over the bundle he'd unwrapped on the hard-packed dirt floor, the wet woolen seemed to wrap itself around his thigh, as if his clothing had orchestrated some special little performance just for her benefit.

Abby snapped her eyes back to the pot in front of her, searching desperately for some distraction from the knowledge that at any second now, Colin would be standing somewhere behind her, not a stitch of clothing on him.

Stir. She needed to stir the oats. With the stick. The stick in her hand.

The stick itself was tapered to a rounded point on one end while the other had been carved into a crownlike design. She recognized it immediately as a classic spirtle, a specialty tool long used in Scotland for the cooking of oats.

From behind her she heard the sound of the wet plaid slapping up against the rail.

If she closed her eyes, she could see him standing there, the firelight flickering over his well-defined body, his long legs covered only in the dark hair . . .

Stop it!

She needed to think of something to do, something to say, anything she could use to distract herself from the image that crowded her thoughts and stirred her emotions.

"I've read that it's tradition to stir the oats clockwise with the spirtle." She kept her attention focused on the little pot while she babbled like some tourist at a medieval fair. "For luck. Is that what you . . ." She turned her head as she heard him approaching, and her tongue forgot how to form words.

He'd changed out of his wet things, but since she wore his dry tunic, he wore only his spare plaid. It hung low at his waist as if he'd wrapped it hurriedly.

If she was the tourist, then surely he was the medieval attraction she'd come to see.

"Lord," she breathed, unable to wrench her eyes from his bare chest. The glow of the fire created shadows and planes over the muscles, highlighting what was impressive enough to start with.

"Stir whichever way you will, woman, but stir you must." He swept the spirtle from her hands, whipping it round and round in the pot. "It's an overdone porridge we'll be having this night," he complained, though the rare grin he'd shown her earlier was back, eliminating any sting his words might have had.

He set the pot between them and tore two chunks of bread from the fresh loaf they'd gotten just this morning from Roderick's cook. After handing one to her, he sat beside her, offering her first go at the pot.

She scooped her bread into the porridge, careful to keep her eyes averted from the man beside her, a task made more difficult by the heat radiating off him.

Or was that heat coming from her?

A quick sideways glance caught a flash of black and she turned her face fully to inspect his arm.

The area from his bicep to his shoulder was covered in a familiar tattoo design. In the center, a snake with a bar crossing over it, a classic Pictish marking. It was the same design she'd seen in the drawing Jonathan had shown her. The same design she'd searched for on the stones at the dig.

"Where did you get that?"

Though she'd seen him without clothing more than once since she'd been here, they had been in relative darkness each time. Only on that first day so many months ago back in Denver had she had the opportunity to really see Colin's body, and she knew for a fact this tat hadn't been there then. She would have remembered something like this, especially when she'd been tasked with finding the same mark when she reached the dig site.

"Mark of the Guardian," he answered, the design appearing to ripple as if alive when he reached out to dip his bread into the porridge. "Earned through my training with the Fae in Wyddecol."

The Faeries again.

Abby made a noise she hoped was acceptably acknowledging and fixed her gaze back on the food in front of her. She might not be able to deny such things existed anymore, but she certainly didn't intend to put any effort into thinking about them, let alone discussing them. Especially not since it would ultimately lead to her having to deal with her own connection to them.

Now that they were finally speaking to each other again, there had to be something better to talk about than Faeries. Taxes, politics, even the horses' bathroom habits were preferable to discussing the creatures responsible for her current dilemma.

"It's a shame you didn't have some vegetables to put in this. Or potatoes instead of oats. Mashed potatoes would have been good with the pieces of meat." Food. Always a safe subject.

"Mashed potatoes?" Colin gave her a blank look as he dipped his bread back into the porridge.

Abby nodded as she swallowed her last bite. "Yeah. You had some at the café that night. Tatties, they called them when they served them with the haggis and neeps."

"Ah yes," he breathed, closing his eyes as if to see his memory better. "Those were excellent."

With the pot emptied, Colin took it to the opening and set it just outside the door. "It'll fill with rain and be easier to clean in the morning," he explained as he sat back down beside her.

The silence between them stretched out once again, broken only by the irregular thump and splash of raindrops filling the pot. Abby attempted to sneak a quick peek in Colin's direction, only to find him watching her, the same serious expression on his face as earlier.

"What?" she asked as she had before. "You have that look again. What are you thinking when you stare at me like that?"

She almost hesitated to ask on the chance that he might choose to embark on another round of the commitment debate that had ended so poorly last night. And even when she did ask, she suspected from his continued silence that he meant to avoid her question as he had earlier.

This time he surprised her.

"I was thinking how beautiful you are."

"Oh. I . . . wow." Not at all what she'd expected to hear. "Thank you." If she'd guessed from now until the end of time, those particular words wouldn't have been anywhere near the list of things she'd have expected him to say.

"You've no need to thank me. It's a statement of fact and no meant to flatter you. It's only that an old friend recommended I make a point of saying aloud those things which are on my mind and in my heart. I'm finding it's no a habit that comes easily to me."

She could only bobble her head up and down like one of those silly glass weather birds her grandmother used to keep on a doily in her living room.

"Chocolate," he said suddenly, breaking the new round of silence that had fallen between them.

"Chocolate," she echoed, not at all sure where he was going with this or how it could possibly fit with their last conversation.

"Yes," he confirmed. "Chocolate would be good to have right now. I rather fancied the kind with the fruit and nuts mixed in."

"Mmmmm," she moaned, remembering that chocolate was only one more of the many things she missed while she stayed here. "A big mug of hot chocolate with whipped cream on top would be so perfect on a night like this."

"We do have cream in this time, you realize. When we return to Dun Ard, we could manage to make the whipped cream you speak of." Colin shifted his position, lying down on one side, his head propped on his arm as he stared at her. "Though we've nothing now to replace the chocolate to go with that cream."

"That wouldn't work. I wasn't thinking of real whipped-in-a-bowl cream." If they were going to compare her century's food with his, he was going to lose. Big-time. "My whipped cream comes in a can that you keep in the fridge. It's cold and sweet, and you shake it up and spray it out in little designs and curlicues. On absolutely anything. Strawberries or hot chocolate or even straight into your mouth if you're having a really horrible day."

She fully intended to expand on the variety of wonderful uses and to make sure he understood that the straight-into-your-mouth thing was unsanitary and totally frowned on in some quarters, but he was giving her that look again. The one that made her throat dry out. Probably because all the liquid in her body was flowing south.

Damn, but he was good to look at.

"I've something I need to tell you, Abby, though it's another that I'm no at all comfortable with the telling."

He reached out to her, tracing the back of his index finger along the curve of her cheek, a move that sent chills racing through her body to places that were nowhere near her face.

"You already told me you thought I was beautiful. You don't have to say it again." Though, heaven knew, it was perhaps the most wonderful thing she'd ever heard. Not just because it stroked her ego, but because it came from him.

"No." His finger moved to gently cover her lips. "What I need to say is more than that. I need to share that which is in my heart."

Abby clasped her hands in her lap, locking her fingers together to prevent his seeing the trembling that was beyond her ability to control.

"You told me once that for the whole of yer life you'd felt the need to come to Scotland to search for something ancient. Something that waited here, just for you to find it. I'd put to you, wife, it was no a thing which called to you at all. I'd have you consider that it was my soul calling out to yers to be found."

His words hung in the air, vibrating in the space between them as he held her gaze, staring into her eyes. It was as if he looked into the depths of her heart to uncover her deepest, darkest desires, examining each one in turn until she had no secrets left from him.

"I believe I ken now the reason the Fae sent me to you in the first place."

Abby couldn't speak, couldn't move, couldn't even think straight. If he'd truly seen into her heart, if he truly knew she believed him to be The One, if he knew that she really had wished him into the future with her, and that she was responsible for ripping him out of his world and putting his kinsmen in jeopardy, what would he think of her then? She'd almost rather have him simply trying to seduce her.

"It's the same reason they sent you here by my side when they returned me to my own time." He moved his hand to cup her chin, his thumb feathering over her bottom lip as he continued. "We are destined to be together, you and I, my Abby. We are Soulmates. Two halves of the same whole. Only together will we be complete. I love you, Abigail. These are the words I need you to hear."

Roderick's advice had eaten away at him all day. Colin knew by this time tomorrow he and Abby would reach the most dangerous part of their journey. Though he'd not hesitate to give his life to save hers, he didn't want to risk either of their lives with so much left unsaid.

He had seen his friend's pain and recognized the truth of the things Roderick had told him. Losing forever the opportunity to share how he felt with Abby would stain even his afterlife with the unending sorrow of regret. Roderick's advice was sound. Once heeded, it had only been a matter of gathering his own courage to act on that advice.

Now that the words he'd struggled to find all day had finally passed his lips, Colin waited, his heart pounding in his chest. If Abby was going to reject him, it would be now.

She covered his fingers with hers, drawing them away from her face and clasping them tightly between her two hands.

"You don't have to say things you don't really mean to get me to sleep with you. You should know that by now. I haven't made any secret of the fact that I'm attracted to you."

Her voice shook even as her hands trembled against his. That she feared rejection as much as he did was clear to him now.

"What you feel is no a matter of attraction, wife. It's the love shared by those souls meant to be together."

As the only physical proof he could think to show her, he opened her hand, brushing his index finger over the healing wound that marred her soft palm.

"An accident with Jonathan's knife," she explained, her voice soft and breathless as he stroked his finger over the spot again.

"An accident I felt in my dreams because of our connection. One that called me to find you. To protect you." He opened his hand next to hers to once again display the twin to her wound.

She caught up his hand, tracing her finger over the mark in his palm. "I'd forgotten this. You were going to tell me about it, but with everything that happened, I forgot. How can something like this be possible?"

Her beautiful eyes had rounded, whether in fear or amazement, he couldn't be sure. He knew only that he wanted to shield her, to hold her as she came to terms with the reality of what he told her. He lifted his hand from her grasp to caress the back of her neck and draw her down to him. Her lips were warm and eager against his.

"We are fated to be together. Together from the beginning of time until the end of time," he whispered before losing himself in her kiss.

His mother had been right. This woman was his destiny. On some level he had known it from the moment he'd first laid eyes on her. His own foolish pride and arrogance had been the barrier that had kept him from recognizing it, from admitting it. Roderick's pain had broken that barrier.

"Thank the Fates," he murmured, trailing his lips down the soft skin of her throat.

She moaned as he slid his hands under the tunic. Urging the fabric up and over her head, he pinned her arms in place, outstretched. Her lightly tanned skin begged for his touch and he obliged, tracing his tongue down a pathway from her inner elbow to her shoulder and lower, to her firm, rounded breasts.

He molded his hands along her sides, down to her waist, tightening his grip to hold her close. Her heart pounded against his cheek, almost a match to his own.

"I still can't commit to staying here with you, Colin." She sounded breathless, as if she fought for enough air to speak the words. "I need you to understand. I think . . ." She gasped as he took her nipple into his mouth, pausing in her little speech. "I can't believe I'm going to say this out loud. I don't think. I know. I know I love you, too. But I can't stay here. I have to go home. I'm not meant to live in this time."

He slid his hand over her abdomen, enjoying the twitch of her muscles responding to his touch, caressing the soft skin down to her inner thigh and over the heat between her legs.

"Just as I must do the things I am meant to do, love. But we have now, do we no?" As Roderick had counseled, this precious moment was not to be wasted.

Though her brow furrowed, she smiled her response, her hands skimming over his chest and lower, down to his waist. Her fingers trailed into the dark hair at his navel and tracked down. When they closed around his manhood, his mind went momentarily blank, all thought erased by the ecstasy that existed in her touch, slowly undulating up and down his shaft.

"No," he growled. He wouldn't last long if she kept that up.

Pulling her hands away from his body, he lowered her to her back and fit himself into the warm cradle between her legs. She lifted her hips to meet his first thrust, locking her ankles behind his back.

"All the way this time, agreed?" Her soft fingers traced a path down his chest as she spoke, her eyes catching and holding his.

"Agreed." By far the most pleasurable bargain he'd ever consented to.

He drove deep, over and over, his face buried in the crook of her neck. She gave as good as she got, urging him to continue, pressing her fingers into his skin as she arched her back and cried out in her pleasure.

Gritting his teeth, he refused to give in to his own release until he had brought her to the edge once again.

Perspiration slicked their bodies when he thrust deeply inside her heat, her little gasps of pleasure lost in their combined groans as they met their climax together.

It was like nothing he'd experienced before. Golds and silvers shot through his mind, melding together in one great shining whole before shattering and splintering in a display that he'd swear shook the ground beneath them.

It was only afterward, as he held her trembling body in his arms and they drifted on the edge of sleep, that he realized the pounding in their chests beat in unison, as if they shared but a single heart.

Thirty-two

~

Colin had awakened early, more rested than he could remember feeling in years. He'd lain there, waiting for the sun to rise, holding Abby in his arms, more content than he could remember feeling perhaps in his whole life.

He'd decided to give himself those treasured moments, like a gift a supplicant would present to his king. All too soon the sun would rise and he'd be ready to face whatever hardships this day would bring.

By the time the sun sank behind the horizon this day, they'd likely find themselves in the place that would be known one day as the King's Field. Whether MacDougall of Lorn already waited there to ambush King Robert or whether he and his men would be arriving shortly, it was the place where Colin would attempt to take the future into his own hands.

It was also where he and Abby would face their

greatest danger, both as he attempted to ascertain the MacDougalls' exact location and to warn his king and his kinsmen of the impending danger.

Those precious moments had flowed by swiftly, like spring runoff from the highest peaks. They had passed all too quickly, leaving him with only the sweet flavor of their memory. Even now, Abby bent to pack her folded belongings back into the bundle she'd tie behind her saddle.

"What do you think yer doing with those wee weapons, my lady? They're to wear for yer protection, no to carry in yer bundle where they're of no use to you."

Abby huffed out her breath and held up one of the knives Ellie had given her for the journey. "Honestly, Colin. Look at this thing. What do you possibly see me doing with this? I'm no warrior. I don't even know how to use it."

"Is that so, wife?" He smiled at her disheveled appearance, remembering how it had been his touch that had brought down the neatly tied-up hair not half an hour past. "I seem to remember yer putting one no larger than that to good use in a moment of need, do I no?" Her bravery in attacking the Nuadian had impressed him more than any other woman's.

"Fine. But I'm telling you right now, if I end up stabbing myself with one of these things, I'm going to be really pissed with you and your sister-in-law." She tied the belt with the longer knife around her waist and shoved the smaller of the two into her bodice. "There. Happy?"

"It will do for now. I'll be happier at this day's end when you allow me the pleasure of retrieving that trinket from its hallowed resting place."

He would be happier when this day had passed and he knew she'd had no need for the weapons. For now, he could but take joy at the flustered blush his words brought to her cheeks as he took her bundle from her hands and secured it to her saddle before lifting her up onto her mount.

He allowed his hand to linger on her waist for longer than necessary before trailing his fingers to her thigh.

If only there were more time.

"Wait a minute. I need your oath, Colin." Abby fit her soft hands on either side of his face, her eyes dark with concern. "Promise me you'll be careful no matter what happens today. Give me your sworn oath that you won't do anything to risk your life in any way."

He'd warned her that their journey would change this day. He hadn't wanted to frighten her, but it was important that she be on her guard as much as he would be. The miles of empty countryside were behind them. Ahead they'd face the roaming bands of English and their toady sympathizers, the traitors who dared call themselves Scots though they rode in support of Edward.

"I'll do everything in my power to see to yer safety and mine, this I swear to you, my love." It would have to do. He could not swear he'd take no risks. Were Abby to be in danger, he'd offer up his life without a second thought to save hers. He had no doubt, however, that this was not what she wanted to hear, so he left those words unspoken.

His declaration seemed to satisfy her. That, or she knew him too well to press for better. Either way, she bent to kiss his forehead before taking up her reins, staring out toward the forest.

"Which way to your friends this morning?"

It was the question she'd asked him each day at the start of their journey since he'd told her how he used his gift to locate the Soul aura surrounding his kinsmen to track them. It had become something of their own private little ritual.

With one last sideways glance at Abby's lovely profile, he closed his eyes and lowered his defenses, opening himself to the onslaught of the other world of Faerie Magic, allowing his senses to seek the visions he needed to follow this day.

Nothing.

The sheer vast emptiness hit him like a physical assault. It wasn't simply the blank comfort of no souls nearby; this was different. This was as if there were no people left in the world for him to find.

Frantically, his mind hunted for the signature auras associated with Dair and Simeon.

Nothing. Not them, not the armies they traveled with, and no one in between.

He concentrated, blocking out everything around him, searching. Not even Flynn's black soul showed itself to him.

His chest tightened and his heart pounded. What had happened to all of them? Either they no longer lived or . . .

He opened his eyes and stared toward Abby, searching the air around her for her now-familiar golden aura.

Nothing.

After nearly a decade of agony, now that he'd come to depend on the Faerie Queen's horrible curse, now that he actually needed it, it was gone.

Proof positive that he'd found his Soulmate.

*   *   *

As if her nerves weren't already shot to hell this morning after Colin's little speech about their having reached the dangerous part of this trip, now he was sitting there like some statue, frozen in time.

"Well? Which way?"

He opened his eyes and turned his face to her, but he wasn't really looking at her. It was as if he were looking through her, around her, but not seeing her.

"Colin?"

He blinked. Once, twice, his face crumpling into a vision of horror. Whatever had happened to him had to be hideous beyond anything they'd experienced so far for him to allow her to see so much unbridled emotion. His mask was completely shattered.

"Oh, my God, Colin! What's wrong?" She pulled her horse as close to his as possible, grabbing for the hand he held clenched around his reins.

"It's left me." His voice sounded so desolate, like a lost child. "I canna feel them. I canna feel any of them."

"Your friends' Souls? What do you mean you can't feel them? I thought you were cursed with it. That the Faerie Queen had cursed you to feel everyone's pain forever."

He'd told her the whole story. He'd described the day it had happened in such detail, she'd felt as if she'd seen the entire event through his eyes, experiencing it along with him.

"Only by joining with your own Soulmate will you cease to feel the horror and pain of the great wanting."

She recognized the words even as he spoke them. They were the ones the Faerie Queen had given him as a way out of the curse. Just before she'd snatched back all hope by informing him his match didn't exist in this lifetime.

"Because I'm your Soulmate," she said slowly, the realization weighing down on her. "Because I existed in the twenty-first century, not here. And we would never have been together had I not . . ."

"Had you not wished for me at your side," he finished for her, his eyes haunted with the knowledge that his gift was gone forever. "It is gone because of our joining."

Colin scrubbed his hands over his face, all expression wiped away when he finished, his mask back in place, firmly shutting her out. That lack of emotion frightened her almost as much as the horror she'd seen in his eyes only moments before.

"I don't understand why you'd lose your gift now. We had sex before. Sort of. What was different this time?" She watched him closely waiting for some sign of how he felt about this.

Only the rhythmic clenching of his jaw muscle gave away the fact that he had any emotions at all.

"Dinna you ken it's no about the joining of our bodies. It's about the joining of our Souls."

The joining of Souls. As in, he was definitely The One.

"There's naught to be done about it now. We'll travel southeast until we reach the area where the road to Oban crosses our path. Once there, our best choice will be to follow the road to the west and hope we can find where John of Lorn lies in wait for my king."

Doing that might guarantee they'd find the enemy all right, but that in itself seemed risky as hell. If she'd thought his plan to change the future was crazy, this was off the charts.

"And how is that supposed to help your kinsmen? I thought your plan was to warn them, to keep them from walking into that ambush in the first place. Instead, what I'm hearing you say is that you're planning on jumping into the fray with them. How's that supposed to do anything but get you killed right along with them?"

When Colin turned to face her, the emotion had returned. His eyes were so haunted and brimming with pain, she almost wished he still wore the mask.

"What would you have me do? From the beginning my choice was to find them first. But I dinna ken the way they will approach, and only the general area of where they will encounter battle. I've no way to tell if my kinsmen yet live. It's gone from me. Can you no understand what I'm telling you? I've no way *to* save them. By the Fates, woman, I've no even a way to track the danger that follows us."

"What danger?"

He turned his eyes from her, staring off into the distance, his lower jaw working as if he ground his teeth.

"You were right that night. Flynn is here. Somehow he managed to follow us. I've been keeping track of where he is, making sure we stayed far enough ahead to avoid him."

"Once again, this is probably the sort of thing you should be sharing with me." She chose her words carefully. "These are the kinds of things I really need to know."

"Now you do, and what's to be gained?" The mask had slipped once again, his raw emotion on display.

"Naught but one more worry on yer head along with the knowledge that I have no more ability to track the demon than I do to find my kinsmen."

And that was her fault. Guilt washed over her in a torrent. She'd brought this hideous pain to the man she loved. She'd stripped his abilities from him now just as she'd stripped him from his world in the first place.

She'd messed this up good and proper, so it was up to her to set things right.

"I can't do anything about Jonathan, but maybe I can help with your kinsmen. I can find them for you."

Colin shook his head, turning away from her to stare into the distance. "It's no use, Abby. You told me yerself that yer gift disna work with finding people. Only things."

"True, but surely your guys have things, right? Some token or something special they always carry with them? A wallet, a necklace, a special weapon. Something. Think." He had to remember something. It was their best hope.

"They carry only what we all carry. Swords, knives. Dair carries a bow and a quill of arrows."

Too general. "What we all carry isn't good enough. Not unless there's something special and different about one of those weapons. I need something you can describe for me that I can visualize. Something I can use to find just that one person who—"

"Dair wears a band of braided leather on his wrist, decorated with a small silver cross. His twin sister made it for him and he never takes it from his wrist."

"Okay. That's good. Really good. Give me a minute."

At least a minute. She'd never before attempted to search for something farther away than the other rooms in her house.

Fighting the self-doubt, Abby cleared her mind of everything except an image of the wristband Colin had described. She sent the delicate tendrils of fluorescent green energy out from her mind in every direction, curling and creeping across the countryside faster than she'd ever seen them move before.

There was nothing, not in any direction. She waited, concentrating on the energy as all of the tendrils receded, slithering back into her mind, shrinking, withering, disappearing. She'd failed him. There was nothing.

Wait!

All the slithering green tendrils had returned save one. One lone wisp of energy remained; straining forward like a leashed dog, it beckoned to her, a shining beacon in the dark mist.

"I've found the wristband."

"He lives?"

Abby wanted with all her heart to say yes, to soothe the apprehension she heard in the question. But she could not lie to him.

"I don't know that for sure. I only know the wristband is somewhere in that direction." She lifted her hand and pointed out the direction she saw in her mind.

By way of answer, Colin pulled on his reins, urging his mount in the direction she had shown him.

If these Faeries really existed, she could only pray they didn't pick now to let her down.

Thirty-three

⁓

Do you hear that? What is that noise?"

Abby had drawn her horse up alongside Colin's, her brow wrinkled in concern.

Even if he hadn't spotted the brightly colored wagons in the distance, the familiar noise of pans rattling against one another assured him there was only one thing it could be.

"Tinklers."

It was clear as the wagons closed the distance between them that their drivers were pushing the rigs as hard as they could.

"Turn back and save yerselves," the first man called, pulling hard on his reins to slow his wagon to a stop. "You and yer lady will no want to be caught in what's to come at the end of this road, lad."

"What lies ahead of us, Tinkler?" Colin asked, even

though he'd read the stories of the battle that would rage in this area.

"An army passed our camp in the night. Desperate men on the run. They warned that the English followed."

His king knew he was pursued, but he knew not of the men who waited in ambush. An ambush Colin would be too late to prevent if he didn't hurry.

"Turn back with yer lady. Yer more than welcome to ride along with us. Unless you'd rather no been seen in our company, that is."

"I've no hesitation to ride at yer side, good sir." Tinklers, long thought to have mysterious ties to the Fae, had always been welcome at his family's home. "But I canna turn back, though I do appreciate yer warning."

"Consider my words well, young sir. Men from all sides of the conflict roam the countryside ahead. It's too dangerous for you and yer lady to—"

The Tinkler's insistence was cut short by a woman's hand to his shoulder as she leaned out from the flap of material covering the opening in the wagon.

"That's enough from you, William Faas. These people chase their destiny. Can you no feel it?"

She turned to face them, her sweet smile seeming to spread a feeling of joy when it lit on him.

"My home is but a few days' journey in the direction you travel now. There is safety at Dun Ard and you'll be welcomed there." Why he felt compelled to offer these people the protection of his clan eluded him at the moment. He only knew that it was something he should do.

"We are well familiar with Dun Ard. The lady Rosalyn is one of my best customers." She smiled again and patted her husband's shoulder. "We must hurry,

William. This is no place for us to be right now. Go forth with our blessings, Master MacAlister."

William snapped the reins he held, urging his team of horses onward as his wife disappeared back behind the flap of cloth. "Go with caution, lad," he called over his shoulder as their wagon pulled away. "Go with faith."

Colin waited, Abby at his side, until both the Tinklers' wagons had passed them by.

"What did she mean about us chasing our destiny?" Abby's voice seemed to blend with the musical sound of the Tinklers' pots.

He shrugged, at a loss for any logical answer. "They are Tinklers."

When he started off this time, he held his mount to a slower pace. They had need to be watchful from here out to avoid any unpleasant surprises.

Abby followed along at his side, silent after the encounter with the Tinklers. He should say something to reassure her after the dire warnings, but he couldn't bring himself to tell her such a falsehood. William Faas had spoken the truth. Danger did lie in wait, both ahead and behind them.

The afternoon sun rode midway down the western sky by the time they reached the crossroads.

They were close now. He might have lost his Faerie abilities, but his warrior senses were as keen as ever. The very air seemed to shimmer with the potential for violence only a great battle could bring.

Without a word, he turned his horse to the west, to follow the path his king's army would have taken.

"That's the wrong way." Abby sat her mount in the middle of the crossroads, making no move to follow him.

"Robert's men travel this direction." West, to their own peril.

"That may be true, but even if it is, your friend isn't with them. He's this way. Or—" She shrugged, her face seeming to pale as she continued. "His wristband is this direction, anyway."

East. Away from where he knew the ambush awaited.

"Yer sure of this. There can be no mistake?"

"Absolutely positive. If you want to find the wristband, we have to travel in this direction."

She waited for him, moving not a muscle, trust shining in her eyes even as indecision rumbled in his gut, an unfamiliar, worthless emotion he had no use for.

East to find the wristband Dair always wore, or west to join his king.

One direction might well be an exercise in futility. The wristband could have fallen from Dair's arm. Or— and this thought set his stomach to a full churn—the band could still be on his kinsman's body. His lifeless body.

The other direction required risking not only his own life but that of his beloved Soulmate as well, and in the end it was possible he'd neither find his kinsmen nor reach his king in time to warn him of what awaited.

And if he did?

He could hear Pol's voice floating through his mind as clearly as if the Faerie Prince stood at his side.

You cannot change the outcome of history. You may only alter the circumstances.

Certainly he had the power to ignore the edict, but at what price? If he was successful in his quest, the world, Abby's world, would be forever changed. Everything she loved and wanted to return to might very well have never existed.

She might never have existed.

"Your call, husband. Whatever you decide, that's what we'll do."

She'd not called him by that name before. Hearing it from her lips set the very foundations of his world to trembling. He would give all that he owned if only he had the faith in himself that she showed in him at this moment.

Abby felt her heart close to breaking as she watched the indecision radiate from Colin. She'd never seen him like this before. For a fact, she suspected this moment was a first for her brave, hardheaded warrior. He was not a man given to vacillation.

How very odd it felt to realize that the whole of her world, the whole of their world together, rested on this one decision. Right or left. East or west. See to his kinsman or attempt to change the future. Colin would choose one or the other and that choice would change everything for them from that moment forward.

"Bollocks," he muttered at last, reining his horse around and directing him toward where she waited. "Let's have at this band you're so sure you can find."

They rode side by side, once again in silence. He was obviously on alert, constantly scanning the road ahead for any sign of danger. Confident in his ability to protect them, Abby allowed herself to sink inward, using the quiet to explore the extent of her ability to find something.

She visualized the tendril, taut and straining, stretching far out into the distance ahead of her. It was a new sensation to find something so far away. She felt as if she floated over this world, outside her own body, carried forward on wings, always keeping one eye on the pulsating tendril far below her.

The deeper she allowed herself to fall into the vision, the more real her surroundings became. Rather than the black mist that normally surrounded the energy she sent out, it was as if the mist coalesced into the countryside through which they traveled. The tendril snaked forward, pulsating its fluorescent light along the very road over which their horses carried them.

Below her, trees formed a canopy over the road, so full and large she couldn't tell where one set of limbs ended and the next began. So dense were the branches she even lost sight of the tendril at times, able to track it here only by the faint pulsing light flickering below the canopy.

There! Movement to the left of the road. That must be the tendril. But no, the light still shone in pulsing blips from the center of the canopy. Curiosity invaded the vision. If not the tendril, then what had she seen?

Abby stopped, hovering above the trees, straining to peer between the leaves, searching for any trace of the movement.

"What is it?"

Like being snatched from a speeding car, Abby's thoughts slammed back into her body.

Colin's hand gripped her arm, his face only inches from hers.

"What's wrong with you? Abby! Answer me!"

She shook her head, struggling to form the sounds she needed to use. "Nothing," she managed at last.

"Nothing?" He sat back, disbelief written across his

face. "You can hardly expect me to believe that. You stop yer horse in the middle of the road and when I try to speak to you, it's as if yer no even there."

"I wasn't there." She took a deep breath, hoping to clear her foggy mind. "I was trying to follow the trail to the band. I told you, I've never done this over such a long distance before. I guess I just got a little carried away. I'm fine now. A little fuzzy, but fine."

Fine if she didn't count the booming headache her unexpected reentry to the real world had brought with it. She reached up to rub her temple, thankful the sun had slipped behind a cloud, leaving only a dappled pattern of light on the road rather than the bright glare they'd ridden through for the better part of the day.

"Stay behind me and keep yer eyes open."

She looked up at Colin's urgent whisper. His attention was directed ahead of them, though he continued to speak to her with the same low urgency as before.

"If anything looks to be amiss, turn yer mount and ride hard. Do you ken what I'm saying? Dinna think about it. Dinna pause to look back. Just do what I've told you and ride."

Abby studied her surroundings closely for the first time in a long while. It wasn't clouds that shaded them but a heavy overhang of large trees on either side of the road on which they traveled, just like those she'd seen in her vision.

In the distance, a man walked toward them, leading a horse behind him. His progress was slowed by a heavy limp, but as he drew closer, he lifted his arm in greeting.

"He seems friendly enough."

"They always do. Until they turn on you."

Suspicion must be an instinctive function of the warrior brain.

"Don't be such a dinosaur, Colin. Look at the poor man. He can hardly be a threat. He can barely walk, let alone—"

A rain of arrows ended her tirade, and the world around her erupted in a cacophony of battle: men yelling, swords clanging, and most immediately, her own horse screaming in response to the arrow sticking out of his shoulder.

Behind her, Colin shouted for her to ride, but fleeing was her last concern at the moment. Her only thought was to stay on her horse's back. When her mount reared in response to the pain, the reins jerked from her grasp. She leaned against the big animal's neck and tangled her fingers in his mane while she clenched her knees in an attempt to keep her seat, all to no avail.

The sensation of this particular flight was both unsettling and short-lived, followed by a bone-rattling crash to the hard-packed earth of the road that left her flattened and gasping for her next breath.

She forced herself to her hands and knees, scrambling backward just in time to avoid the vicious kick of her terrorized mount. She pushed up to her feet and lunged for the side of the road, slamming her shoulder into a tree in her urgency to escape the big animal's frenzy.

On the far side of the road, Colin fought off at least three men, his sword flashing in the dappled light as he kept his back to the forest, drawing them farther away from the spot where she clung to the tree. His sword slashed in a blur of movement, and one of his attackers fell with an ear-piercing scream.

Down to two men. He could handle only two.

Three men.

"Behind you!"

She screamed the warning too late as the third man emerged from the forest, swinging a club that struck Colin in the back of the head. He crumpled forward and fell to the ground, motionless, as an eerie silence filled the air.

"Colin!"

Pushing away from the tree, she ran to reach him, as uncaring of the men standing around him as about the pain searing through her body.

She had almost reached him when arms clamped around her like a vise, sweeping her off her feet. She clawed at the hands holding her and kicked the air, connecting with flesh hard enough to make her captor yelp.

Her efforts earned her a head-rattling shake. "Be still, shrew, else I'll make you wish you had, I swear it!"

The smelly beast who held her slipped his meaty arm around her throat, leaving just enough space for her to dip her chin and sink her teeth into his forearm.

He yelled out in his pain and slammed her to the ground at his feet even as his companions' laughter echoed in her ears.

She would have continued to fight, useless though it might be, but from here her view of Colin was unobstructed and what she saw shattered her will.

Not Colin. Colin's body.

Lifeless, unmoving, he lay not six feet away from her, on his back, his face turned away from her, his head pillowed in a pool of his own blood.

A scream curdled up from the depths of her soul,

primeval and ancient in its pain. Nothing mattered but reaching his side.

Ignoring the men around her as well as the one who approached on horseback, she clambered to her feet and threw herself toward Colin.

The man he'd felled lay in her path, but he was no obstacle. Turning her face from the gaping wound in his chest, she climbed over him to get to Colin as if the man's body were nothing more than a large rock in the road. She tightened her fingers around a handful of the material of Colin's tunic, pulling his arm toward her as she reached him. Even her hand to his face brought no sign of life.

"Colin?"

This couldn't be happening. She'd only just found him; she couldn't lose him so soon. It wasn't right. How could the Faeries who'd worked so hard to bring them together allow this to happen?

"Send us back," she whispered as she bent over him. If ever she'd needed to believe in the Magic, this was the time. "Please send us home. Get us out of here, now! I wish to go home!"

She waited, holding her breath. Waited for the mysterious Magic to manifest itself and whisk them to safety. Waited for the green glow of lightning or an earthquake or whatever form it wanted to take.

Waited until unfriendly hands fastened around her waist and dragged her from Colin's side.

"Goddamned freaking worthless Faeries!" she screamed, kicking with everything she had left as the man who held her lifted her up to the newcomer on horseback.

She tightened her hand into a fist and drew back, swinging wildly at her new captor, but he caught her wrist, easily deflecting her blow.

"I'd recommend against any more of your useless hysterics, my good woman. If you continue, I'll have one of these men slit your throat and dump your body on the road along with his. Do you understand?"

Whoever he was, he spoke with a distinctly British accent.

"We'll take her with us to rejoin the company and add her to the other prisoners. A woman, a lady by the looks of her in spite of her behavior, will likely bring MacDougall a fair ransom."

"Or a fair bedding," one of the men shouted, to the laughter of all.

"What about him?"

"Leave him," her captor ordered. "If he's not already dead, he'll bleed out soon enough. We've our hands full with the lot we already hold."

If he's not already dead . . .

In spite of these animals, in spite of the betraying Faeries, those few words gave her something to hang on to as the horse picked up speed, carrying her away from the other half of her Soul.

Her heart lay behind her on the road, but those five words gave her hope that her heart might yet live, if only she could figure out some way to escape these men and get back here.

Flynn bided his time in the trees, watching the drama play out on the road ahead of him.

When the soldier had lifted Abigail to his mount, he'd considered using the weapon he'd brought with him. Briefly considered.

He reached for the weapon tucked in his waistband, clenching his teeth in irritation as his fingers passed right through it.

The blood he'd taken from Abigail had worn off.

Once again, his body had returned to the insubstantial state that had cursed his people since their banishment to this half-existence on the Mortal Plain. He could neither commit nor experience violence. The only ability left to his people in their punishment had been the Compulsion, an ability to control the weaker-minded among the Mortals to do their bidding.

But that was before the discovery of the consequences of taking blood. Through the ingestion of fresh blood, he could do anything.

Too bad the only blood available to him at the moment was wholly Mortal. Though it would restore his ability to act as he needed to, it would not carry the sweet tang of Magic. For that, he needed to find Abby.

Ah, well. For now, Mortal blood would suffice.

"Come to me, blacksmith."

He waited impatiently while the big man he'd taken in the last village lumbered over to him, eyes blank, waiting to be told what to do.

"Take your knife from its sheath. I'd have you draw its blade across your finger. Do it now."

Without hesitation, the blacksmith did as he was told.

Large of body, small of mind. It suited his purposes to have one such as this under his Compulsion.

Flynn lifted the man's finger to his lips, fighting the revulsion he felt in taking the filthy Mortal blood into his mouth. It couldn't be helped. He needed what the blood would give him. He needed to be solid and whole to take Abigail from the soldiers.

"Mount up, blacksmith. Follow with me."

Flynn directed his horse forward to where the two bodies lay on the road.

Good. The soldiers had saved him the effort of dealing with MacAlister. It made his task of recovering Abigail much easier.

Once again, he'd follow. He'd wait and watch for the inevitable opportunity to make her his.

Thirty-four

❦

Abby landed hard, pushed from her perch on her captor's horse to the ground below. She stumbled and fell to her knees, completely ignored for the moment, as the men were greeted by their companions.

So much for all that medieval chivalry she'd read about.

"You'll want to collect that wee weapon that dangles at her hip," one of them pointed out as another pulled her to her feet.

Her weapon!

She grabbed for the knife too late. The man who held her twisted her wrist, breaking her hold on the weapon.

"Sir Stephen's got the right of it on this one. Who but a fine lady would forget to use the weapon she wears for decoration, aye? It's a fine ransom our laird will demand for her return."

He dragged her through the waiting, jeering soldiers toward the far side of their encampment, back to a line of bedraggled and wounded men kneeling on the ground. Their arms were held high up above their heads, their wrists tied together over a rope strung between two trees. Clearly, these were the other prisoners Sir Stephen had mentioned.

"On yer lovely arse, lassie," her captor ordered, pushing her to the ground.

"Have a care with the lady, you oaf," the man on the ground next to her growled. "I'll remember you well when my bindings come off."

"Remember this," her captor offered, sending a well-aimed foot into the prisoner's midsection that would have doubled the man over had he not been held up by his ties.

He jerked her to her knees and roughly pulled her arms above her head, then halted his efforts, turning to call out.

"Angus! There's no enough of her to reach the line when she kneels. Should I let her hang?"

"Bind her by one hand. It's no like she's much of a danger to any of us. Perhaps she'll find use for that free hand in fending off admirers, aye?"

"Or in pleasing them," someone else shouted, drawing another round of laughter.

"It is my order that the lady will remain unmolested." Sir Stephen approached on foot, one man with a sword drawn on either side of him. "Your laird made quite clear his desire for captives who would bring him a healthy ransom. Despoiling her would only lessen her value. I can't think he would go easy on any one of you who ended up costing him silver."

Perhaps she'd judged too soon. Maybe chivalry was only in intensive care and not completely dead after all.

"She's spoils of war," the one named Angus countered. "Our laird has never denied us what we claim from battle."

Sir Stephen stared at the man, his eyes as cold and hard as they'd been when he'd stared at her and threatened to have her throat slit.

"That may be so. But until we reach Dunstaffnage and I turn her over to your laird, you'll do as I say or I'll skewer your hide to the nearest tree and leave you for the wolves to dine upon. Do I make myself clear enough?"

He waited for a scattered round of ayes before he spoke again. "Give her a bucket to kneel upon, but tie both her hands. Our guest is . . . spirited." With a formal nod of his head in her direction, he turned and, along with the men on either side of him, disappeared into the small tent at the far end of the encampment.

"Arrogant English bastard," the man holding her arm muttered as he tied her hands over the rope above her head. Then he leaned in close, his fetid breath flowing over her face. "When we reach Dunstaffnage, I'll be having you as payment for my cousin what yer man gutted back there on the road. Just you remember Fergus, my fine lady. We'll be seeing a lot of each other."

"I'll certainly be remembering you, Fergus," the man next to her taunted, earning himself another kick to the stomach.

"You'll no have an unbroken bone left in yer body if you dinna cease yer constant aggravation of these brigands." This from farther down the line of prisoners.

"Mayhaps," Abby's neighbor replied after he sucked in his breath. "But bones will heal and what I intend for that man when my bindings come off will no, that much I swear."

Fergus returned with a bucket, which he slammed to the ground beside Abby. He pushed her down to kneel on it and proceeded to tie her ankles just as the men with her had been bound. With another leering promise of what awaited her at Dunstaffnage, he left, joining his companions around a large campfire to share in the skin of drink they passed among them.

Night had arrived, bringing with it a curtain of darkness barely pierced by the sliver of moon hanging above them.

It brought desperation along with it as well.

How long had Colin lain in that road, blood seeping from the wound in his head? Hours. How could any man survive that?

They couldn't. He couldn't.

She was on her own. The only man she'd ever wanted, the one she'd waited and wished for her whole life, taken from her by these filthy, warmongering, piece-of-shit excuses for men.

Desperation faded into despair.

Slow, hot tears tracked down her cheeks. Once they began, there was no stopping them. Her breath caught in her throat, jerking her chest in little coughing sobs. She clenched her teeth together to hold back any sound, determined not to let her captors see how they'd defeated her, but her pain was too great to control for long.

"Did they harm you, my lady? Where are you wounded? Are you in pain?"

Unending, horrible pain such as she'd never imagined. But she could hardly tell the man next to her it was no wound he could see, only her heart that had been torn to pieces. Not with him looking as if he'd been beaten over every inch of his body, anyway.

"I'm not . . . no wounds," she managed at last.

"The blood on your gown?"

Abby looked down, unable to make out any but the barest markings on her gown in the dark. If her gown was bloodied, it must have come from Fergus's cousin when she'd climbed over him to get to Colin.

"Not mine."

The thought of Colin lying in the road brought a fresh round of pain and with it a fresh round of hot, salty tears. She couldn't fight it any longer, it hurt too badly.

Her head lolled against her arm as she gave herself over completely to her misery. The stars twinkling above her were magnified by the prism of tears she viewed them through, as if the fates controlling her world had decided to make them extra beautiful just to mock her pain.

"You should try to get some rest. They'll have us marching at first light."

Rest? Tied up like this? No chance in hell. Besides, how could she sleep? Her heart hurt too much. She'd never sleep again.

Her head pounded and her nose stuffed up and

still the tears flowed. She didn't care. It didn't matter. Nothing mattered anymore. Not her years of education wasted, not the damn betraying Faeries, not even being stuck in this horrible time. Without Colin, nothing mattered anymore.

The soldiers had drifted off to their blankets, many of them well inebriated by the sound of it. Now only the sounds of snoring filled the night air, adding to her desolation. She was alone. Completely alone in this awful world.

Her shoulders ached and her shins hurt where the rim of the bucket dug into her skin. Her face stung where she'd scraped up against the tree, and every muscle in her body bore witness to her fall from her horse.

Worst of all, guilt consumed her that she could sit here cataloging her aches and pains while Colin . . .

Another round of tears ran down her cheeks, raw now from the light breeze blowing over the tear-stained skin.

Above her, her hands had gone numb and she tried straightening her back to relieve the pressure from her bindings. She glanced at her neighbor to see how the others managed to avoid cutting off their circulation.

A twinkle at her neighbor's wrists caught her attention and she blinked several times to clear her vision. Moonlight sparkled, reflecting off something metallic.

Maybe he had something they could use to free themselves from their ropes? Freed, she could make her way back to Colin. If there was any chance he lived, any chance at all, she wasn't about to let it pass her by.

"Hey," she hissed, leaning his direction. "Hey, you!"

She couldn't tell in the dark whether his eyes were open or shut, though how anyone could sleep like this was beyond her ability to imagine.

"Hey!" Louder this time.

"Lower your voice before you bring the guards down on us."

Good. He was awake at least.

"What's that on your arm? Is it something we could use to get loose?"

"Is she daft or just stupid?" The question floated from the other side of her neighbor.

This was not the response she'd hoped for.

"Do you honestly believe that if I had the means to cut these bindings, I'd still be hanging here next to you?"

His tone sounded just a tad snotty to her. "I was only trying to help. I want out of here as much as anyone. More, even."

His response sounded very much like a snort.

"Think what you want. Those bastards left my husband on the road to die. I don't know if he's . . . I have to get back to him." This time she willed herself to hold back the tears. She needed to fight this, not give in like some quitter. Even with her new determination, her voice still broke when she continued. "If you had something we could use, I only . . . I only wanted to point it out."

When he answered her this time, his tone had changed completely. "It's naught but a cross, my lady. A trinket given me by my sister meant for nothing more than protection."

"That would be spiritual protection," the man on his other side added. "No actual protection."

A cross given him by his sister worn on his wrist?

According to her visions, there was only one of those out there. If this was Colin's kinsman, she'd have an ally to assist her in trying to get back to her husband.

And Ellie had told her there were no coincidences when it came to Faerie Magic. Could it be that this was the Faerie way of trying to make up for having failed her back there on the road?

"Are you Dair Maxwell?"

Her neighbor stilled at the question. "I am. But I dinna recall having met you before, my lady. Might I ask how you come to know my name?"

"You're my husband's kinsman. We were searching for you when we were attacked. They smashed Colin in the head and left him bleeding, lying there in the road. I have to get back to him."

"Colin? MacAlister? Yer claiming to be wife to Colin MacAlister?" The other voice again.

"I'm not claiming anything. I am his wife. We married at Dun Ard a few days ago and then set out to find the two of you. Assuming you're Simeon, that is?"

Silence again.

"Aye. Simeon MacDowell, at yer service, my lady. How badly was he wounded?"

"How badly do you think?" Dair interjected before she could answer, his disembodied voice sounding bitter. "How badly would he have to be wounded to allow this lot to carry his woman away? It's Col we're speaking of."

"Too bad they took the wee weapon you carried at yer waist." Simeon spoke wistfully, as if he thought aloud.

"Too bad," she agreed. They'd done exactly what

Ellie had predicted, overpowered her and taken the knife she had worn. All the more reason for the second . . . "Shit!"

She was an idiot. A total freaking idiot.

"I have another one. Hold on a minute."

She scooted off the bucket, teetering dangerously when she landed on her feet. Her leg muscles screamed out in agony, shooting pains pulsing in every direction. A moment to make sure she wouldn't tip over, and then she attempted to retrieve the little knife stuffed discreetly in her bodice.

No matter how she tried, she couldn't reach it. Her arms were too short. She couldn't climb up onto the bucket to get closer to the rope because of the binding around her ankles.

Someone else was going to have to retrieve her knife.

"If you were to stand, Dair, do you think your arms would be long enough that your elbow could bend over that rope?"

"Aye. If I could but get to my feet. Why do you ask?"

That was it, then, her only choice.

Shuffling bit by bit, using the limited slack available in the rope that bound her ankles, she slowly worked her way across the ground between her and Dair. Never had twelve inches felt like such a vast distance to travel.

"Balance against me and work your way up to your feet."

"I'll brace you on this side," Simeon offered.

"Get to yer feet, the woman says, like it's nothing at all to accomplish." The last of his complaint was lost in a grunted whoosh of air as he made it to his feet. "What now, my lady? What is it you need of me?"

"There's a knife hidden in my bodice. I can't reach it. You're going to have to do it for me."

"In . . . yer . . . bodice . . ." He repeated the words slowly, as if he didn't really believe her.

"Just do it."

She turned her head and lifted her chin trying to clear a path. His hand was cold, eliciting an involuntary shiver the instant his fingers dipped below her neckline.

"Sorry, my lady."

He apologized but pressed on. His hand was large, too. Large enough it required him to work his fingers back and forth between her skin and the tightly laced bodice in his attempt to reach lower.

"I'm no finding any—" His words bit off suddenly as his fingers brushed across her nipple. "Apologies, my lady."

"Under the boob." God, could this get any more embarrassing?

"What?"

She'd never heard a whisper sound strangled before.

"My breast. It's underneath my breast."

Was that stifled laughter she heard coming from Simeon?

"One thing I must ask of you, my lady. When we find Colin, you must never speak of this moment. Agreed?"

"Or if you do, make sure to give Dair a day's head start." Simeon was definitely laughing.

"I never thought to see the day I'd find myself wishing for a woman with smaller breasts."

"Just get the damned thing." Someday perhaps she'd be able to see the humor in this moment, too. But today was not that day.

She lifted onto her tiptoes, offering as much access as possible, and Dair dipped lower, his fingertips at last grazing the little knife. Cautiously he worked it across her skin until he could grasp it fully.

"Got it."

Once his hand was out of her dress, she dropped back onto the balls of her feet. Just in time, too. Her calf muscles were already cramping from the time spent up on her toes.

It seemed forever before she felt the pressure of the ropes at her feet relieved. Dair shoved the little blade into the knot binding her hands and began a sawing motion, stopping when, in the dark beyond them, a stumbling, scraping noise captured their attention.

"We canna afford to bring down the whole camp. We canna fight them all unarmed, aye?"

With the whispered warning in her ear, Dair left the knife tangled in the rope while he and Simeon scrambled back to their spots, dropping to their knees and lifting their hands to the bindings as if they were still securely bound.

An instant later, a figure stumbled into view. It was Fergus, her tormentor from earlier.

"What's this, my bonny? Did you fall from yer wee perch? Is that the noise I heard?"

He leaned his face into Abby's, and the smell of stale whisky turned her stomach.

Moving her hands back and forth above her head, she continued to work the little blade against the knot that held her.

"All strung up here, you are, yer wares finely on

display like market day in Edinburgh. Makes a man hungry, it does, to taste a sample of what's to come."

"Leave her alone, Fergus. I've warned you before." Dair's voice sounded positively evil coming from the shadows.

"*Pfft*," Fergus dismissed him. "You can watch if you like. I'll show you how a real man does it."

He walked behind her and grabbed her skirts, lifting them and pressing his erection up against her bottom, obviously surprised when he encountered the riding pants. "What the hell?"

The extra moment was all Abby needed. The blade broke through the knot and her hands were free. Without a thought, she ran.

Fergus ran, too. Much faster than she'd have expected from a drunk. He tackled her from behind, bringing her down with a jarring thud.

"I likes my women to be lively," he said, as he pushed up to stand over the top of her. A drunken grin split his face and he grasped the hem of his plaid to lift it upward, revealing his swollen manhood.

Beyond him, Abby could just make out the figures creeping in their direction. Dair and Simeon. They'd want to take him without any noise. All she had to do was keep Fergus distracted until they reached him.

Clutching the little knife in her hand, she remembered her encounter with Jonathan in another forest, seven hundred years away. If it had worked once, it could work again.

She rolled to a crouch, and the man in front of her laughed.

"Aye, lassie, I like the idea of you on yer knees even more. Fergus has a surprise for you."

"And I have a surprise for you, too." She lunged forward, slicing the little knife downward toward his thigh.

"You whore!" he hissed, spittle flying from his mouth.

Unlike Jonathan, Fergus moved. The blade sliced along the side of his leg, but didn't imbed in the flesh. Instead of falling to the ground as Jonathan had, he drew back his leg and kicked.

Abby rolled to protect herself, taking the full force of the blow in her side rather than her face. Pain, white-hot in its intensity, blazed through her chest, driving the air from her lungs as his foot connected a second time.

"You'll pay for that, you little—"

His voice abruptly silenced in a snap and a gurgle. Abby could only assume her husband's kinsmen had reached her tormentor.

"Can you stand?"

Dair lifted her to her feet, even as she fought to catch her breath. It felt as if the knife she'd held had been driven deep into her side with each breath she took, and only when Simeon picked up the weapon from the ground beside her was she sure she hadn't stabbed herself.

Within minutes, Simeon returned, the other prisoners he'd freed slipping past them to melt away into the inky night.

Dair took her hand to pull her forward and the pain nearly doubled her over. He ran his hands quickly down her arms and around her middle.

"Ribs," he announced. "We'll need a mount. She won't be able to keep up on foot."

"Leave me," she panted. "Go find Colin. See to him. These guys won't harm me. They want me for a ransom."

Simeon snorted his reply before disappearing into the dark.

"Obviously, my kinswoman, you have no concept of what yer husband would do to us if we left you behind."

Gently, Dair lifted her into his arms, but even *gently* hurt like hell.

They waited under cover of the trees until Simeon returned, leading two horses.

Only the knowledge that she'd know Colin's fate within the hour was enough to get her up on that horse. Anything, even the searing pain she felt with each breath, was a small price to pay if there was any way to save him.

Thirty-five

━━━━⊙━━━━

*I*t was the mother of all headaches awaiting Colin's return to consciousness. He lay very still, knowing there was something important he should remember, something urgent, something just beyond his ability to pluck from his memory.

An incessant buzzing plagued him, finally forcing his eyes open.

Memories swam before him, clicking into place sharply.

"Abby." Her name was on his lips though he struggled to make any sound.

He rolled to his side, struggling to push to his knees. He had to find his wife.

"Abby!" He could hear his own voice this time. That had to be a good sign.

His foot slid, jamming against something heavy, and he swung his head to investigate.

Big mistake.

The world swam around him again, the fly-infested body of the man at his feet the last thing he saw before the dark overtook him once more.

The sun hovered halfway down beyond the horizon the second time Colin awoke. Fortunately, this time his memory returned more quickly. Very slowly, he pushed up to his knees and crawled the few feet to the nearest tree. He propped himself against it and surveyed the road while he waited for his strength to build.

The only body he could see was that of the man he'd killed. The man's companions likely hadn't thought much of him to leave him there in the road.

Of course, they'd left his body here, too.

There was no sign of Abby. He hoped that indicated she lived. And as long as she lived, he'd find her.

For now, he had to get off the road. If the men who'd ambushed them had been here once, they might well return.

Using the tree for balance, he pulled himself up to stand. A wave of nausea swept over him and he bent from the waist, waiting for the sickness to pass. Once he felt strong enough, he headed into the woods, stumbling from tree to tree to keep himself upright.

Dusk had settled over the land by the time he heard the first noises. A rustling, as if someone carelessly made his way through the brush.

He scanned the area at his feet, searching for anything he might use as a weapon, finally deciding on a stone the size of his hand. Clutching it tightly, he dropped to his belly, inching his way forward until at last a small clearing lay ahead of him. There he found the intruder.

His own horse stood next to a small stream, nibbling at the leaves of a small bush. Dried blood streaked the animal's flank. He remembered that now. An arrow. It had caused his horse to rear, unseating him.

He waited, overly cautious perhaps, to make sure the animal was the only occupant of the clearing. Satisfied at last, he again pushed himself to his feet and joined his mount at the bank of the stream.

Dropping again to his knees, he dunked his head in the cold water. Once, twice, a third time, the swirling waters carried the last traces of his blood away.

For once he was thankful for his Faerie heritage. Without it, he'd likely have died of his wounds. As it was, he'd live. He'd live to find Abby or her murderers. If the latter, he'd pluck their eyes from their heads and stuff them down their throats.

The vision gave him determination and with that determination, strength.

With the discovery of his horse, he had the means to travel. Now he needed only to decide where to travel to.

Considering where they'd been assaulted, the attackers were likely MacDougall's men, waiting to pick off any of Robert's stragglers who might try to turn back to escape the ambush awaiting them at King's Field. That being the case, any captives would likely be taken to the MacDougall stronghold, Dunstaffnage.

The likelihood of his success if he single-handedly stormed the keep at Dunstaffnage? None at all. He could not do this alone. Then again, he wouldn't have to.

His brother Andrew resided not too far from the MacDougall castle. He needed only to make his way to MacQuarrie Keep. From there he could send a messenger to Dun Ard, requesting that his laird send men to assist him in confronting the MacDougall.

He pulled himself up onto his horse and set out. If he kept his distance from the main road, he should be able to avoid any other men the MacDougalls or their allies the MacNabs had left on watch. If he rode hard, by this time tomorrow he would reach MacQuarrie Keep.

For now, he wouldn't allow himself to consider how his laird would react to his request for men. He wouldn't think on whether or not Abby had been hurt in the ambush. For now, he would simply concentrate on his plan and on staying on his mount.

It was the best he could think of. It was his only hope.

Thirty-six

⁂

"Of course I'm sure this is where we left him. How many places do you think there are with dead bodies lying around opened up like a can of beans?" Abby held her arms tightly around her middle, trying her best to glare at the two men on the ground.

It wasn't her fault Colin wasn't lying in the middle of the road where she'd seen him last. In fact, she was thrilled he wasn't there. Certainly no one had come along and moved him, or they'd have moved the hideous, disfigured body that lay at her horse's feet.

No, his not being there meant only one thing.

"He's alive. He must be."

Though the dark pool of blood where he had lain did give her pause to worry.

"For a fact he lives, my lady. That's no ever been

in question. We only need to find where he's gotten off to."

Simeon looked around, rubbing his hands together in a way that made Abby think of some cartoon detective.

"This way," Dair called from farther back in the trees. "He came back through here."

Simeon pulled on her reins, leading the horse she sat astride as well as his own. Each pounding tread of the horse's foot sent another stabbing pain through her chest, but she panted through it, clamping her arms tightly around herself. She couldn't allow them to stop their search for Colin because of her.

"Looks like he found a horse wandering here. He's no longer afoot." Dair squatted by small, swift-moving stream. The orange rays of the rising sun formed a glowing backdrop behind him as he scanned the area.

"Mounted. Where would he go, do you suppose? He's bound to be half-crazed with worry over this one, aye?" Simeon jerked his head in her direction. "And we've no doubt he dinna come in our direction, for a fact."

Oh, that was classic. More guilt. Just what she needed.

"Drew's, do you think? MacQuarrie Keep is within a hard day's ride. That would give him a place to recover and decide what to do next. It's no like he'd have any way of knowing who had taken her, so he'd no have a direction to head."

She had to tell them. The more they knew, the better their chances were of finding Colin. Though whether they'd believe her fantastic tale was anyone's guess.

"He might have more of an idea than you think." He had known who would be waiting for his king's army, after all. "I probably can't explain all of this well enough to make it make sense. I'm not even sure it makes sense to me, but you need to believe me when I tell you Colin knew where to look for you because he knew what would happen after Methven. He already knew the laird of the MacDougalls would be waiting in ambush for your army as you tried to make your escape."

One side of Dair's face quirked up in a grin and he shook his head. "You've no a need to explain that which canna be explained, lass. It's clear the Fae have had a hand in this."

"How do you know about—"

He stopped her, his hand held up like a crossing guard's. "I've seen their work in this family often enough. Besides, there's naught else to explain Col's disappearing in a burst of color one day and his showing up a fortnight later, with a wife, no less. That smells of Fae if ever I smelled them."

Beside her, Simeon climbed into his saddle. "That's it, then. He's no fool enough to attempt Dunstaffnage on his own. He'd want men at his side, especially if he calculates his odds. I say we'll find him at MacQuarrie Keep, petitioning Drew for aid to march on the MacDougall."

They thought he intended to gather an army and go to war? Over her? "No! You can't let him do that."

"Dinna fash yerself over it, my lady." Simeon's smile was as bright as the morning sun. "He'll have no need for such once we deliver you safely to him."

A hard day's ride, Simeon had said. Abby tried for a deep breath to calm herself, but settled for a series of short, panting intakes when the pain was too much.

Apparently her discomfort wasn't as easy to hide in the daylight as it had been in the dark.

"We'll have to do something about her, aye? She canna travel like that." Again Simeon jerked his head in her direction.

"Aye," Dair answered, rising to his feet and lifting his arms to her as he approached. "Off of there with you, lassie."

A bolt of panic speared through her. They were going to leave her behind? She tried to ignore the fear when Dair lifted her down from the saddle, concentrating instead on the pain.

"You're right. It's for the best," she managed between gasps for air. "I'd only slow you down and you have to get to Colin to stop him from getting himself killed."

"For the best?" Dair echoed. "What? You think we'd leave you behind? Yer daft!"

"It's no her fault." Simeon shrugged his shoulders. "She's no ever seen a MacAlister in the defense of his woman as we have."

Once she was on her feet, Dair leaned over and caught up the hem of her overdress. With a "pardon me, my lady," he proceeded to rip a good foot off the bottom.

"It feels to me as though yer ribs are broken. We'll have to bind them or you'll no be able to bear the ride. It needs to be tight, you ken? Up against yer skin."

"Fine. Whatever will help." Abby did her best to lift her arms, not very successfully.

Behind her, Simeon coughed. "That's no quite his meaning, my lady."

"Not his meaning . . . oh, crap." Against the skin, he'd said. Over her dress, and the binding would twist and slide, useless. Too bad she hadn't landed in Scotland a few hundred years down the road when every lady's stylish longer bodice would have served as a rib binding on its own. "Then you're going to have to help me. I can't get these things off by myself."

"We'll just lift them, aye? Sim, yer assistance?"

Simeon was at her side in an instant, gathering her skirts and lifting them up around her face. Dair placed the band of cloth against her ribs and began to wind, pulling it tight. He finished by tearing off another strip of cloth and tying it over the binding to hold it tight.

"There. That should help."

Simeon dropped her skirts, fluffing them into place, his face a mottled pink. "A reminder, my lady. Just as you've promised no to share with yer husband the details of Dair's adventure in retrieving yer wee knife last night, I'd take it as a personal boon if you'd keep this moment just between us, as well, aye?"

Whether Simeon was actually worried about Colin's reaction or simply trying to ease her tension, she didn't care. It worked.

Getting back on the horse was pretty much as painful as before, but once she was settled, she found, amazingly enough, the binding actually did help a little. She was still forced to take only short, shallow breaths, but at least it no longer felt as if razors slashed into her with every move.

Dair fixed one arm around her middle, pulling her back up tightly against his chest, and they were off, their horses pounding across the ground as if another wildfire chased them.

Within seconds Abby knew if she could last out this day, she'd be able to do anything. And *anything* was what she'd sworn she was willing to do to keep Colin from riding off to get himself killed.

Thirty-seven

*I*t's no far now."

If Abby didn't hurt so bad, Dair's words might have made her smile, wondering if his *not so far* was anything like Colin's.

As it was, the best she could manage was catching her next breath without passing out.

"Halt!"

Dair and Simeon both pulled their mounts to a stop as two men moved out of the forest to block the road ahead of them.

"No," she managed between pants. It couldn't be. She blinked slowly, struggling to focus on the men ahead.

What couldn't be, was.

Jonathan Flynn sat on one of the horses, his gun pointed directly at them.

"Abigail, dearest," he called. "I've found you at last. And with new friends."

How wrong was this? She'd traveled seven hundred years to escape staring down the barrel of that bastard's gun, suffered more than she ever had in her whole life, and how was she ending up? Staring down the barrel of the bastard's gun. Again.

"You ken who this man is, do you?" Dair asked.

"Yes. He has a gun. Don't do anything stupid."

"Gun?" Next to her, Simeon snorted. "That wee bit's hardly bigger than the knife you had stuffed down yer front, my lady. It's of no consequence."

They didn't know about guns. They didn't understand the danger they were in.

"Not big," she panted. "Bad. Very bad. Trust me."

"You'll climb down off that man's horse now, Abigail, and join me over here. Otherwise, I'll have no choice but to start eliminating your new friends."

"The lady stays where she is," Dair growled.

"Wait." She remembered all too well what Jonathan was capable of when he started carrying on about not having any choices. "You don't know what he can do."

"I say we show him and that wee gun of his what we can do, aye?" Simeon grinned and kneed his horse forward.

"No!" Her warning was too late.

With a loud *crack*, Jonathan fired his weapon and Simeon jerked back. Disbelief colored his face just before he doubled over and slid from his mount, crumpled on the ground.

"What in the name of the saints . . ." Dair's arm tightened around her waist.

"On second thought, Abigail, you stay on the horse. Tell your friend he needs to get off so you can join me."

"I canna allow—"

There was no point in letting him continue. "Get off. Now." She wouldn't be the cause of another man's getting shot. "Find Colin. Stop him. Keep him safe."

As soon as Dair dismounted, Abby pulled on the reins, encouraging her horse toward Jonathan. When she reached his side, he took the reins from her hands, leading her horse as he headed back into the forest.

"You've no seen the last of me!" Dair called out from behind them. "I'll hunt you down."

Ahead of her, Jonathan chuckled. "I doubt that. Not unless he has his own little time-traveling woman, eh, Abigail? Not once you whisk us back home where we belong."

That was what he expected? If she could just catch her breath, she'd laugh. Or cry.

If that's really what he expected, they were both in a lot of trouble.

Thirty-eight

❧

Y̶ou said it yerself, Colin, the MacDougall has over a thousand men. Be reasonable. We've perhaps fifty here at best, and that's if we include Hugh and old Walter."

Colin stared into his food, doing his best to ignore the logic of Andrew's argument. He wanted nothing to do with logic at this moment. He wanted only to storm Dunstaffnage and rescue Abby. The thought of her being held captive in a time and place not her own was more than he could tolerate.

"Abby is my wife, Drew. My Soulmate. I canna leave her there."

Drew rose from his spot at the table and moved to kneel beside his brother, placing a hand on his shoulder.

"Believe me, Col, I ken the depth of yer feeling. We've already sent a messenger to Dun Ard. We'll gather the men we need. You must be patient."

"I've no taste for patience!" he yelled, banging his fist against the table. He knew it was a childish, petulant act that would serve to accomplish nothing, but his anger was all he had left standing between him and total despair.

"Sit down and calm yourself, or you'll bust that wound open again." Drew's wife, Leah, marched toward him, her expression clearly brooking no argument. "Lean over here and let me have a look at—"

"Dinnna touch it!" both he and Drew cautioned at the same time.

Leah's exasperated sigh expressed her irritation every bit as much as the exaggerated roll of her eyes. "How about you give me credit for a smattering of good sense, yes? I have absolutely no intention of touching this wound. I only want to see for myself that he's healing properly."

His sister-in-law's touch carried with it the ability to heal, but she paid a heavy price for the use of her gift. What she healed, she took upon herself for a time. Neither he nor her husband wanted to see her go through that process.

"My head is fine. The wound will heal in time."

"Your head is hard, that's what it is," she countered, taking her seat next to her husband's chair. "As you say, it will heal on its own. Unless you bust it open having one of your temper tantrums."

Drew patted his shoulder again before returning to sit next to his wife. "I ken yer need to do something, Col. But realize, there is a safer way. Safer for you and safer for yer lady. Blane will likely arrange an emissary from the MacKiernan to the MacDougall to negotiate for yer Abby's release. Once we hear word of—"

"Begging yer pardon, laird Drew." A small boy ran into the great hall, stopping only when he reached the table across from Drew. "The wall guard asked that you come down. We've riders asking access to the keep. They say they're kinsmen of yers. Two men, but one is injured."

Colin was out of his seat and halfway to the entry door before the boy had finished speaking. It could be anyone. He had no reason to believe it was Dair and Simeon.

No reason but blind faith in the power of the Fae.

Drew was close on his heels as he hit the steps leading to the wall walk. He practically flew up the narrow spiral stairs, bursting through the door and not slowing until he could peer over the wall.

"Dair!" He recognized his kinsmen immediately.

"Thanks be to each and every one of the saints," Dair called back. "Let us in. Sim needs attention, and I've news of yer wife."

Colin took no note of the stairs he skipped over in his rush to get down from the wall walk. He threw himself headlong into the race, stooping to clamber under the rising gates to meet the horses inside the gate wall.

"Where is she?" He grabbed the reins that had fallen from Simeon's hand, noticing for the first time the blood soaking the other man's shoulder.

"Perhaps an hour's ride from here. We were bringing her to you when she was taken from us."

They'd reached the stairs, and others crowded around now, hands reaching up to help Simeon from his mount even as Dair swung his leg over his horse and turned to face Colin.

"Taken by whom?"

Dair shook his head, his mouth drawn in a hard line. "I dinna ken the bastard's name, but he was no a stranger to her. He did that to Simeon with some wee weapon he carried. Yer lady called it a gun."

"Flynn." Colin spat the name, cursing the very air the filthy Nuadian breathed. "Can you take me there?"

"Oh, aye, I can. I've only the need of a fresh horse and a good sword." Dair laid a hand on his shoulder, none of his usual humor in evidence. "But I must warn you, Colin, she's been hurt."

Colin's stomach knotted. "What happened?"

"One of MacDougall's men attacked her when we made our escape. She fought him and took a boot to her ribs for her trouble."

A white-hot rage gripped Colin's guts, twisting and writhing inside him, pressing him to action.

"I want the man. I'll have his bowels for dinner for what he's dared. Once she's found, you'll lead me to him and I'll make him pay for what he's done."

"Sorry, my friend." Dair shrugged. "Any payment you take from that one will have to come in the next world. I had the pleasure in this one."

Colin clenched his teeth together to hold back a primal bellow of frustration. "Painfully, I hope?"

"Oh, I'd imagine so," his friend answered, lifting his hands in front of him to mimic the quick gesture of snapping someone's neck.

It would have to do.

"Drew!" Colin yelled, but his brother had already reached his side.

"I heard. I've sent for the stable master. My men are at yer disposal, brother. My men and my own self as well. We'll find her and we'll bring her home."

Colin broke toward the stables at a run. They'd find her. He just prayed to whatever gods cared to listen that they'd find her in time.

Thirty-nine

⸺⁓⸺

*H*er body had given up flinching. It simply hurt too much now.

Abby struggled for anything even resembling a deep breath as Jonathan paced in front of her, stopping to lean down where she sat, her back against a tree.

For perhaps the tenth time he screamed at her, ordering her to "Try again!" with his face a mottled purple-red, spittle settling at the corners of his mouth.

"Tried," she rasped. "Nothing happens." Maybe it was eleven times. She'd lost count.

When her eyes drifted shut, she could almost will herself into that spot in her mind where the dreams took over. So close to the place she wanted to be. The dream place where Colin waited. She'd be safe if she could only run fast enough to reach his arms. He'd catch her up and hold her tight and none of this would hurt her anymore.

"Try again. Say the damn words out loud. There'll be time enough for rest when you've got me back where I belong."

Her head jarred back against the tree when he slapped her, and a fresh new wave of pain flowed through her body.

Twelve.

"Move away from her, Nuadian."

Abby forced her eyes open, surprised that her dream place had come to her, but in a bizarre déjà vu sort of way. It was like reliving those moments in the glen.

Colin entered from the trees, just as he had that day, but this time he carried an enormous sword in front of him.

"The only place yer going is to hell, on the end of my sword."

Just as he had before, Jonathan lifted his arm, aiming the gun he held at Colin.

This was wrong somehow. The words were different and she couldn't play her part this time. There was no knife for her to use.

"Or will it be on my sword?" Across the clearing, Dair stepped from the trees. "I did promise you'd no seen the last of me."

Jonathan's head swiveled in his direction, his arm swinging to aim at the newcomer.

And then, just like in all her other dreams, everything happened at once.

Two shots cracked from the gun, one after another.

Colin's sword flashed down toward Jonathan, the sun glinting off the blade as if wielded by some avenging warrior out of mythology. Both the gun and Jonathan's hand fell to the forest floor, bouncing when they hit like a poorly inflated rubber ball.

The air reverberated with his screams until Colin's blade flashed again. Then there was only silence, and her magnificent dream warrior was at her side, gathering her into his arms.

Forty

～

"Colin?" Abby's eyes fluttered open, dark and deep-set in her oddly pale face.

"I'm here, love," he answered, just as he had all those other times she'd awakened on the ride back to MacQuarrie Keep.

When they entered the bailey, Leah waited at the head of the stairs, quickly taking charge and directing him to follow her to the nearest bedchamber.

"Leave us for a moment. Allow my maid and me to see what ails her. You can wait right outside the door if you like. It'll only be a moment, I promise."

"She's strong. She'll survive this." Dair's attempt to reassure fell short of its mark.

Colin nodded wordlessly, noting the look that passed between his brother and his friend. An unmistakable look of sorrow. Of pity. For him.

The bedchamber door opened, and Leah stepped into the hallway, pulling the door shut behind her before she spoke.

"I'm not liking what I'm seeing in there one little bit. At least two of her ribs are broken. She's short of breath and there's a wet, wheezing sound that's really worrying me. I'm afraid the rib has punctured her lung."

Colin felt as if he'd taken a tumble from a horse, falling, falling, waiting to hit the ground, knowing how bad it would hurt when the moment came.

"What can I do?"

He should have done something sooner. Should have insisted she go back to her own time. Should have gone with her if that's what it took to get her to go. Instead, he'd dragged her deeper into danger and this is what it had gotten them: Abby lying in a bed behind that door, fighting for every breath like it was her last.

"Nothing. There's nothing you can do." Leah sighed, crossing her hands over her stomach. "But there is something I can do."

"No!" Drew stepped between them, taking her by the shoulders. "I can't allow you to put yerself through that, Leah."

"Allow me?" She pushed away from her husband, glaring at him. "I thought we'd had this whole *allow* conversation worked out some time ago. You don't get to forbid me to do anything, dearest. That's not part of our arrangement."

Colin knew he should step in. He should say something now, insist that Leah not take this risk. But her risk could mean life or death for the woman he loved.

"And what about the babe?"

"First off, we don't even know that there is a baby. We only suspect that I might be pregnant. And second, healing that woman in there isn't going to hurt my baby. What do you expect me to do? What would you have me tell the child I might be carrying? 'Oh, yes, little one, you did have an aunt once, but she died because I was too concerned about a little pain in my side to save her life'? I don't think so, Drew. You should know me better than that."

"Indeed, my dearling, I do." Drew placed a quick kiss on her cheek. "And since we ken each other so very well, you'll no be surprised when I say that if you insist on doing this, I must insist on being at yer side when you do."

"I would expect nothing less." She placed a hand on his arm before turning her attention to Colin. "I don't want her to suffer any longer than she already has. Let's do this thing now."

She pushed open the bedchamber door, allowing him at last to rejoin his wife. Abby's eyes were closed, her skin pale except for the swollen scrapes on one cheek.

Colin laid a hand over her breast, reassured that even though she fought for each quick breath, her heart still beat in rhythm with his own.

"Once I begin, I need to make sure you don't touch her, do you understand? No one can touch either of us. The connection must be only between her and me."

Colin nodded, his throat too tight to allow words. He stepped back from the bed to stand beside his brother to await what was to come.

Leah held her hands over Abby's chest, fluttering them back and forth, hovering just above her ribs. From the movement of her lips, he knew she spoke to Abby, likely explaining what she was doing, reassuring his beloved that all would be well. A low humming filled the room, obscuring her actual words.

He glanced at the ceiling, wondering for a moment if his brother had been negligent and allowed bees to take up residence in the keep, but there was no sign of any insect, even as the pitch and volume of the noise grew. Only when he was forced for the second time to drag the hair from his eyes did it occur to him that a wind had whipped up.

A wind inside the room.

The air between where he stood and the bed where his beloved lay began to shimmer and sparkle, as if it thickened and solidified before his very eyes. Tiny streaks of color shot through the air, dancing around him like the insects he'd sought only moments before.

But these were no insects. He recognized them well, even before the sphere of green light surrounded them. They were the shards of Faerie Magic Leah called on to do her bidding.

It took all his will to keep his distance, especially once the Magic materialized. His worst fear was that when the Magic receded, Abby would be gone, taken from him back to the time where she belonged.

No, that was a falsehood. His worst fear wasn't losing her to her own time. It was losing her to death. At least if she were returned home, he'd have the comfort of knowing that she lived.

Thunder rumbled from a nearby storm, so close to the keep he'd almost swear it was inside the room with them. Once more the thunder boomed and the sphere surrounding the two women shattered, sending shards of flickering colors shooting toward them, through them, beyond them.

Instinctively, he hit the floor, embarrassed that he had until he saw his brother crouching next to him looking as discomfited as he felt.

Drew was on his feet first but reached the bed only a step ahead of Colin. Leah slumped over Abby, her brow damp with perspiration, her eyes closed. Abby appeared as one asleep, her breathing deep and regular, the color returned to her cheeks, the markings on her face gone.

Not gone, transferred to Leah's cheek.

"Is she . . ." He couldn't bring himself to ask the question of Drew, not with his brother's distress so evident as he lifted his wife into his arms.

"I'm fine," Leah answered, her shallow panting attempts at breathing belying her words. "Need sleep."

"And sleep you'll have, dearling." Drew started for the door, stopping to turn briefly. "Abby will likely sleep through the night as well. You'd be wise to do the same."

Sleep? With his beloved's life hanging in the balance? His brother had lost his sense of reason.

Very cautiously, Colin climbed onto the bed with Abby, taking great care not to jostle or move her in any way as he lay down next to her.

He would content himself with simply watching her, with counting each long, slow breath she took. He would use the time to send a prayer up with each and every one of those breaths that she still lived when morning's light graced their world.

Forty-one

Abby dreamed of warm places, safe and tidy little spots in a perfect world. The dreams were short, fractured, hopping from scene to scene, barely allowing her time to settle into one before it morphed into another. All had one thing in common: in each and every location, Colin awaited her, his arms open wide to gather her in and hold her close.

She opened her eyes, not at all surprised to find Colin next to her, fast asleep. He held her hand sandwiched between his callused palm and his heart.

There wasn't a more perfect combination to represent Colin, tough and tender, rugged man and sweet lover, all at the same time.

Watching him sleep, her dreams came back to her in a rush and she realized with a start she'd completely deceived herself as to the locations in her dreams. Many had been dark and dank and had she encountered in them in real life, they would have terrified her.

So why hadn't they seemed threatening in her dreams?

Because Colin had been there with her.

Colin had been there to hold her, to protect her, to give her that sense of warmth and safety. Together they formed one, a whole being that needed nothing from the outside world to complete what they had together.

Ellie had been absolutely right. There were things in this world much more important than toilet paper. What she felt each time she lay in Colin's arms was definitely one of those things. For the first time since she'd arrived in this century, she knew, absolutely without any reservation, that she belonged at Colin's side, no matter where—or when—he chose to be.

A light knock sounded on the bedchamber door and his eyes flew open. His face creased into a smile when he saw her, the rare smile that always burrowed deeply into her heart when it lit his features.

He stroked his fingertips down her cheek. "Good morning, wife."

"Good morning, husband." She returned his greeting, rolling to her side toward him to accept the kiss he offered.

Again the knock sounded at the door.

"Bollocks," he muttered with a sigh, pushing up and out of the bed to answer the door. "A pox on all of them that would bother us."

Leah entered the room first, Drew directly behind, his hand protectively guiding his wife.

Colin caught up her hand, kissing it and bowing low. "Yer an amazing woman, Leah, and I'm honored to have you as part of my family. How can I ever repay you for what you've done?"

"Don't be silly. It's what I do. Now." Leah hurried to the bedside and tossed back the covers to prod at Abby's side. "How does this beautiful morning find you? Well, I'm predicting from your husband's reaction."

"I feel great." It was no lie. She'd all but forgotten yesterday's horrible pains. They seemed as blurred as her memories of arriving at this place. "What did you do to me?"

"Just a little Faerie Magic," Leah said with a shrug, turning a big smile toward her husband. "Will you two join us for the morning meal, or would you prefer to have food sent up here?"

"No food, thank you," Colin announced as he returned to her side. "We'll be leaving shortly."

"Leaving?" Abby swung her gaze around to him and pushed herself up to sit on her knees, searching his face for an answer. They'd only just arrived. Besides, wouldn't a meal make sense before they started their journey to . . .

"Oh, Colin," she groaned. Even after all they'd been through, he hadn't given up on finding his king. "You're still determined to change the world, aren't you?"

"Only your world, wife," he said, brushing the hair from her forehead. "It's time to return to your century, Abby. This is no the place for you to be."

Her mind reeled with confusion. If he thought he was going to get rid of her that easily, he'd better think again. "I'm not going anywhere. I'm staying right here. I'll adjust. I can figure out how to make the best of this world. As long as I'm with you, that's all that matters."

"As if you think I'd let you go anywhere without me," he scoffed. "We go together."

"But . . ." Had she missed something important in the past twenty-four hours? "You said you belonged here. That you were determined to make a difference."

He nodded slowly, catching up her face in his two hands. "And you said I'd no right to try to change yer history. I see now that you had the right of it. My pig-headed stubbornness nearly cost yer life."

"And yours," she added, placing her hands over his. "I was so afraid I'd lost you."

From the doorway, Drew cleared his throat. "We'll leave you now to do whatever it is you need to. If you dinna join us by midday, I'll pass yer farewells along to Mother, aye?"

"I'd appreciate that, brother." Colin answered without taking his eyes from hers.

"If you really want to repay me, there is something you can do. When you get back, find my sister and tell her how happy I am."

Beside Leah, Drew cleared his throat again.

"And yes." Leah hooked her arm through her husband's, her face glowing with happiness. "Let her know she's going to have a new niece or nephew in a few months."

"The first of many," Drew interjected with a laugh.

"You have my word upon it," Colin promised.

Abby waited until the door closed before broaching her fears.

"Would it be so horribly bad if we stayed here?" She prayed he'd say no, her failed attempt at wishing them out of this time when she'd thought him dying still ripe in her memory.

"It would be."

His answer sent her stomach plummeting to her feet.

"But you said—"

"I've said many things," he interrupted. "And now I'm saying I choose to go forward with the woman I love. I choose cars and potatoes and libraries full of books. I choose air travel and hot showers and cream that comes in a can."

"What if I can't do it?" Her heart already ached at the thought of disappointing him.

"There's nothing you canna do, wife. I believe that with all my heart. Together, there's nothing that *we* canna do. Wish us home, Abby. Wish us to our home, together."

She threw her arms around his neck, sinking into the love he offered as he tightened his embrace.

"I wish us home. To our home. Together."

"Forever," he added.

The heavy bed began to rock and bump against the stone floor as the air around them shimmered like a bright green curtain of rushing water.

When thousands of multicolored sparkles began their dive-bombing maneuvers around their heads, Abby buried her face in Colin's shoulder.

"You see? What did I tell you!" His triumphant shout was barely audible over the buzzing and hissing.

With a hand to her cheek, he lifted her face and covered her mouth with his. The sensation of his kiss felt like the world dropped out from under them, and they fell, endlessly locked in each other's arms.

Abby could imagine no better way to go forth into forever.